Enamel

TIM SABADOS

For Mary, Mackenzie and Zoe

1

THE UNRELENTING DOG bark punched through the thick night air, slid amongst the maze of darkened alleys and rolled over the pungent stench that festered from the grime-coated streets. It was the same kind of disgusting stink that had burrowed into the walls of Aryssa's apartment. No matter the scent of the candle, the type of air freshener, or how much she scrubbed, the acrid odor always managed to out-muscle her efforts.

The bark clung to the air—air as searing as a demon's oven-like breath—and rose the several stories into the once-calm nocturnal sky, only to slip past the tiny window above Aryssa's kitchen sink.

An elbow on the kitchen table, her hand lethargically braced her head. Aryssa halfheartedly tapped the pestle against the rim of the marble mortar, then blew the strand of blonde hair that had been obnoxiously rubbing against her forehead. It flew to the side, only to creep back to its rightful spot and tempt her to try to shoo it away once again.

Two thirty-six struggled to light up on the stove's clock, except the six looked more like a five. The lower left red hash that made a digital six look like a six, or for that matter an eight like an eight or a two a two had long ago stopped working. The torn curtain that hung from a rod speckled with the sores of rust silently fluttered. Aryssa hoped the breeze would survive the short journey across the kitchen to where she sat. She yearned for its cool touch to ripple across her skin, whisk away the glaze of sweat that coated her body and relieve the monotony that was caked like gelled lotion inside her head. It never came. Instead, the apartment's stagnant atmosphere coiled around the draft of her desire and devoured it.

Above her the ceiling fan with its dust-coated blades strained to spin, even though the switch was on max. Aryssa slowly exhaled and rubbed her ear, hoping to soothe the persistent ring, a ring as relentless as the slow descent of nails on a chalkboard. Once again the speakers closest to the stage had been turned up past their limits. How many times had she bitched about it to Ariek? A dismissive flick of her hand. It never did any good. She had chosen to stay quiet be-cause...well, she hadn't been in the mood to hear the same empty rhetoric. *It comes with the territory. The needs of the customers come first.* And on and on and...

A tiny bead of sweat broke away from Aryssa's neck and dribbled down her chest. She swiped it away with her finger before it could pass the border to her breasts. There was a similar kind of dew coating her glass of bourbon. She took another swig only to realize there was no burn down her throat. It didn't matter though because it wasn't helping. It wasn't enough to appease the predator inside her head, push away that unquenchable lust as it seductively circled its tongue around the clit of her prudence and insistently urged her to drink more. Not enough to pacify the orgasmic fix her body craved. Not enough to shut up that damn dog, stop the dripping faucet, dial down the heat, soak up the humidity, obliterate the memory of work and appease the sandman so she could finally succumb to the gentle rhythms of a deep slumber. A frustrated grunt. There was something that possibly could and it was lying on the table right in front of her.

She grabbed the purple Crown Royal bag and fingered the stuff inside. Were there three, or maybe four of them? Whatever the number, it was the last of her stash. The smaller, less potent ones. The ones that were constantly shoved aside for those that were slightly better, and now those last few were all that remained.

Another sigh. Aryssa needed to find more. It was still dark outside, which meant there was plenty of time before sunrise. The night's take was balled into a loose wad next to the bottle of Elijah Craig. It would be enough. At least she didn't have to turn a...

Vrrrr. Her cell vibrated. She glanced at the caller ID. Huffed. What does he want now?

"Yeah," she said sharply.

"Glad to hear from you too," Sammy responded. "Is that any way to greet your number-one fan?"

"Greet?" Aryssa glanced at the stove's clock. "It's only been a couple of hours."

"Does it matter? I wanted to make sure you made it home in one piece."

Aryssa rolled her eyes. "As you can see, I did."

"How was I supposed to know? It's not like you called."

"Didn't know I was obligated to do so."

"You aren't," Sammy responded. "Doesn't mean I can't be concerned."

Who's he trying to kid? "I'm a big girl. I can take care of myself."

"Damn. Who suddenly pissed on your parade? You weren't anything like this earlier."

What had gotten into her? A twinge of remorse injected itself into her discretion. Aryssa mustered the strength to say it. "Sorry." She sank back into her chair, looked up at the ceiling and exhaled the waste of her discontentment. "It's been a long night, and I'm beat."

"I believe it," Sammy said in an optimistic tone. "With the way you were moving, you had the whole place in an uproar."

Aryssa curled her knees to her chest and rubbed her shin. The soreness along her bone wrinkled under her touch. "I didn't do anything different from any other night."

"Are you kidding me?" Sammy replied. "Your sets were out of this world. Hands above the others."

A flame of pride flickered inside Aryssa. It grew warmer. Glowed brighter. "Thanks." She was good. Dancing was in her blood, and she used it as a way to escape the drabness that had infected her life. "I had to find some way to help me tune out the speakers. Ariek had them blasting again."

A brief moment of silence. "Now that you mention it, it was kind of loud."

"Kind of?" Aryssa questioned incredulously. "I'm surprised my ears are still attached to my head."

Sammy chuckled. "Everything was fine from where I was sitting."

"That's because you spent all of your time way over at the bar. There's nothing there but TVs."

"Doesn't mean I didn't hear the music," Sammy retorted. "Besides, I didn't spend all my time at the bar."

"You what…broke away to go upstairs."

"Isn't that what you ladies are there for?" Sammy said. "It just so happens that I enjoy it." A pause. "You're not jealous, are you?"

"Of what?" She couldn't hide the annoyance in her voice.

"You not being there and providing it for me."

Aryssa scoffed. "Not at all."

"I think you are," Sammy said with an air of confidence.

"We've been over this," Aryssa reiterated. "I'm not giving you a lap dance."

"Why not?" Sammy asked. "You do it for other guys."

"It's how I make money."

"And I'm not a paying customer?"

Aryssa tightly squeezed her hand into a fist. "That's not what I'm saying."

"Then what are you saying?"

She slowly exhaled, hoping to smooth the sharp edges of her frustration. "You and I both know that you'd expect more."

"What makes you say that?" Sammy was trying his best to sound naïve.

"Oh come on," Aryssa countered in a tone that dripped with contempt. "I can't believe you would ask me something like that."

"I've never placed any expectations on you."

"So you say," Aryssa replied. "It doesn't matter, because things are different."

"All because of that one night?" Sammy asked in a way that implied it shouldn't matter. "You can't tell me you didn't like it…'cause I know you did."

Aryssa bit her tongue to stave off the impending barrage against Sammy's smugness. She silently expelled a breath, trying to relieve the pent-up aggravation that was building inside her. Yes, it was all because of that one night. The one night she wished she could delete from her memory. Try as she might, she couldn't. No amount of liquor or the long shower where she relentlessly scrubbed every inch of her body had helped. Neither had snorting that extra crush.

That night she had been in a mood. God only knows what had put her in that mood, but something inside her made her bust loose. Had it been stress? Boredom? Some strange desire to shake things up? Whatever it was, Aryssa would never fully understand it. She did know it had been lurking. Stalking. Patiently hiding on the fringes of her awareness. Waiting for the right time to seduce and take control.

It started off as one of those nights when she had somehow chosen to break one of her cardinal rules. A rule she rarely breached, but on this particular night she did. She allowed a customer to buy her a drink. The Tanqueray and tonic was the spark. One led to two, which turned into two more and then several after that. Her mind went blissfully numb. The thin layer of inhibition that covered her desire had evaporated and left her discretion free to do as it pleased.

The music had been hypnotic. It had tantalized her carnal appetite. The rhythm deviously slipped through her flesh and grabbed her hips. Her pelvis gyrated. Flirted with the fiendish beat. The fire of lust burned in her groin, spread upward into her chest, passionately caressed her breasts and made her heart flutter with passion.

That night she had danced her heart out. She lit up the stage with hips that thrust and contracted with unrestrained vigor. She enthusiastically twirled around the brass pole. Courted the catcalls. Eagerly took on the privates and ground into those patrons for that little extra. The money came, but it wasn't enough. She wanted something more. Needed a way to squelch the inferno that burned between her legs. Appease the juices that had lubricated the quivering walls of her lips.

Sammy happened to be there. There was something about him that had made him especially good-looking. Was it the charming twinkle that swam in the clear blue lake of his eyes? The teeth that were as white as a snow-capped mountain? Maybe the masculine stubble that covered his face? Or the way his confidence propped his undaunted demeanor? Maybe it was a combination of it all? It didn't matter, because she had been in a mood. He said the right things, smiled in the right way and most importantly flashed a wad of cash.

It wasn't the first time she had given him a lap dance, but that time it had been different. She hungered to be touched. To be grabbed by a pair of thick, muscular hands—his hands. She had urged him with the subtle movements of her body. He responded by stroking her back and then running his fingers over the curves of her ass. He had grabbed her cheeks and pulled her close. Instead of resisting she had plunged her chest into his face. Ground into him even harder which made him thrust back. The moment was ripe. Her sensuality was a fleshy fruit bursting with the warm liquid of desire. Sammy suggested it and she readily agreed. A race to his place and then...

"It was decent," Aryssa said. "Nothing to get overly excited about."

"I beg to differ," Sammy replied. Was there a tinge of hurt in his voice? If there was, it quickly disintegrated. "The moaning, screaming and the way you clawed me betray you."

The heat of embarrassment rolled through her core, up into her neck and singed her cheeks. If memory served her, she'd had him gasping. "Think what you want. It's never going to happen again."

"How can you be so sure?" Sammy replied arrogantly. "Never say never."

"Trust me." Aryssa reassuringly countered.

"Suit yourself." Sammy paused. "So be it, if you want to

live in denial."

Aryssa sprang upright in her chair letting her feet smack the floor. "Are you kidding?"

"I saw the way your eyes glimmered when you looked at me across the bar," Sammy said in a voice full of certitude. "Your cute little smile spoke volumes."

"Is that why you're calling me?" She shook away the wave of astonishment. "Thinking you're going to get a piece?"

"You say it so crudely," Sammy answered. "I would never think of you and what we did in such a crass way."

"And this coming from the person who said, "'never say never'.""

"Ha, ha. You know what I mean."

"I know what you're trying to do." Aryssa grabbed her glass and took a swig.

"I can easily pick you up in about twenty minutes."

"You don't even know where I live."

"I will once you tell me."

Aryssa shook her head. "Not going to happen."

"Why not?"

"Because it's late." She ejected her frustration with a quick breath. "I'm tired, and I'm going to bed."

"Are you sure?" Sammy asked with a honey-coated voice. "It sounds like you doubt yourself."

Aryssa nudged her slackened jaw back into place. "I don't doubt myself at all. And trust me when I say that I'm very sure."

"Well then, how about dinner tomorrow night? There's a great Italian place that just opened…"

"Sammy," Aryssa said pointedly. "I'm going to bed now."

"So it's a yes."

Sammy's overbearing ego played havoc on the circuitry of

her mind. It jumbled her thoughts. She just wanted him off the phone. Needed him to go away. "Whatever you say."

"Good. I'll call you later in the afternoon."

"I've got to go," Aryssa said. Why had she ever given him her phone number?

"Trust me; you're going to love…"

"Uh-huh. Talk later, bye." Aryssa abruptly hung up then tossed the phone on the table.

As if Sammy's pompous conviction wasn't enough, her ears suddenly rang louder. The thick air seemed to become heavier. The room seemed to shrink, the walls appeared to close inward and compress tighter and tighter as if a giant python had wrapped itself around her apartment and tried to squeeze the life from it.

Aryssa ran her hand through her hair. Her heart thumped anxiously against the bars of its claustrophobic cage. She had to get out of here. Somehow escape the confining space and find a spot outside to simply breathe.

She snatched the purple Crown Royal bag and held the opening over the mortar. The last three white rocks tinged then pinged inside the bowl. Definitely time to get more.

Aryssa grabbed the pestle and mashed the rocks until the last bits were pulverized into a fine powder. Tapping the pestle on the mortar, she then lifted the glass vial from her little black box and carefully filled it with the white contents from the bowl. It filled only about two-thirds of the vial. Not as much as she'd hoped for, but still enough to be effective.

A tingle swept through her. The predator inside her head chuckled with anticipatory pleasure. He would soon get what he craved. So too would Aryssa.

2

THE AIR WAS still. The place hollow. From the floor to the ceiling, the stage to the speakers, the entrance to the beer taps and everything in between, it was all drained of life. A little over an hour ago the club had been crammed beyond capacity. The walls had practically buckled from the surge of customers who had packed themselves like sardines. Money flowed from one hand to another as if it were a rapidly running river. The current was aided by the thumping music, gyrating lap dances, the carnal odor of overzealous desire mixed with the musky scent of sexual yearning and the faint whiff of false hope. In the end, it wasn't enough to stop the unfailing hands of Father Time from pushing the clock to two in the morning. Closing time always showed up, no matter how much Sammy wished it would take a night off.

Even though Sammy wanted the party to keep going, the club had had enough. It rebelled against the mind-numbing chatter, the ear-splitting music, the dancers' unrelenting need for drama, the spilt drinks, the liquor-soaked washcloths and the empty beer bottles that lay across the bar like fallen soldiers. It rebelled like anyone who had had too much of a good thing. It got sick. It opened its mouth to the parking lot and regurgitated the night's excitement, leaving stillness in its wake.

Sammy reached for the black thong draped over the railing near the stage. How it got there was anyone's guess, but the thought made him quickly pull away. That thing was probably teeming with some kind of STD. Who or what it had been in contact with was anyone's guess. Just another article vomited from the guts of the night's festivities. Besides, this was Ariek's place, not his. Better to let him and his cleaning crew deal with it.

He slid into the booth off to the side of the bar and anxiously tapped the edge of the table with his finger. It wasn't the most pleasing of sounds, but it was better than the alternative. Silence. It lay across the club like a thick wool blanket and soaked up any last bits of the once-energetic evening.

Sammy despised this time of the night. The early hour both pushed him out the door and held him prisoner. He could never shake away that ear-numbing quiet that clung to every molecule in the air. He hated being alone with only his thoughts to entertain him. Hated the absence of music, the lights, the crowd, the striptease, the clop of stilettos against the stage floor. Hated not having the drinks, the pills and occasional line to stimulate his brain into a frenzy. He reached into his pocket for his stash, but thought otherwise. It just wasn't the same without his senses being thrown into overdrive.

He gazed around the room, hoping another drink would magically appear. A sigh. No such luck. Sammy bowed his head and stared at his phone. Aryssa would call back. She wanted him. He was sure of it.

"Sammy," Ariek called.

Startled, Sammy looked up and tipped his chin. "I've been waiting for you."

"What the hell are you doing here?" Ariek walked toward the booth. "Thought you were long gone."

Sammy shook his head. "Soon." Slid his phone into his pocket.

Ariek clicked his tongue. "You weren't talking with …?"

Sammy sheepishly shrugged. "What's it to you?"

"You need to let it go." Ariek gestured toward the stage. "This place is crawling with potential and yet you cling to the one you can't have."

Sammy slashed Ariek's suggestion with a slice of his hand. "I've had it and I'll have it again."

Ariek gestured toward the phone in Sammy's pocket. "She turned you down, didn't she?" His tone was a little more mocking than usual.

"How do you know that she didn't?" Sammy questioned defensively.

"I know you all too well," Ariek countered. "That gloom in your voice is a dead giveaway."

Sammy grunted. "She'll come around."

"If you say so," Ariek mumbled.

"Mark my words," Sammy retorted. He watched Ariek lower himself into the booth and sit directly across from him. "When she does, she'll be all mine."

Ariek purposefully rolled his eyes. "You're dreaming if you think you can land a woman like Aryssa." He paused. "She's one of a kind."

"Don't you think I know that?" Sammy smiled. "And amazing in more ways than you realize."

"Count yourself as lucky to even have had the chance."

"It wasn't luck," Sammy said optimistically. "She wanted it and she liked what she tasted."

"If she liked it so much, how come she hasn't been back for seconds?"

Sammy grunted. "She needs time to digest the first to

realize she wants another."

"I think she's had more than enough time to realize her mistake." Ariek softly exhaled his discontent. Lifted his glass. "You want one?"

The conversation had curdled Sammy's mood. "I'm good."

"Suit yourself." Ariek sipped and kept silent for a few seconds. "You'll have plenty of distraction when those new recruits come."

"We both will," Sammy replied halfheartedly. He gazed at the table, allowing his thoughts to drift to Aryssa. The way she could move her body. Shake that tight...

"Could be well worth your time to individually inspect each of them."

Sammy shook to the negative. "I want nothing to do with retreads."

"This is supposed to be a clean batch." Ariek advised enthusiastically. "You could break them in. You know...satisfy that overly active libido of yours. Forget all about..." He cringed. Did his best to hide his expression. "Well, you know..."

Sammy sighed sharply. "Maybe." He paused to mull over the idea. Would it quench his lust for Aryssa? "You know they don't like it when we dip into the newbies."

"Hey." Ariek held out his hands. "Who's going to know?" Tapped his chest. "I'm not going to say anything." Pointed at Sammy. "Doubt you would either. And the newbies..." a huff of dismissal, "who's going to believe them? That's even if they open their mouths."

"None of that helps me right now," Sammy said in an unadorned tone. "That's still a couple of days away."

Ariek held up his palm. Fingers glued together. Thumb

spread away from the rest. "There's always the internet and Miss Michigan." He snickered as he lowered his fist to his crotch. "It'll tide you over."

Sammy staved off the dig by harboring the thought. "I just might." A pause. "I don't know if it'll be enough after watching her." He bit his lip to contain his hunger. "God, does she have a body made for..."

"Easy now," Ariek interjected. "You're just going to get yourself all worked up over nothing."

"Easy for you to say."

"It's not like I haven't watched her," Ariek admitted. "But our plates are going to fill up real fast. Got to keep our eyes on the prize." A tip of his drink. "You'll have to deal with that issue later."

Sammy huffed. "I'd rather deal with it now."

"It's all too obvious that she doesn't..." Ariek waved the sentence away. "You sure you don't want a drink?"

"No. I need to get up early."

"Early? You?" Ariek questioned with a bit of surprise in his voice. "How come?"

Sammy's brows crinkled. "My morning manager is out sick and the nephew will be there by himself." He hesitated. "I've told you...not the brightest bulb in the pack."

"I thought you were getting rid of him."

"I can't." Annoyance coated Sammy's words. "I promised my sister."

"So you're going to keep letting him screw things up?"

"That's why I'm going in early." Sammy pressed the pads of his fingers into the tabletop. "I've got to watch over him."

Ariek scratched his ear. "How long has it been?"

"Not even a month."

"And he's caused you this much grief?" Ariek sipped his

Scotch. "How much worse can it get?"

"I don't know, and I don't want to find out," Sammy replied. "My patience can only last another week or two."

"Then what?" Ariek tapped his glass. "Your sis will blow a gasket if you fire him."

"And my mom and uncle and…" Sammy massaged his temple. "I can't keep letting him tear my business to shreds." Cleared his throat. "And to think that she wants me to train him to be a manager."

Ariek leaned back. "Thank God that's your problem, not mine."

"Very funny," Sammy said sarcastically. "At the moment he's near the bottom of my list of problems." Ran his finger over his brow. "We've got other more important things to worry about."

"I'm well aware." Ariek pinched his thumb and forefinger together. "I still haven't come up with a solution to our other problem."

"I haven't either," Sammy confirmed. "We need one soon."

"Yes, we do," Ariek agreed.

Dread zipped across Sammy's nerves. He shivered. "Yes, we do." They needed to find a solution to their problem sooner rather than later.

3

THE WATER WAS as smooth as polished granite. The efferves-
cent glow of the skyline and the city's numerous lights were
mirrored in the river's glossy varnish.

The bow of Charlie's speedboat was lifted to the level of
his eyes and almost blocked the view of everything in front of
him. It didn't matter though. His jet-black hair excitedly
ruffled behind him. The twin engines thundered like the
hooves of two thoroughbreds sprinting across a field. His heart
galloped wildly inside his chest and fed off the whine that
jettisoned from the motors. All those weeks of rebuilding and
then the relentless hours of tinkering had finally made them
behave the way they were meant to behave.

Charlie filled his lungs with Mother Nature's untainted
breath. The same nimble breath that seemed to chip away at
humidity's obesity drifted out over the river, climbed into the
expansive atmosphere and disappeared into the dark and
bottomless bowl above his head.

Things were better out here, especially on nights like this.
Just Charlie and his boat, racing across the middle of the wide-
open river. Free from the confines of the city. Free from the
blackened fumes of car exhaust. From the claustrophobic
crowds of people. From the stuffy enclosure of his apartment.
He exhaled. And most importantly, free from the passengers

that made it a point to lurk over his shoulder and ask all those stupid questions. *How much longer? What's it like over there? How come it's so expensive for such a simple boat ride?*

Charlie grunted to chase away the thoughts. They have no idea what it takes to keep this thing running. No idea what it costs to dock it. The marina fees. The gas. On top of it all, he had to somehow scratch out a living.

He banked starboard, away from the small lighthouse jutting from the tip of Belle Isle Pointe. Reluctantly left behind the dark throat of the river's horizon, passed through its jaws of solitude and sped toward the twinkling lights of the marina.

The marina was well over a mile away, but closing fast. Its lights becoming brighter. The slips and countless boats bigger. A half mile. Quarter mile. Charlie didn't want to give up the freedom, the ecstasy of speed as he zipped across the river's expanse. Three hundred yards. It was time. Nearly one hundred yards. He cut the engine.

The bow dropped. The boat slowed, then bobbed as the trailing wake caught up and rolled under the custom flat black hull. Charlie swiped his hair from his face, then tapped his pocket to make sure the four coins were still there. Felt like it. He sighed. Another slow night.

The gas gauge was under of a quarter of a tank. He opened his wallet and ran his thumb over the bills. Several twenties. A few fifties. Money was getting tight, but there was enough to fill the tank. He'd have to pawn those coins sooner than he wanted.

As it should be, the light was on in the dockmaster's shed. Charlie aimed his boat toward the pumps, slid sideways next to the dock and let his boat gently tap the rubber bumpers.

Honk. Honk.

Charlie waited nearly a minute. Nothing. He hit the horn

again and kept his hand on it a little longer that he should have.

Another thirty seconds passed. He relentlessly tapped the steering wheel. Huffed a glob of his impatience. He was ready to lay on the horn once again, but hesitated.

The door to the shed swung open. A plump silhouette, the one that looked like that new guy, stepped out. It didn't take long for Charlie to realize that it was him. The one who moved at the speed of cold molasses. The one who now slowly made his way down the steps and lumbered across the dock.

"What you need?" the dockmaster's voice was as flat as a pancake and dry as sand. Even though sleep slackened his cheeks, annoyance burned in his eyes.

Charlie gestured toward the pumps. "Need to fill up."

"Now?" the dockmaster glanced at his wrist. "It's after four o'clock."

"What difference does it make?" Charlie halfheartedly tried to cloak his aggravation. "You're supposed to be open twenty-four seven. Or have things changed?"

The dockmaster didn't say a thing. He hesitated a few seconds, then shook his head. "Nothing's changed." A long sigh. "You know you're practically the only one who does this."

"Does what?" Charlie questioned in a manner that suggested he already knew the answer. "Get gas this late?"

"Yeah." The dockmaster nodded.

"I don't like fighting the traffic and the crowds." Charlie paused. "Besides, I pay for the convenience."

The dockmaster rubbed his belly, set his gaze on the shed and then let it drift back to Charlie. He thumbed over his shoulder. "I need to get the keys."

Charlie tipped his chin in acknowledgement. He watched

the portly man trudge across the dock and up the sidewalk. If only that man was more diligent, maybe he…

There was another set of footsteps. Not as heavy as the dockmaster's, but definitely a little more quiet. Hard soles on wood planks and moving in his direction. Who could it be at this hour?

A man stepped into the cone of light from the overhead lamp. Overweight and barrel-chested. Feet turned out as he walked. A chugging breath that gurgled with each exhalation.

The man stepped up to Charlie's boat. His lips were a faint shade of blue. "You the man I'm looking for?" he boldly demanded.

Charlie cocked his head. "Sorry, I'm done for tonight."

"I'm supposed to give you this." The overweight man thrust out his hand.

Charlie eyed the coin. "That you are."

"Well," the man said firmly. "Aren't you going to take it?"

"I will. But not now."

"Why not?" The man scoffed. "I was told to come down here and give it to a man with long black hair in a black boat." He pointed at Charlie. "Can't miss him, I was told. Said I would be taken care of right away." He looked up and down the dock. "Sure looks like that person is you."

"Who said that?"

The man's eyes squinted as if annoyance itself tried to squeeze them shut. "Some man with dark eyes. Black suit with a red tie." A pause. "Does it matter?"

Charlie bit his tongue. The pressure inside his lungs bellowed with irritation to the point that his chest was like a boiler that cracked at the seams of his ribs. "You've been misinformed."

"Are you kidding me?" The man's impatience spewed out

of his mouth. "What kind of crap operation are you running?" He pointed behind him. "I don't have time for this. I was told I'd be taken care of, so I expect that…"

Charlie had had enough. He jumped out of his boat and stood toe-to-toe with the man. Towered over him as rage quivered across his nerves. He resisted the urge to wrap his large hand around the man's fleshy throat and squeeze until his head popped like a grape. Instead he jabbed his thick finger at the man's forehead. "I told you that I am done for tonight."

The man's eyes went wide with fright. He stooped under Charlie's rage. "But…but…hey." Held up his hands, "It's…it's cool."

"What part of 'I'm done' do you not understand?"

The man stepped backward. "What…what do I…I do in the meantime?"

Charlie pointed at a bench down the dock. "You wait until I come back."

The man nodded. Another step backward. "When will that…"

"When I come back," Charlie answered. "Not a moment before. I get here when I get here."

"What do I do with this?" The man glanced at the coin.

"You'll give it to me, and only me, before you step foot on my boat."

The overweight man nodded even faster. More steps backward.

"Now go!" Charlie demanded in a tone as hot as molten steel. "I don't want to see your face until the sun is setting."

The man turned and ran. More like waddled. His heavy footsteps slapping the wooden dock. Charlie took a deep breath to cool his throat.

"Who were you talking to?" the dockmaster asked from somewhere behind Charlie.

Charlie waved his hand dismissively. "Some prick was demanding that I ferry him across right this very minute."

The dockmaster stared down the dock with skepticism spilling from his eyes. "I'm not seeing…"

"When it's time to be done, it's…" Charlie turned toward the heavyset man scampering down the dock. Then back to the dockmaster, only to realize that he wouldn't understand. Charlie brushed away his blunder with a flick of his wrist. "Forget it."

The dockmaster uneasily rubbed his hands together. "Umm, how much gas you want?"

"Top it off," Charlie answered as he stepped back onto the boat.

The dockmaster silently gazed up and down Charlie's boat. "I heard that when you first got this thing it was a total piece of junk."

Charlie twisted off the gas cap. "It was." Motioned at the opening.

"You've done some damn good work." The dockmaster inserted the nozzle into the tank. "This thing's cherry."

"Thanks."

"No, really. It gets all kinds of looks," The dockmaster confirmed. "Got to be a blast to drive."

"Best part of my day," Charlie confirmed.

"How fast have you had it?"

Charlie flattened his hand and smoothly swiped it away from him. "Don't know. Don't really care." A pause. "All I know is that it's best when I'm out there by myself. Wind in my face. The sound of those engines. No one bothering me." Became lost in the thought of the open water. It abruptly shattered. "Sometimes those customers can ruin it, but I always find a way to recover when I make my way back."

The dockmaster slowly nodded. "Right, those customers," he seemed to patronizingly agree.

Charlie looked at him doubtfully. "Yeah, those customers." Again realized that the dockmaster probably wouldn't understand. "They can be a pain in the…"

"Business must be good," The dockmaster said in a tone dabbed with mockery. "I see you've been out a lot."

"It's been slow. Too slow. Should be better." Charlie looked out onto the horizon, wondering if the reason for business being so sluggish was hidden in its shadows. "It's not like I'm being paid an hourly wage or getting any benefits."

The dockmaster sighed. "The joys of being in business for yourself."

Charlie circled his finger around his ear. "Whoever said that running your own is rewarding had to have been a little crazy."

"There's something about the service industry that can drive even the most stable person mad."

"You got that right," Charlie agreed. "Always having to be the professional one. Play nice so you don't ruffle anyone's feathers."

The nozzle clicked off. "Cash or credit?"

Charlie pulled several bills from his wallet. "Keep it."

"I appreciate it," the dockmaster replied. "Umm, I hope things pick up for you."

"Me too." Charlie started the motors, pulled away from the dock and aimed for his slip.

He yawned, ran his hand across the small lump of coins in his pocket and then sighed. Why had business been so slow? He scratched his chin with reassurance. At least he had a guaranteed customer later on. But one wasn't enough. He needed several more. Something was off, but what? If things didn't pick up soon, how much longer would he be able to hold it all together?

4

THE DOOR CREAKED open like an old man's arthritic joint struggling to straighten. Aryssa stopped, worried that she might wake someone. Everything stayed silent, so she slowly pushed the dilapidated door even farther. She cautiously glanced down the hallway, along the scuffed and dented walls and up to the ceiling, where a few of the working lights labored to regurgitate a gritty glare over the cracked tiled floor.

She slid inside her apartment building and braced herself against the wall. Giggled. Why had she been so worried? No one cared who came and went. They didn't care who was awake or sleeping. What could possibly happen? Get grounded to her apartment? She giggled again.

Aryssa clutched the purple Crown Royal bag that was filled with a few new rocks. Her replenished stash. She braced her free hand on the wall and used it to guide her down the hallway. A faint mist hung on the edges of her vision. Her mind blissfully numb. She bit her lip only to discover that it was numb too. Another giggle.

She somehow found the stairway at the end of the corridor, placed her foot on the step, grabbed the railing and hoisted herself up. Repeated the movement over and over until she reached the first landing.

Aryssa gripped the handrail and spun a half circle, stopping a few inches short of the next flight of steps. A contented sigh. Just like being on stage and spinning around the pole.

Again she snagged the railing, placed her foot on the step and hoisted herself up. Again and again. A sharp exhale. Why couldn't this place have a working elevator?

She contemplated the thought as she became lost in the mountainous ascent. Time passed. The echo of a heavy stomp somewhere below broke her concentration. She smiled ever so slightly, having made it to the fourth floor. Her floor.

The pounding boots grew louder. Drew nearer. She glanced over her shoulder to see someone approaching with a gaze focused on his own feet. A silent giggle. She waited for him to get closer.

"Hey Charlie," Aryssa said abruptly.

Charlie twitched in surprise. His eyes narrowed with alarm. Jaw tensed with irritation. Shoulders postured. It all softened the moment he realized it was Aryssa. "You just scared the hell out of me."

Aryssa laughed playfully. "Sorry." Bit her lower lip. "Thought you knew I was standing here."

"Wasn't...I guess I wasn't paying attention." Charlie's voice cracked with shyness. The way it usually did when she made it a point to talk with him. "My mind was elsewhere."

"Where was it?" Aryssa tapped her temple teasingly. "It's not missing, is it?"

"No, I still have..." Charlie flustered. "I mean I..." His brow scrunched with exasperation. "I was...I was thinking about work. Just work."

"Work is work," Aryssa commented sarcastically. "Everything okay?"

Charlie scratched his scalp as he leaned against the railing.

"Can't figure it out," he said, looking toward the ceiling. "It's been slow. Unusually slow." Rubbed his chin. "Not in all my years have I seen..." Charlie stopped. His voice hung apologetically. "Didn't mean to dwell on..." absently motioned his hand, "I'm sure you find this boring."

"Not at all," Aryssa said. "I wouldn't have asked if I didn't want to know." She braced herself against the wall to stop from swaying.

Charlie didn't say a word for several seconds, allowing his awkwardness to paint itself on the walls and evaporate into the surroundings. "You're um..." a pause, "kind of out late, aren't you?"

Aryssa tucked the purple bag behind her back. "Couldn't sleep," she answered. Leaned harder against the wall. "One of those nights I couldn't sit still."

Charlie slowly nodded. "I know the feeling." Another pause. "You have a good night dancing?" His face crumpled with embarrassment. "I mean at work?"

Aryssa silently giggled. "Yeah, decent." She gripped the purple bag more firmly. "It's never as good as you want it to be."

Charlie smiled. "No matter how much you make."

"It's never enough." Aryssa finished. "I can't believe we still say that."

"Neither do I." Charlie chuckled. He let a couple of seconds drift by. "You didn't walk past," he thumbed over his shoulder, "that factory, did you?"

Anxiety shook Aryssa's head. "No way." She shuddered. "I try to stay clear of it."

"Place gives me the creeps," Charlie added. "Always cross to the other side of the street."

Aryssa folded her free arm over her waist, hoping to find a

sense of comfort. "Do you really think that it's haunted?"

"As in ghosts?"

"Yeah." Aryssa cocked her hip. Raised her eyebrows incredulously. "What else could there be?"

Charlie hunched ever so slightly. "I have no idea." His voice grew sharper. "Have no desire to find out."

Aryssa reeled backward. Her tone must've been harsher than she realized. This wasn't Sammy she was talking to. She softened her tone. "Me too." Flipped a stand of her hair behind her shoulder. "You back to work tonight?"

"Yeah." Charlie shifted his weight. "You?"

"Unfortunately," Aryssa answered. "No rest for the weary."

Charlie wiped his palms over his thighs. Leaned forward. "Um, I was wondering if you would…" He paused as if to collect his thoughts. "I was wanting to know if…" Something snared his attention. He spun to gaze down the steps and appeared to wave something away. "Not now," he muttered.

Was Charlie talking to someone? Aryssa blinked. Tried to use her lashes to slice the haze that covered her periphery. "Is everything okay?"

Charlie's shoulders stiffened. He turned back around to face Aryssa. "Yeah, um…just fine." Clasped his hand behind his back.

Was Aryssa hearing things? She shook her head. There was no one on the landing below. "What did you want to ask me?"

CHARLIE'S HEART THUMPED against his chest. The nervous sheen of sweat glazing his palms wasn't going away. He desperately wanted to ask Aryssa out. Had wanted to for a

long time. For some reason he had chosen this moment to do
it. What was he thinking? Reason had somehow abandoned
his thoughts and there was no going back. He rubbed his
hands over his thighs again. "Um…yeah." That was a great
choice of words. He winced. Cleared his throat. "I was
wondering if you would like to…?"

"You ARE the person I'm supposed to talk to, aren't
you?" the woman interrupted.

Charlie's thoughts derailed. He desperately tried to wave
the woman away.

"If I would like to…?" Aryssa's tone was brimming with
curiosity.

"Why are you waving me away?" the woman questioned.
"A simple yes or no would suffice."

"I'm kind of busy," Charlie whispered out of the corner of
his mouth.

Aryssa scratched her head. "You wanted to ask me if I'm
busy?"

"No, that's not it," Charlie said uneasily.

"So, you're not the one?" the woman stated.

"I am the one," Charlie mumbled, desperately trying to
project his voice behind him.

"You're the one?" Aryssa cocked her head. Squinted uneasily as if trying to adjust her vision. "Are you talking to
someone else?"

Charlie cleared his throat and did his best to appear nonchalant. "Only to you. Why do you ask?"

"If you're talking to me, then why is your back turned?"
the woman asked callously. "This would go a lot easier if
you…"

Aryssa halfheartedly pointed down the steps. "It looks like
you're trying to…" She flicked her wrist to dismiss the

thought. "Um, never mind." A sigh. "It's been a long night."

"It has," Charlie agreed.

Aryssa motioned down the hallway. "I think I'm going to turn in."

"It has?" the woman questioned. "What are you talking about?" She paused. "That's all you can say? You still haven't…"

Charlie couldn't let Aryssa leave. Couldn't let this opportunity pass. "Not yet," he blurted a little louder than he meant to.

Aryssa's eyes widened.

"I mean…" Charlie tempered his tone in order to keep Aryssa close. "I mean…before you go I wanted to know if…"

"I'm not going anywhere until you tell me what I'm supposed to do."

Charlie ran his hand over his head. Tensed his jaw. Tightened his gut in order to prevent the ball of stress from exploding out of him. "Will you excuse me a minute?" Held up his forefinger. "Please. I'll be right back."

Aryssa appeared hesitant, but nodded her acceptance.

Charlie tiptoed down the steps as quietly as he could. He grabbed the woman by the elbow and led her around the landing, away from Aryssa's view.

"Yes, I'm the one you're supposed to meet," Charlie said with a growl.

The woman folded her arms. "Why couldn't you have just told me that?"

"I'm kind of busy."

The woman leaned back, looked up the flight of steps and shrugged with indifference. "All I know is that I'm supposed to find you and give you this." She pulled a gold coin from her pocket and thrust it forward.

Charlie held up his hands defensively. "Put that away."

"I was told to give it to you," the woman advised. "Do you want it or not?"

Charlie nodded. "Yes, you give it to me. Just not right now." He exhaled slowly. "Meet me at the marina at sundown." Gestured toward the coin. "Give that to me when you get on my boat."

"Tonight? That's a long time from now." The woman swiped her lower lid then sniffled. "What am I supposed to do in the meantime?"

Charlie's insides recoiled. Gut quivered. Couldn't handle a crying woman, especially right at this very moment. "Do what it is you like to do. Grab a coffee. Read a book. Walk around a store." He paused "Trust me; it'll go by fast."

Another sniffle. "I don't see why you can't take care of this…"

Charlie glanced up toward Aryssa. He couldn't keep her waiting much longer. "What is with you people today?" he mumbled so only he could hear. "I'm not a twenty-four-seven service." Rubbed his eye to try to blunt his frustration. "I've got to go." Spun away from the woman. "I'll see you tonight."

"But…but I don't think I can wait until…"

Charlie refused to listen to the woman any longer. He had a more pressing issue to take care of. He marched up the steps to once and for all confront Aryssa.

Aryssa was standing on the landing, right where he had left her. She looked down on him and smiled. "Is everything okay?"

He opened his mouth, but no words came out. His throat seemed to have swollen shut. Heart bashed against his ribs. Thoughts began to unravel and became jumbled. His momentary confidence started to disintegrate and blow apart like sand in the wind. Palms once again glazed themselves with sweat. "All's fine," he struggled to say.

Charlie took a deep breath and let it out. Hoped the very act would calm his shaking nerves. How could this one person mess him up so much? Would he finally have enough guts to ask Aryssa out?

5

MARJORIE WALKED OUT of the apartment building into the bright morning sunshine. She sniffled, then wiped away the last remnants of the tear that had crawled over her lid. Purposefully squeezed the coin to try to quell her swelling annoyance. Why wouldn't that man just take the coin? She had done what she was told. Why did she have to wait until tonight to give it to him? Didn't he realize that she had things to do?

Never mind work. There were letters that had to be mailed. The grocery store for brownie mix. Laundry that was piled high. Kids that would have to be picked up from school. Dinner that would need to be started. Marjorie didn't have the time to wait around.

She glanced up and down the quiet street. Readjusted her jacket as a way to steady her frustration. There was that café near the marina. The thought nestled into the folds of her mind. A cup of coffee would be nice, especially before she had to deal with the stress of work and then all those damn errands.

It was settled. Marjorie took off down the sidewalk toward the river. The abandoned factory loomed in the immediate distance. A car pitted with rust rolled by. She rarely made it to this part of the city because, well, she never really had a reason to. Still, there was something strange about being here. She scratched her cheek with uncertainty. Shouldn't she be on her way to work right about now? An image of herself driving on the freeway zoomed across her vision. Fiddling with the radio. Cell phone ringing. A sea of red taillights suddenly illuminating. She slammed the brakes and...

"A pass up the side of the field," a male voice rang out. "Blows by the first defender. Then another." Something solid bound across the cement. "He passes toward the center."

The image in Marjorie's memory disintegrated. She looked up to see a man dressed in dirt-stained jeans and an overstretched shirt. He chased a tumbling rock along the side of the road.

The homeless man kicked the rock forward. Passed it from one foot to the other. "The evil number six tries to slide into his ankles." The man sprang upward. "But no! His dirty play didn't work!"

Marjorie leaned against a cinder-block building and waited for the man to pass.

"All that stands between him and destiny is one thing. One gigantic thing...the goalie!" The vagrant spun. Edged the rock onward. "The crowd's going crazy!" The rock bounced along the street as the make-believe screams of thousands of people echoed from his throat. "Time's running out."

The homeless man jammed his foot into the ground, causing the rock to shoot forward. It bound relentlessly over the cement. "Goal! It's a goal!" He raised his arms in triumph. "Unbelievable!" Jumped up and down. Started to sing. "We are the champions." Spun in a circle. "We are the..." Stopped right where he was standing when he spotted Marjorie. Arms fell. Mouth hung open.

Marjorie smiled. Waved sheepishly. "Don't mind me." She

pointed in the direction of the marina. "Just passing by."

The vagrant clasped his hands together. "Tough game, but we managed to pull it out."

"I see that," Marjorie said as she shuffled sideways.

"This game…well, it suddenly came around on my way to work." The man ran his hand over his hair. "Well…it's kind of like work. I get paid to help." Gestured down the road. "You ever been to Differ and Sons Hardware?"

"Can't say that I have," Marjorie answered cautiously.

"You got to go. Mister Differ is a great boss." The homeless man tapped his chest. "Tell him I sent you. The name's Johnny. Tell him that. He'll know." Johnny tapped his chin inquisitively, then cocked his head as he looked hard at Marjorie. "You've come a long way."

Marjorie hesitated. "Like I said, I'm just passing through."

Thankfully Johnny kept his distance. "You know this isn't a good place to be." Shook his head. "Not at all."

Small waves of panic rippled from Marjorie's core. "Noted." She turned away from Johnny. "I really should be going."

"Make sure you stay away from that place." Johnny pointed toward the abandoned factory. "No one should ever go there."

"Okay," Marjorie said in an appeasing tone as she walked a little faster.

"No, really," Johnny stated. "And make sure you give that coin to the right person."

How'd he know? Marjorie had it cupped in her hand and out of sight. She clutched it even tighter. Looked over her shoulder at Johnny, but kept her mouth shut.

Johnny had his hands on his hips. "It goes to one person and one person only." He paused. "Very important. Very, very important. Very, very, very…"

"I get it," Marjorie said in a way to block Johnny's repetitiveness. "I'll make sure."

"Hope so," Johnny said. "Mostly good people get 'em. Not always, but most of the time." He coughed. "Certain people want them and some of them are no good. Just make sure you give it to the right one."

"I'll make sure," Marjorie said reassuringly. Was Johnny spewing a bunch of nonsense? Sure sounded like it. That factory. The coin. It wasn't like that guy she was supposed to give it to was willing to take it. At least not until tonight. She scoffed. What's wrong with everyone?

Marjorie kept walking, causing Johnny to fade into the distance. The factory loomed larger. The marina and that café had to be close. A few cars passed by. Two men in business suits were walking toward her. Well-dressed. Clean-shaven. In fact, they were both decent-looking. They appeared deeply engrossed in a conversation. Maybe this side of town wasn't so bad after all.

She tried to keep her attention forward, but she couldn't help but smile as the men approached. The taller of the two, the one in the light gray suit, smiled back. "Hello." His voice was smooth. "How are you today?"

Marjorie slowed her pace. "I'm well." She hoped she had covered the shyness in her tone. "And you?"

The man in the gray suit took a deep breath. "Can't help but feel good on a morning like this."

Marjorie glanced at the blue sky. "I agree." A brief image of the radio, her cell phone, the taillights, her slamming the brakes flashed across the screen in her mind. She shuddered.

"Are you okay?" the shorter man asked. He tucked his hand into his pocket. "It looked like you were thinking about something."

Marjorie scratched her brow with doubt. "It's nothing. Been a busy morning."

The man in the gray suit slowly nodded. "I hope it gets better." His voice was sweetened with reassurance. "Where are you headed?"

"That way." Marjorie gestured down the street. "Heard there's a café near the marina."

"There is," the man in the blue suit confirmed. "The Coffee Bean." A smile. "Just keep following this road and you'll run right into it. Definitely worth the stop."

"Thank you," Marjorie replied gratefully.

"You're welcome."

"Are you sure that's where you want to go?" the man in the gray suit questioned.

Marjorie nodded. "Yeah." Cocked her head with uncertainty. "Is there someplace better?"

"I wouldn't say it's better," the man in gray responded. "But, more fitting for a woman in your position."

A tiny shock rippled through Marjorie. "More fitting?"

"Yes," the man in blue answered. "I'd say better suited for your situation."

"My situation is just fine," Marjorie responded.

"Do you even know why you're taking this road to that cafe?"

"Of course I do." Marjorie stepped forward uneasily. "I'm supposed to meet...meet someone." A pause. "In fact, I'm running a little late."

"I don't think your someone is waiting for you," the man in the gray suit said firmly. "In fact, the person you want isn't going to be there until later tonight."

Dread clenched Marjorie's throat. How'd he know that? "I don't know what you're talking about." Her tone undulated with indecision "I know who I'm supposed to be meeting."

The man in the gray suit chuckled. "I don't think you do." He stepped sideways to block her path. "I'm guessing you haven't fully grasped everything that's happened to you this morning."

Panic trembled through Marjorie's legs. "I'm well aware of my morning and the things that I need to get done." Was she really aware, though? Uneasiness cramped her gut. There was something off about the morning. Something off about walking in this part of the city. Something she couldn't put her finger on. She crossed her arms to keep it all contained. "If you'll excuse me, I've got things to do and places to be."

The man in the blue suit pointed at her hand. "And what about that?'

"What about what?" She could feel the edges of the coin pressing against her palm.

Both men chuckled. "You know very well what I'm talking about," the blue-suited man said.

"It's none of your business." Marjorie tried to weave around the men, but the man in gray became an unmovable barrier. "You're in my way."

The man in the gray suit momentarily hesitated, and then stepped aside, extending his arm to allow her to pass. "As you wish."

A faint huff squeezed past Marjorie's lips. Her heart thumped wildly, but she refused to let it influence her hardened expression. She lifted her chin, straightened her shoulders and stepped forward. Took another step. And another. Each one successively filling her with a little more confidence.

Marjorie was nearly untangled from the situation when suddenly each of her arms was snatched. "I think you'll find your situation better with us," the gray-suited man hissed.

"Let me go!" Marjorie screamed. She desperately tried to wrangle free from the two men. Their grasp only became tighter.

"Stop fighting," the man in the blue suit demanded.

She remained defiant. Kicked the blue-suited man's shin. He barely flinched. Marjorie crouched toward the ground, dug her heels and yanked. It didn't work. Instead, the men effortlessly hoisted her upright and dragged her toward the abandoned factory.

"Help me!" Marjorie shouted. She attempted to catch her feet so she could stand. So she could resist. "Someone help…!"

A truck drove within a few feet of her, but didn't stop. A man smoking a cigarette never bothered to look up from his phone. What's wrong with everyone?

"Somebody!"

The gray-suited man snickered. "Scream all you want. They can't hear you."

Marjorie refused to believe him. "Help me!"

Nothing.

The factory got closer. Marjorie couldn't stop their unrelenting progress. The man in the blue suit ripped open her hand and snatched the coin. "You won't be needing this."

"Give it back!" She tried to wrestle her arm free to get it. "That's mine." What was that coin for, anyway? Why was no one willing to help her? "Somebody…I need…!"

"Damn it!" The blue suited man yelled. "It happened again."

"Forget about that thing right now," the man in gray said. "I don't even know why you bothered."

Somehow the coin was back in Marjorie's palm. She squeezed it for reassurance even as her strength waned. The factory loomed over her. The dark, foreboding entrance drew nearer. Her children, husband, work, those errands blazed across her thoughts. Something had happened to her this morning. But what?

The static of screeching tires burst from the speakers inside her head. A flash of her cell phone falling from her hand. Crunching metal. Shattering glass. Air bags exploding. Pain piercing her head. Her back. The world spinning uncontrollably. Had she been in an accident? If so, what exactly had happened? Could she be…?

The two men thrust Marjorie through the door and into a cavern of darkness. She was heaved into the void's throat and swallowed into the abyss of nothingness.

6

CHARLIE YAWNED, TRIED to rub the sleep from his eye, but instead fingered a small crust from the corner near his nose. He dragged the jagged piece over his cheek, gripped it between his fingers and flicked it away.

He sighed. It was barely past one in the afternoon. A stagnant haze dulled the edges of his mind and numbed his consciousness. It was a rarity for him to be awake this early, even rarer still to be up and moving. Charlie put his hand over his stomach. His gut squirmed with nervousness, which was one small reason he hadn't slept that well. The bigger one was her.

Charlie gazed at his reflection in the glass door. At his long, black hair. Dark clothes. Thick features. Glaring eyes. Chiseled cheeks. Stocky frame. No doubt he looked menacing, even scary, if he felt like projecting it. But still, how was Aryssa able to turn him into a babbling ball of melting Jell-O? A sigh. He still had an hour or so before they were to meet for lunch.

He reached for the door to G.G's Pawn and Coin Shop. Faltered. What happens if she doesn't show? Charlie fought the sag in his shoulders, clenched his jaw and shoved doubt aside. Aryssa will show up. She said she would. For God's sake, just be confident.

Charlie stepped into the glaring fluorescent lights and

stood before the counter. Some talk show blared on the television off to the side. The same scruffy, bald guy was behind the glass case. He sat on a worn-out stool, blankly stared at the television and absentmindedly chewed on a piece of a bagel. Charlie knew this man by sight. He could easily pick him out of a crowd, but just couldn't remember his name. A silent scoff. Did it matter?

Charlie took the six gold coins out of his pocket and laid them on the glass countertop.

The counterman drank something out of a mug and smacked his lips. "Sellin'?"

"Like I do every time I come here," Charlie answered.

The man grunted. Picked up one of the coins and held it before his eye. Turned it back and forth. "Cash or credit?"

"Cash, like always," Charlie responded impatiently.

"You know," the counterman sucked on his teeth, "these things aren't exactly easy to sell."

"What do you care?" Charlie questioned. "You melt them down for the gold."

"It's not that easy." The counterman placed the coin on an electronic scale. "I just can't drop these off any ol' place." He cleared his throat. "You think I want the cops wandering in here and asking questions?"

Charlie kept quiet as he pushed the remaining coins across the glass.

"There's a ton of risks playing the middle man." The counterman took another coin and placed it on the scale. "In all the years we've done business, have I ever asked where you get these things?"

Charlie shook his head.

"And I'm not going to," the counterman advised. "Truthfully, I don't want to know."

"So don't ask," Charlie blurted. "You get well paid for your time and trouble." A tense pause. "In all the years we've known each other, have I ever tried to rip you off?"

The counterman shook his head.

Charlie rested his fists on top of the case. "And I expect the same in return."

The counterman's brows arched. "You know damn well I give you the best deals." He gestured toward the exit. "You can always try some of the other guys and see what that gets you."

Charlie tipped his chin. Puffed his chest. "I've been faithfully coming here for years. Don't take too kindly to being suckered."

"Neither do I," the man argued.

"At least we agree on something," Charlie said.

The counterman finished weighing the coins. He punched the buttons of a calculator, slid it in front of Charlie and waited.

Charlie swallowed the bitter annoyance that coated his tongue. The number was lower than he had expected. He opened his mouth to complain, but bottled the words in his throat. Nitpicking wouldn't do any good. This guy didn't have to buy the coins, and he could easily tell Charlie to go somewhere else. Then what? Could he trust those other pawn shops? He had tried a few of them in the past and had never made out as well as he had here. No way was Charlie going to humiliate himself and come crawling back with his tail between his legs. He desperately needed the money. Bills were due. Besides, this place was close to home and too familiar to leave. Charlie sighed silently and nodded his acceptance.

The counterman disappeared into the back of the store and within a few minutes returned with a small stack of bills.

He extended it to Charlie. "Here you go."

Charlie counted the money, purposely laying each bill on the countertop as he went. No way was he going to get ripped off. When he was finished, he stuffed the cash into his pocket. "Until the next time."

The counterman tipped his head. "Later."

Charlie stepped outside the pawn shop and exhaled sharply. Anxiety sank its claws into his gut and twisted. A glance down the street in the direction of the Penn Bar and Grill. It was time to meet up with Aryssa. Hopefully she'd show up.

THE COUNTERMAN PALMED the six coins. Gazed at the way the gold sparkled lustily under the lights. He watched Charlie in the security cameras as he left through the front door. Fidgeted in his chair. Waited until Charlie was well down the street before picking up his phone. He punched the number he had scribbled on a scrap piece of paper taped to the side of the case. The phone rang. It rang again. And again.

"Hello," answered Sammy.

"Hey it's me, over at G.G's," the counterman said.

"You got something for me?" It sounded as if Sammy were trying to contain his enthusiasm."

"Yeah. Just got 'em."

"How many?"

The counterman hesitated. He opened his hand and gazed at the six coins. "Five."

"Sounds like it's been a slow week," Sammy commented.

"Must have been." The counterman clicked his tongue. "You want 'em?"

"Of course," Sammy said. "Usual price?"

The counterman wavered for a couple of seconds. "Yeah,

the usual price."

"I'll be there in a bit," Sammy's voice was rushed. "Thanks for calling." The line went silent.

The counterman set his phone on the counter and stared at the six coins. Why was Sammy so eager to have these? What made them so special? He slid one of the coins into his pocket. The other five he placed in an envelope and locked it in a small box. There was no doubt Sammy would be by soon. He'd have to watch him closely and find out why he was so desperate to have these.

7

SAMMY STEPPED OUT of his car and eagerly slid his cell phone into his pocket. "Finally," he whispered. It had been a few weeks since he had last heard from G.G. Sammy needed coins. Any amount would do. Still, only five? It was something, but not nearly enough.

He exhaled sharply, trying to quell the stress that rattled his nerves. It didn't help; there was too much to simply blow it all away. Those new recruits were arriving sometime soon, and that meant the next payment was due. The Network had been ratcheting up the pressure to get their money. If only things hadn't gotten so screwed up following the last shipment. Sammy uneasily pinched the bridge of his nose. And the time before that hadn't gone so smoothly, either.

An image of the coins dangled in his vision. The Network loved them. Practically craved them. It had to be the reason Sammy and Ariek were still alive and breathing. If only he could figure out a way to gather those other coins, then his problems would be solved tenfold. Sammy squeezed his frustration into his fist. All the things they had tried hadn't shown any promise. What the hell was he supposed to do now?

Sammy unintentionally brushed his hands over his crotch. The burning ache intensified. He walked even faster across the lot to try to quench the fiery lust. Aryssa should have just given him what he wanted. She had eagerly done it before, and she had to be more than willing to do it again. Why was she making things so difficult?

If only he could have slid his hands across her smooth skin and taut body. Gripped her luscious hips. Run his tongue across her slim belly and along the inside of her yearning thighs. Up toward the inviting warmth of her...

Honk!

Sammy shuddered. Sprang sideways away from the grill of the black SUV. The man in the car raised his hands in irritation and mouthed something unpleasant.

Sammy scowled. "Why don't you watch were you're going!"

The SUV sped by. The driver extended his middle finger.

"Same to you, asshole!" Sammy shouted. Swung his arm to brush the moment away. "Hope you get in an accident." He grabbed the door handle to his convenience store and yanked it open.

His nephew was behind the counter, exactly where he was supposed to be. Thank goodness for the small things. Except he still had that dopey expression painted across his face. Jaw slowly chomping on a piece of gum as if it were a cow's cud. Cheeks drooped. Eyes glazed in a sheen of boredom.

"Hey, Uncle Sam," his nephew called out sluggishly.

"How's things?"

"Yeah." His nephew slowly exhaled. "Good."

Sammy quietly sighed. He shook away the last pieces of his irritation that the SUV driver had given him, but his nephew's presence immediately filled the void. "How was the morning rush?"

His nephew shrugged. "Fine." Stared at Sammy as if he

was going to say something else, but his lips failed to move.

Sammy bit his tongue to prevent the barrage of expletives from exploding out of his mouth. "Better than bad news, I guess," he said in his best positive tone. "By the way, did you get those boxes of gum out onto the shelves?"

"Umm…" His nephew bit his lip. "Been kind of busy."

Sammy glanced over the aisle and down the glass coolers along the walls. A single customer was looking over the bottles of chilled coffee. There were two, maybe even three, cars at the gas pumps. Plenty of time to get the gum stocked. Not like the task required any large degree of intelligence. He opened his mouth, but instead swallowed the sarcasm that was ready to rifle out of his throat.

"Can you please get them stocked sooner rather than later?" Sammy flicked his wrist. "And maybe straighten this place out a bit. You know, make it clean and presentable."

His nephew was reluctant to speak. "I suppose."

Sammy quietly grumbled. Exhaled slowly. "I'll be in my office for a moment, then I have to run an important errand."

"Sure." His nephew lethargically turned as if he were an old clock running on rusted gears. He grabbed the microphone. "Umm…pump five." A sharp scoff. "Like, you need to press one of those blinking buttons if you want it to work."

"Do you think you could be a little friendlier when you do that?" Sammy questioned.

"I was," his nephew countered. "How is it my problem if they can't understand something so easy?"

"It's not how you do business," Sammy replied. "It's called customer…" His nephew was back to gazing over the lot. Sammy silently growled again. "Just keep the place running while I'm gone."

"Uh-huh," his nephew responded absently.

Sammy stomped into his office and nearly slammed the door, but caught himself before it launched out of his hand. He glanced at the boxes stacked in the corner. Boxes of cups and lids for the soda and coffee. Candy and gum. Cell-phone supplies. Cigarettes. Lighters. Cleaning supplies toward the bottom. At the very bottom were the animal banks. Stuffed animal banks, to be exact. The kind meant for kids. A box he had gotten for dirt cheap from one of his suppliers, but had never bothered to display in the store. There were elephants, raccoons, dogs and cats. Only one bear, but it was one special bear. He purposely kept the box on the bottom of the stack, because, well, who would want to rummage through something like that?

He walked over and knelt before the safe at the side of his desk, punched in the combination and took out the money he needed for G.G's. When he was finished he locked the door, solemnly tapped the top of the safe with his fingers and let loose a drawn-out sigh.

There was so much that needed to be done. He and Ariek couldn't afford to screw things up this time; he shivered over the thought of what would happen. But this was not the time to dwell on such things. First things first, he needed to buy those coins. He stood and tucked the money into his pocket.

Sammy slid his hand over the box of animal banks, walked out of his office and headed for the exit. His nephew was holding the microphone with his fist and staring out at the gas pumps, seemingly waiting to pounce on another customer. A restrained grumble rattled Sammy's throat.

The morning manager was out sick, the afternoon one couldn't make it for another few hours and his nighttime staff had already gone home. Of all days, why today? Could he trust his nephew to keep things running smoothly while he was gone? Avoid any unnecessary controversy? At least his nephew couldn't burn the place down. Could he? Sammy's heart anxiously pounded against his ribs. A shake of his head. He'd make it a point to get back as soon as possible.

8

STICKY GLOBS OF sweat slumped off humidity's fleshy extremities and slathered Aryssa. Dewdrops percolated on her forehead, her neck, her back and crawled down her skin like bugs overdosed on Xanax. The sun's overly bright rays relentlessly drilled into her eyes and pounded her skull. She massaged her temples to try to relieve the headache. How had she managed to forget her sunglasses, yet again? Last night's bourbon was partially to blame. The bottle exposed itself like a second-rate cabaret dancer from behind the thick curtain hanging inside her head. That extra hit of crush hadn't helped matters, either.

Aryssa's stomach churned on a sea of melted cheese. Her arms hung like decaying branches from the knotted sockets of her shoulders. She slipped under the awning of a jewelry shop and slowly exhaled. Fought back the vomit that wanted to rocket from her gut. She was running late and the Penn Bar and Grill was only a block away. Still, she needed to rest. Needed this brief reprieve to give her that final nudge to make it the rest of the way.

After a few deep breaths she heaved herself toward the bar and was soon standing in front of the door. She reached for the handle, but stopped when a twinge of anxiety tumbled across her nerves. A sheen of sweat glazed her palms. How long had it been since she'd been on a date? Six months? A year? Longer than that?

She ran her hand over her hair, then flipped a few layers behind her shoulders. Was this even considered a date? Maybe it was nothing more than a simple get-together. She nodded her head in agreement. Just two neighbors talking. Despite the mental justification, the nervousness wasn't going away. Charlie had always been kind of cute. A little gruff, but then again, he was someone who could make her feel safe.

Aryssa sighed, opened the door and stepped inside. The acrid odor of the decades-old building swirled around her head and crawled into her nose. The geriatric scent seemed to ooze from deep beneath the walls, maybe from the building's skeleton itself. She reflexively sniffed. Got a whiff of stale body odor mixed with the stench of decomposing alcohol, dried grease and endless conversations of counterfeit optimism.

The smell made Aryssa's head teeter. Made her belly want to purge itself of the caustic veneer clinging to its sides. She tightened her gut to keep from retching. Took a deep breath and momentarily held it. Somehow managed to extinguish the launch out of her stomach.

Charlie stood and waved from the far end of the place. The dark jeans and white dress shirt he was wearing made Aryssa's heart skip a beat. Damn...he looked even better cleaned up.

Aryssa's anxiety trickled down her legs and puddled in her feet. Her steps became heavy. Balance a little off. Shoes seemed to unnecessarily clunk across the floor. The hangover wasn't making it any easier. Still, Charlie looked good...well, very good. Wasn't this supposed to be a simple get-together?

"Hey," Charlie said shyly. "Glad you made it."

Aryssa smiled. "No problem." Ugh. Did she really just say

that? Could she sound any more conceited? "I mean…thanks for inviting me." An awkward pause. "Sorry I'm running a little behind. Hope you weren't waiting too long."

"Not really," Charlie tucked his hand into his pocket. "Did you get some sleep?"

"Sort of." Aryssa rubbed her temple. "I forgot to set my alarm."

"I can never sleep when I have to use one of those." Charlie gestured at her head. "Headache?"

Aryssa nodded. "Rough night."

"That sucks," Charlie said. "I never see you up when I'm coming home."

Aryssa dropped her arm. "You…you know how it is. Work was so busy that I left all wound up. I get home and my place is scorching hot. Nothing's working. The fans suck. So, of course I couldn't fall asleep." She sighed. Was she complaining too much? "Anyway, I had to get out of my apartment and…and one thing lead to another." A pause. "Basically, I had to get out and get some air."

"I know the feeling." Charlie sat down. "Working nights can mess with your rhythms."

"It does." Aryssa slid into her chair. The sudden change in altitude made her head throb harder. "Don't get me wrong, I love the nights. But I don't mind the daytime either. It's just that on some days it's too bright." An exasperated sigh. "Sometimes I wish I could turn off that burning ball they call the sun."

Charlie chuckled. "That's why I chose to sit way back here." Tipped his chin toward the windows in the front. "Hope you don't mind?"

"Not at all," Aryssa answered with gratitude. "If only it was that easy to get my fans to work."

"I can take a look at them."

"You know how to fix things like that?"

"Yeah." Charlie nodded. "I know my way around a toolbox."

"That would be amazing if you…"

"I can come over before I go to…"

"Hi folks." The waitress stepped up to the table. "Can I start you off with something to drink?"

Charlie looked at Aryssa. "You want a beer or something?"

Aryssa moaned silently. Her gut grumbled with annoyance over the thought of being doused with alcohol. Temples thumped in agreement. "I think I may have to pass."

"Not feeling it?" Charlie asked.

"Not really." Aryssa tapped her belly.

"Too much last night?"

Irritation singed the edges of Aryssa's voice. "How'd you know?"

"You looked a little tipsy in the stairwell."

"I did?"

Charlie uneasily rubbed his forehead. Pinched his thumb and forefinger together and then softened his voice. "Well, just a little."

Aryssa said nothing for a few long seconds, allowing her irritation to dissipate. "Ugh." Squinted. "Was it that bad?"

Charlie shrugged. "I just happened to notice."

"I guess the bourbon looked too good to pass up." Aryssa flicked her hair. "Like I said, one thing led to another and well, you know."

"I hate when that happens," the waitress interjected. "It sneaks up on you."

"It does," Charlie chimed in.

The waitress tipped her chin as she looked at Aryssa. "You know what they say?"

"No, what?" Aryssa curiously asked.

"A little hair of the dog goes a long way."

"Hair of..." Aryssa mumbled. She braced her elbow on the table and then her head in her hand. "Where did that come from?"

"The middle ages," Charlie said a little too eagerly. His enthusiasm downshifted. "At least I think it did."

"Did you read that?" Aryssa questioned.

"I think so," Charlie said. "In fact, I must have. All I know is that they believed if a dog bit you, you had to get some of that dog's hair and rub it on the wound."

The waitress scrunched her face. "That's gross."

"Why in the hell would they do that?" Aryssa said with disgust.

Charlie shrugged. "They thought it was the only way to make sure the wound didn't become infected. Hence, hair of the dog." A pause. "It somehow found its way into the belief that drinking would cure a hangover."

"I'll be damned. I've never heard that," Aryssa commented. "Kind of makes sense."

"Which part?" Charlie asked with a sly smile. "Rubbing dog hair on a wound or drinking for a hangover?"

"Ha ha," Aryssa said. "I'm just saying that it kind of makes sense how that saying came about. Do you think drinking really works?"

"I think it does," the waitress answered. "I have friends who swear by a Bloody Mary."

Aryssa bit her lower lip. "As long as it's not too spicy."

"Trust me, you're going to love it." The waitress turned to Charlie. "And you?"

"Pint of Oberon and a glass of water."

"Make that two waters," Aryssa added.

"No problem. Let me get those for you."

Charlie looked at Aryssa. She briefly gazed back. Awkward silence. Some announcer was going over last night's sports highlights on the nearby television. The hum of several conversations echoed throughout the place. Ice tumbled into a glass.

"So..." Aryssa said hesitantly. "Did you do anything productive with your morning, or did you sleep late, too?"

"Believe it or not, I was up kind of early," Charlie said.

"How come?"

"I just woke up." Charlie leaned back into his chair. "Don't know why, I just did. I hate when it happens."

"I do too. I end up feeling like crap for the rest of the day."

"Part of being a night-shifter."

"One of the few drawbacks," Aryssa added. Her stomach quietly rumbled. Still, the conversation was going much better. More relaxed. She nestled into her chair and did her best to suppress the hangover. "When it does happen, I usually just lay around. Then I feel guilty for not doing anything, but at the same time I'm too tired to get up and actually do something about it."

"I've done that," Charlie agreed. "Not this morning, though. I managed to pry myself out of bed."

Aryssa softly clapped her hands. "Kudos to you. However, the bigger question is, did you get anything done?"

Charlie chuckled. His stone-chiseled cheeks crinkled into a smile. A smile that made him...dare she say it...even better-looking. "Not really. A couple of errands. Nothing special."

"At least you did something."

"True, but I was too tired to..."

The waitress stepped up and placed the drinks on the table. "I'll be back in a few to get your order."

"Take your time," Charlie said. He raised his glass. "Cheers."

Aryssa grabbed her Bloody Mary and clinked Charlie's glass. "Cheers to you, too." She took a long drink through the straw.

The acidic tomato juice flowed across her taste buds. A tinge of saltiness swam beneath the current. The burn of vodka quickly followed. It all sloshed together, swirled down her gullet and swam into her stomach. Her gut buckled in revolt. The door to her memory swung open. That time she had drunk so many vodka-and-tonics that she'd barfed over and over again in her friend's backyard.

A waitress delivered a couple of burger baskets to a nearby table. The heavy, grease-laden odor crashed into Aryssa's olfactory sensors and triggered another distant memory. That cheap diner on Forest Avenue. A sweltering afternoon. Undercooked beef and the way it sat like a rock in her stomach.

Aryssa's head spun like a merry-go-round. The noise in the bar intensified. So did the hammering against her temples. Heartbeat echoed in her ears. The oven in her core flicked on and instantly set itself to broil. A trickle of sweat dribbled down her back. She struggled to get her mouth to move. "Where's the bathroom?"

Charlie pointed. "Over there."

"I'll be right back."

"Please, go and..."

Aryssa was up and running before Charlie could finish his sentence. Stars swirled in and out of her vision. She tightened her gut, desperately trying to keep it all in, despite her stomach's unyielding retching.

She burst through the bathroom door and slapped her hand over her mouth as if it were a cork trying to clog the rumblings in her gut. It wasn't enough. The contents roared upward, churned through her throat, burst into her mouth and exploded between her fingers before she could lean over the toilet. The red liquid splashed across her shirt. Dribbled onto her jeans.

Another wave struck. She made it over the toilet just in time. Except the vomit crashed onto the rim and splattered across her pants. She retched again, and again, and again, until her stomach was completely drained.

She quickly cleaned off the porcelain with toilet paper and looked at herself in the mirror. "Oh crap," she mumbled. "I look like shit." A glaze of sweat varnished her pale skin. What little mascara she had managed to put on was streaking down her cheeks as if she were a psychotic extra in a horror movie. The circles beneath her eyes looked like the decaying carcass of road kill. Of course those red stains splattered across her clothes made her look like she had taken part in a damn axe murder.

Aryssa exhaled sharply. How could she face Charlie looking so...so repulsive? There was no way he would find her attractive. Embarrassment singed her cheeks. She bowed her head and braced her hands on the edge of the sink. The chill of panic swept away all doubt, leaving her with only one option. She needed to get out of here and it needed to be now.

Aryssa opened the bathroom door and gazed out at the crowd. Charlie was watching the televisions with his back to her. Everyone seemed focused on their conversations. It was now or never. With her head down, she slipped out of the bathroom, scampered across the bar and out into the piercing bright sunshine. Next stop, home and bed.

9

SAMMY HOISTED HIMSELF out of his car, leaned his elbows on the roof and glanced over at the gas station. There were cars parked by the pumps. People were doing what they were supposed to be doing, and that was filling them with gas. It was as simple as that. Could things really be going this well?

The drab voice of his nephew wasn't blanketing some unsuspecting customer with its condescending overtones. There were no flames licking the entrance or tarnishing the windows. No plumes of smoke billowing through the roof. The *open* sign was still lit. A sigh of relief. Everything appeared to be perfectly normal.

Sammy strolled across the parking lot, fiddled with the coins in his pocket and cautiously opened the door to the store. Business as usual. A couple of people were browsing the coolers. One of them grabbed a bottle of Coke. To his left his nephew was ringing up a sale for a customer. He still wore that dimwitted expression, though. Moved as if he were a sloth on Ativan. "Change…fifty-two cents," his nephew said.

"Thank you," the customer replied.

"Want the receipt?"

The customer shook his head.

His nephew lethargically ripped the strip of paper from the register, crumpled it and dropped it into the garbage.

"Have a nice day," Sammy mumbled. Why couldn't his nephew say the words? Instead, he slowly exhaled and proceeded to stare off into space. Still chewed that damn piece of gum like a calf eating out of a trough.

Sammy squeezed his fists to contain his frustration, then unfolded them, effectively releasing the tension. "Everything seems to be running fine."

"Yep," his nephew replied.

"Any issues?"

"Nope."

"Phone calls?"

"Nope."

Sammy bit his lip with uncertainty. Dare he ask? "Did you get those boxes of gum stocked?"

His nephew sighed sharply. Shoulders stooped. "Yes."

"You did?" Sammy did his best to contain his surprise.

A huff. "Uhh…yeah."

Sammy shook away the wave of disbelief that had crashed over him. He glanced down the candy aisle. It was true. Boxes were filled. Organized. His nephew had done what was asked of him. "Nice job." A point toward the back of the store. "I'll be in my office."

"Uh-huh." His nephew turned and grabbed the microphone. "Umm…like, pump three." Sarcasm molded itself into his tone. "You need to like push one of those blinking lights if you…"

Sammy's frustration boiled over. He stepped toward the counter and reached. First he'd choke the life out of the microphone. Then maybe his nephew. Thoughts of his sister and mother flashed across his mind. Of the endless scolding he would receive from his family. The difficulties of trying to hide his nephew's body. All he had to do was turn around. Let it go. Just walk away.

Sammy silently huffed. Let his head sag, then dropped his arm. There were matters more pressing that needed his attention. He reached into his pocket, gripped the coins and headed into his office.

The boxes appeared to be a little disheveled. Sammy shrugged his indifference. It was to be expected, since his nephew had to rummage through them to get the gum.

He pulled a box off the top of the pile and casually set it on the floor. Took another one off. Then another. Something wasn't right. A tinge of worry crawled over his back. He tried to shudder it away, but it clung too tightly.

Sammy lifted another box and gently set it on the stack next to him. It still wasn't adding up. Was it the way his nephew had restacked the boxes? Something was missing, but what? The label on the bottom box snared his attention. Cigarettes. What were they doing there? It should be the...

"No, no, no!" Sammy yelled. The moorings to his heart broke loose and sent the beating organ free-falling into the pit of despair. He frantically peeled away the boxes until he got to the last one. Tore open the lid. Cigarettes. Cartons and cartons of them. It should be...be...

He ran out to the counter and angrily jabbed his finger toward his office. "Where are...?" Struggled to get the words to roll off his enraged tongue. "Where in the hell are...are the...the animal banks?"

His nephew's eyes widened. He pointed to the shelves behind Sammy.

Sammy smacked his forehead with the palm of his hand. "What are they doing there?"

Nephew shrugged. "As good a spot as any. They're a perfect fit."

"Are you kidding me?" Sammy repeatedly stabbed his finger into the counter. "What did I tell you to do while I was gone?"

"Watch the store and stock the packs of gum."

"And that was it." Sammy nodded his head violently. "Nothing else but stock the gum!"

"That's not entirely true," his nephew stated simply.

"Not entirely true?" Sammy hissed through the valve of his lips that tried to contain his boiling anger. "How's that not entirely true?"

His nephew's eyes narrowed. "You said to straighten up the place. Make it look clean." A pause. "So I did." Tipped his chin toward the shelves. "The thing was empty, so I filled it." Folded his arms over his chest. "Empty shelves don't make money."

Sammy eyed the banks that were crammed on the shelf. "Is this all of them?"

"Yes." His nephew exhaled his displeasure. "They were sitting back there doing nothing. You should be happy."

"Why should I be happy?"

"Because I sold two of them."

"You what?" Sammy squeezed his gut in order to contain the lava of irritation that was about to spew out of his mouth.

"I said," his nephew articulated firmly. "I sold two of them. I don't know why this is such a big deal. I moved the merchandise and made you money."

"Big deal? Do you realize that…?" Sammy gritted his teeth. Let the explanation drop. Looked over at the banks once again. Where was the bear? The one holding all the coins? "Tell me that you didn't sell the bear?"

"The first one," his nephew said proudly.

The weight of the world fell across Sammy's shoulders.

Clamped his chest. Was this really happening? He fought to keep his breathing steady. Struggled to fill his lungs with air. "Who bought it?"

His nephew shrugged. "Some little girl."

Sammy sliced the thickened atmosphere with the side of his hand. "There's no way that some little girl could afford to buy that. No way." He tensed his entire body. "She had to be with a parent." Tapped his forehead to jar his thoughts. "Think Sammy," he mumbled. "Did they use a credit card?"

"Who…the little girl?"

"No," Sammy answered pointedly. "The parents. Her parents or someone looking responsible. You know—the damn adult she was with. No little girl is going to wander in without one."

"No one used a card," his nephew advised. "Paid in cash. It was her allowance money. Her sister bought one of the dogs."

Sammy gripped the sides of his head. "How am I going to find them?"

"Why do you want to find them?"

"So I can get them back!"

His nephew cocked his head with uncertainty. "You want them back?"

"I was supposed to…they were to go…" Sammy scratched his scalp. He couldn't come up with a reasonable-sounding explanation except, "They weren't supposed to be for sale."

"Why didn't you say so in the first place," his nephew said. "Or else I wouldn't have put them out."

Sammy threw his hands on the air. "A little late for that, don't you think?"

His nephew clicked his tongue. "It'll break their hearts if you take them back. You should've seen how excited they were." A gesture with his hand. "I don't think anyone could've pried them away."

The door leading to Sammy's compassion locked shut. "I'll give them double, no triple their money back." A grunt. "That's if I can find them."

"Their mom bought some gas."

"Did she pay with a card?" Sammy questioned with a twinge of hope rising in his chest.

"No. Cash."

The bottle holding Sammy's hope shattered. A scoff. "How's that going to help me?"

His nephew thumbed over his shoulder. "You've got all kinds of cameras pointing at all those pumps. If you're really that desperate you'll find them getting into their car." A slow exhale. "You should be able to see their license plate. It can't be that hard to figure it out from there."

That bottle started to mend itself. Sammy grabbed his cell from his pocket. Found the contact and dialed. He bound into his office and studied the tiny monitors on his desk. The phone line clicked on. "Hello Ariek. We have a problem. A huge fucking problem."

10

"Mom!"

Mary kept her hands glued to the steering wheel, her head and eyes forward. If she ignored them, would her daughters give up?

"Mom!"

Of course they wouldn't. She sighed. "What is it, Mackenzie?"

"Zoe's picking at her tooth again."

"You're being a tattletale," Zoe said. "Mom, make her stop."

Mary rubbed her temple. "Mackenzie, we've talked about this."

"You told her not to do that," Mackenzie stated firmly, "but she's not listening. Do you want me to lie and not say anything?"

Mary glanced in the rearview mirror. Mackenzie was hugging that dog bank. She gazed back with determination painted across her face. "Never lie."

"See Zoe...Mom agrees."

"Mom!" Zoe demanded. "She's doing it again."

"Mackenzie," Mary stated definitively, "leave your sister alone."

"Why are you yelling at me?" Mackenzie questioned innocently. "She's the one who's not being a good listener."

"Just..." Mary silently grumbled. "Zoe, didn't I tell you to stop messing with your tooth?"

Zoe was silent for several seconds, then meekly answered. "Yeah, I guess so."

"Then why do you keep doing it?"

Zoe shrugged. "Maybe you changed your mind."

"Mom's not going to change her mind," Mackenzie said.

"How do you know?" Zoe fired back. "You're not Mom."

"Mom!" Mackenzie called out. "Did you change your mind? Zoe thinks that you did."

The ends of Mary's nerves were frayed. She swallowed her frustration before it could spew out in a violent ball of fire. "Will the two of you just...just..." A scream through clenched lips. "Just settle down!" She exhaled sharply. "No one talks for the rest of this trip. And I mean no one."

Mackenzie buried her face in her dog bank. Zoe zipped her lips shut, looked out the window and wrapped her arms around her bear.

Seconds, then a minute passed without as much as a peep. Ahh, the sweet sound of silence. Mary sighed with relief. Her internal furnace clicked off and the heat of irritation dissipated. She happily nestled into the driver's seat and loosened her vice-like grip on the steering wheel. She could actually hear the voices drifting from the radio.

"...*enjoy the sun while you can. We've got a big storm system heading our way and it should reach the listening area by this evening. Expect...*"

A gasp rifled from the backseat. "You can't say that, Zoe."

"Why? It's not a bad word."

"Yes, it is," Mackenzie said.

"No, it's not."

"Yes..."

"Mom. Is shits a bad word?" Zoe asked.

Shock zipped through Mary and smashed the quiet she had been enjoying. How did Zoe learn that word? "Umm, Zoe, I think that..."

"Shits is not a bad word, Mackenzie," Zoe informed her sister confidently.

"Stop saying that. It's bad." Mackenzie slapped her hands over her ears. "Mom, tell her it's a bad word."

Mary rubbed her eye. She'd have to make it a point to stop swearing in front of the kids. "Zoe..."

"It's a dog," Zoe interrupted.

"A dog?" Mary asked uncertainly.

"Shih Tzu," Zoe stated. "It's a type of dog."

Mackenzie gasped. "I forgot about that. Mom, how can shits be a bad word if it's a name of a dog?"

Mary shifted in her seat. "Are you saying it correctly?"

"Simone's grandma has one," Zoe said. "I heard her call it a little shit."

"I did too," Mackenzie added.

Mary sighed. "When we get home we'll look it up to make sure that's how you say it."

"How will you know if you have the right kind of dog?" Zoe questioned. "Do you know how to spell shits?"

"Mom knows how to spell," Mackenzie said.

"I'm just asking." Zoe adjusted her shoulder belt. "There's all kinds of dogs out there."

"Mom," Mackenzie summoned. "Tell Zoe that you know how to spell..."

"Okay girls; let's not use that word until we look up how to say it for real."

"Why, Mommy?" Mackenzie asked cautiously. "Is it a bad

word?"

Mary slowly exhaled. "Let's just not use it, okay." A pause. "Not for a while."

"I said a bad word, didn't I?" Shock filled Mackenzie's voice. "Zoe, you're the one who made me..." Another gasp. "Mom! Zoe's picking her tooth again."

"Zoe, what have I...?"

"I'm not picking at it," Zoe informed. "It's out."

"It's out?" Mary asked.

"Gross! She's bleeding," Mackenzie said with disgust. "Look, Mom."

"I can't...I can't right now." Several cars had boxed Mary into her lane.

"Don't swallow it," Mackenzie stated.

"You swallowed the tooth?" Mary asked frantically.

"No," Mackenzie answered for Zoe. "Her spit."

Mary's gut churned. "Where's the tooth?"

"Right here." Zoe held up her clenched hand. Blood-tinged spit seeped though her fingers. "What should I do with it?"

Mary reluctantly reached behind her. "Give it to me."

The goop-encrusted tooth plopped into her hand. The blob of spit oozed across her palm. Her stomach retched.

"Is there a napkin or something?" Zoe asked with urgency.

"Hold on, honey." Mary reached for the box of tissues tucked in the space between the seats. She managed to snatch one with the tips of her fingers and held it out for Zoe. "Wad it up and put it in your mouth where the tooth used to be." Snared another one to wrap the tooth. Another to wipe her hand.

"Don't lose it," Zoe commanded.

"I'm not going to lose it," Mary verified.

"Are you sure?"

"Yes, I'm sure."

"Can I give it to the tooth fairy?" Zoe asked.

Mary nodded. "We'll put it under your pillow before you go to bed.'

"Will she come? What if she decides not to?" Zoe's voice brimmed with concern.

"She'll come." Mary answered. "You better make sure you're sleeping, or else she might not."

"How do you know?"

"I just do."

"Even if it storms?" Zoe questioned matter-of-factly. "The man on the radio said it was going to storm. What happens if she doesn't want to go out in the rain?"

"Trust me," Mary said. "She'll be there to take your tooth."

"I wonder what she does with them." Zoe said to no one in particular.

"Maybe she gives them to people who need them," Mackenzie commented.

"Does she, Mom?" Zoe bounced her bear on her lap. "Does she give them to people who need them?"

Mary tapped her finger on the steering wheel. How to answer that? "She might. I'm not sure."

"Is that why she leaves money?"

"I think so," Mary answered vaguely.

"How does she know how much to leave?"

Mary sighed. "She just does." A pause. "That's her job."

Zoe slowly nodded her understanding. She looked out the window. "I sure hope she comes and leaves me a whole bunch of it."

11

LAST NIGHT'S HANGOVER was the tick that had burrowed into Aryssa's core and sucked the vitality out of her soul. Her gut bobbed on unyielding waves of nausea. The headache felt like the relentless clash of a sledgehammer against a steel girder. It pounded from somewhere deep in her brain and reverberated against the walls of her skull. Aryssa quietly slipped into the dimly lit dressing room and rubbed her forehead, hoping to soothe it away. It wasn't working. She sighed feebly.

Behind her the music boomed from the speakers. As usual, they were turned up louder than they needed to be and easily competed with the clamor from the crowd—an energetic crowd, to say the least. Drinks were guzzled. Shots drained. Money flowed. Lights flashed. Men...well, they were being what men are in this place. At least she could find some semblance of peace here in the dressing room.

Aryssa grabbed a nearby chair, slid it just inside the closet and sat. Let the coats, gowns and other stage paraphernalia drape over her. She needed a moment away from the people. The racket. The persistent innuendoes and scummy propositions. She placed her elbows on her thighs and braced her head in her palms. An image of Charlie swirled across her mind causing a brook of embarrassment to trickle through her veins. How could she have left him like that? What had she been thinking?

She could feel the thumping music roll through the dress-ing-room door. See the flashing lights bounce off the walls. Hear the endless chatter, cheers and sexually infused banter. Did she really have to go back out there? Her desire to dance had left hours ago. Her mood had been trending on a downward slope to *screw this shit.* Besides, she had already made a few hundred bucks. Wasn't that good enough?

Aryssa could just go home, take a hit of crush, a swig of bourbon, make some popcorn and maybe even watch a movie. Then again, maybe she should take the time to gather some more rocks before completely calling it a night. The thought nestled against the edges of her sensibility. If she did, then she could get up at a reasonable hour and start her day on the right foot. Clean her apartment. Go to the gym. Buy a few groceries. She sighed gently. Be an adult and apologize to Charlie. A slow nod. Yes, she'd have to do that for sure.

She leaned forward to stand up, but a sudden presence made her stop. The silhouettes of two men appeared at the doorway. One of them motioned into the dressing room.

"You see anything?"

Aryssa slid back in the chair, allowing the clothes to fall over her. She sat as still as she could, barely filling her lungs with air. Anxiety injected itself into her heart and made it beat a little harder.

"It's empty," the man said.

Despite all the background noise, Aryssa thought she rec-ognized the voice. Was it Ariek?

"You sure?"

That voice sounded a lot like Sammy.

"I know an empty room when I see it," Ariek said with a huff of discontentment. "I still think we should use my office."

He pointed down the hall.

"I told you," Sammy replied. "Can't trust it."

"I'm in there all the time. There's no way that it's been bugged."

"Do you really trust the Network? Do you think they trust us?" Sammy paused. "And what about the cops?"

The Network? The cops? Aryssa bit her lip. What were they talking about?

"I think you're overreacting."

"Excuse me for being cautious," Sammy said defensively.

"Cautious? It's a little late for that," Ariek said condescendingly.

"Enough already. I've owned up to it and I'm taking care of it, too," Sammy said with a hint of strain in his voice. "Don't need the constant reminders." A pause. "If it wasn't for my nephew, we…"

"There's no *we*," Ariek interrupted. He jabbed his finger. "It's *you*. What were you thinking by cramming them into some toy bank for anyone to come and grab?"

"Need I remind you how you fucked up the last shipment?" Sammy exhaled through his nostrils like an angered bull. "They almost cut our heads off. I don't know about you, but I want to keep mine." A sharp inhale. "There's no room for this to get screwed up again."

Aryssa swallowed hard. If they were talking about being killed, what did that mean for her if she was caught listening?

"And you think that I don't know that?"

"I'm just saying."

"I don't need any reminding," Ariek shot back.

"Neither do I," Sammy retorted.

They both went silent. Stared at each other. The atmosphere became so thick with tension that it seemed to buckle the walls. It crept into the closet and pressed on all sides of Aryssa, causing her to shift in her seat.

Ariek broke the silence. He sighed. "Look…I agree with you. We need to get this right, or else we're both as good as dead." His tone softened. "Have you figured how you're going to get them back?"

"The brothers," Sammy answered.

Ariek's eyes seemed to widen. "Are you sure that's a good idea? I know they're good, but they come with a price."

"Forty percent."

"Forty? Are you kidding me?"

"I wish I was," Sammy answered.

Ariek folded his arms across his chest. "Will we have enough?"

"It's tight," Sammy replied. "Very tight. But," he gestured with his hand, "they have no idea how many are actually in there. And I'm not going to be the one to tell."

"Don't look at me to say anything." Ariek slid his hands into his pockets. "What happens if they decide to count them?"

"They won't. They know their job and their place."

"Still, I don't like the way this is playing out."

"Neither do I," Sammy agreed. "We've got to get them back. You and I are in no place to do this ourselves. Besides, if things get ugly…" He slashed his hand near his throat. "That's why I've made arrangements for it to be taken care of tonight."

"As in now?"

Sammy glanced at his watch. "In a few hours."

Aryssa clamped down on her finger to stifle her gasp. Fright dried her throat and made her heart thump against the bars of her ribs. Did Sammy and Ariek want someone killed?

Did they really have the means to do it? She worried she might be found so she did her best to quietly wriggle deeper behind the clothes.

Ariek slowly nodded. "I get it. But, I wish…I," he drew a long sigh, "things would be so much easier if we knew how to get them away from the others."

"It would." Sammy leaned against the wall. "I'm at a loss."

"So am I," Ariek concurred, then huffed, "Why is it that he can get them and we can't?"

Sammy shrugged. "I've been wracking my brain for months." A pause. "Maybe we'll have to get him to tell us."

"More like beat it out of him." Ariek gazed at the floor as if lost in thought. "Except we don't even know what this guy looks like."

"I know that he docks his boat at one of the marinas."

"You've mentioned that before," Ariek said. "That's like looking for a needle in a haystack."

"Almost, but not quite," Sammy replied. "We just have to do the proper legwork."

"That's a lot of legwork in a short amount of time." Ariek uneasily shifted from one foot to the other. "Where are you getting them from, anyway?"

"What's that got to do with anything?" Sammy asked defensively.

"Look, I know you're buying them from a pawn shop," Ariek said guardedly. "All I'm saying is that maybe they can give you some kind of description. Or maybe even a name." A point at Sammy. "They could even have this guy on one of their security cameras."

Sammy shook his head. "Believe me, I've asked." A drawn-out exhale escaped from his lips. "He's protective of all his clientele."

Ariek rubbed his finger and thumb together. "You offer him something?"

"If you mean like money, then yes, I've suggested it." Sammy shook his head. "Wouldn't budge."

"Everyone has a price."

"Wasn't going to push it and risk losing what's been established." Sammy kneaded his cheek. "He calls me when he first gets them. Can't expect anything more than that."

"Maybe we need to expect more."

"That's not…" Sammy sighed. "Maybe as an absolute last resort."

"Don't you think that things are getting to that point?" Ariek stopped shifting his weight. Shoulders became taut. "That shipment will be here in a couple of days and we're scrambling to secure payment. I want this to go down without so much as a hiccup."

"So do I," Sammy said determinedly. "We're both under a lot of pressure." He held out his arm and motioned downward with his hand. "We need to take a step back and see the entire picture." He paused. "Once I get that damn bank back, we'll have just about enough. I've got some cash put aside for emergencies and I'm betting you do, too."

What did Sammy mean by getting a bank back? Why were they so desperate for cash? A faint whiff of perfume mixed with the dry scent of dust, stale wisps of cigarettes and the decaying odor of sexually infused testosterone wafted from the clothing in the closet and swirled into Aryssa's nostrils. She desperately tried to quell an impending sneeze by scrunching her nose. Squinting her eyes. The burn flared along her nasal passages. Tears fanned out across her lashes. She bit the inside of her cheek and looked up to try to make it all go away. After a few seconds the sneeze drifted harmlessly back down her throat.

Ariek verified with a nod. "Not enough to pay everything off."

"Between you, me and those coins, I'm positive we can make this work," Sammy stated confidently. "Now is not the time to panic."

"Who said anything about being panicked?"

"It's a figure of speech."

"Whatever," Ariek said bluntly.

The two men fell silent. The driving music and the chatter of the crowd continued to pour through the door. Aryssa remained glued to her chair. The only thing that dared move were the questions that spun through her mind like the reels of symbols in a slot machine. What was the shipment coming in a couple of days? How did coins figure into it? How much money were Sammy and Ariek talking about?

Ariek broke the silence after several long seconds. "Those new cameras are up and running."

"Concealed like we talked about?"

Ariek nodded. "Can't even tell unless you know where to look."

"About time," Sammy said. "Now we'll know if anyone comes snooping around."

"Don't think anyone is brave enough," Ariek commented. "Except for the occasional stray bum or strung-out addict." He rubbed his shoulder. "Still, let the rumors keep everyone thinking the place is haunted."

Sammy chuckled. "It kind of is."

Ariek's lips thinned to a smile. "We should get it cleaned up before the newbies arrive."

"Does it matter?"

Ariek shrugged his indifference. "Some of those mattresses

are disgusting."

"Our resources are better focused on…"

"Hey you two," a woman said. "What are you doing way back here, when all the action's up front?"

"Hey Monique," Ariek said. "Had to get away for a few."

"I know the feeling." Monique glanced back and forth between the two men. "Something's up with the two of you." Clicked her tongue. "Kind of looking stressed out."

Sammy waved the comment away. "It's nothing." Tipped his chin toward Ariek. "I was telling him how my family forced me to hire my nephew and now he's screwing things up."

Monique scoffed. "Family." She scurried into the dressing room. Her heels shuffled across the floor. "I've got to pee." She waved her hand in the air. "I know, too much info. But when you got to go, you got to go." She was too focused on the bathroom to even realize Aryssa was sitting nearby.

Another dancer passed by Sammy and Ariek. She rubbed her ear. "That music is too damn loud."

The bartender yelled from somewhere down the hall. "Hey, Ariek. Do you think you can find the barback and get me a case of lager?" A brief pause. "Oh yeah, I need another fifth of bourbon too."

"I'll take care of it," Ariek advised. Turned to Sammy. "We're not done talking about this."

"No, we're not" Sammy said.

"Closing time." Ariek pulled his keys from his pocket and took off toward the stock room. Sammy headed out front.

Aryssa waited nearly a minute before spreading apart the clothes that had been draped over her. She cautiously stood and stretched the kink out of her lower back. What in the hell was she supposed to do now? Pretend like she hadn't heard a thing? A nod. Of course she would. She had too many of her own problems to get involved in something like that. Whatever *that* was.

"Hey Aryssa." Melissa pranced up to a mirror. She turned her head from side to side, puckered her lips and finally adjusted the sequined bra that barely fit her burgeoning boobs. "How's your night?"

"Good," Aryssa simply answered. "You?"

"Eh. Making some money." Melissa scrunched her nose. "Some jerk-off tried to grab my ass during a private." She scoffed. "You know what he tried to do when I was done?"

"No, what?"

"Stiff me. Claimed that I didn't live up to the agreement, so therefore he didn't have to pay."

"Agreement? There's no agreement," Aryssa stated derisively. "They know that going in. Why can't they simply follow the rules? Show a little respect."

"Who the hell knows?" Melissa ran her finger across the corner of her mouth. "People think that they can do whatever they want when they come in this place."

"Entitlement."

"Amen to that. That's the problem with our society." Melissa stepped toward the bathroom.

Aryssa pointed at the door. "Monique's in there."

"Oh, damn." Melissa slapped her hands onto the hips. "She almost done? I've got to go."

"Should be," Aryssa answered. She glanced out the door and silently sighed. It was time to go back out there, make some more money and use it to stock up on crush. Maybe even buy a small gift for Charlie so she could make amends. She uneasily flipped her hair behind her shoulder. How was she going to explain herself to Charlie, anyway?

Aryssa slowly made her way toward the exit. That conversation between Sammy and Ariek uneasily paced in the back of her mind. Nothing about it sat right. What in the hell were they talking about? What had they gotten themselves into? Dread tingled across her skin. She tried to brush the conversation away, but it gripped her thoughts even tighter. What did they mean by, "Let them keep thinking the place is haunted?" Could they have been referring to that old factory?

"Hey Aryssa," Monique called out.

Aryssa looked over her shoulder. "What's up?"

"Can you cover my turn on stage?" Monique plopped onto a chair. "I need a few moments away from that crap out there."

Aryssa bit her tongue. That wasn't how she wanted to finish her night. A grunt that quietly stuck in her throat. It couldn't be that bad, could it? "Yeah, I can do that."

Monique gestured with a finger. "I owe you."

Aryssa tipped her chin and left the dressing room. She'd make it a point to get out of here sooner rather than later.

12

CANDLES SHIMMERED. THE flicker of lightning lit up the window and flooded the bedroom. With a patter of feet, Zoe scampered into the room cradling her bear bank. Her fingers were curled around something in her hand. She kneeled on the end of Mary's bed.

"Can I sleep with you?" Zoe whispered softly.

Mary laid her cell phone on her lap. "What's wrong?"

Thunder, like the deep bass booming from a speaker, rolled from somewhere in the distance and shook the house.

Zoe clutched her bear tighter. "I can't sleep."

"Neither can I." Mackenzie was standing in the doorway holding her dog bank by the leg.

"Please," Zoe pleaded.

Mary sighed. "It's a school night."

"Can't we break it this one time?" Mackenzie walked toward the bed.

"Yeah, can we? It's dark," Zoe added.

"Just because the power is out doesn't make it any darker than any other night." Mary did her best to rationalize the rule, but deep down the reasoning was cracking. On a night like tonight it would be kind of nice to have the girls curled up on either side of her.

"But it is darker," Mackenzie said firmly. "My butterfly

light isn't working."

"And my bunny lamp isn't lighting up," Zoe said.

Mackenzie sat on the edge of the bed. "You're the one with all the candles."

"Why don't *we* get any?" Zoe questioned halfheartedly.

"It's not safe," Mary answered.

"It's not safe when our rooms are super dark," Zoe replied.

"Yeah, Mom." Mackenzie lay down on her back. "It's better in here with you."

Lightning flickered again, followed by a loud crack of thunder.

Zoe nudged her way farther up the mattress. "Come on, Mom."

Mary couldn't stop her daughters' methodical push into her bed. Then again, did she really want to?

"Can we watch television on your phone?" Mackenzie snuggled into Mary's side.

"Yeah, can we?" Zoe chimed in.

Mary shook her head. "This is still a school night." She buried her smile. "And it means you still have to get up at your usual time."

Both girls cackled with delight. Zoe curled up on the other side of her mother.

Mackenzie yawned. "Are you sure that we can't watch…?"

"What did I just say?"

"That it's a school night," Zoe answered. "School's dumb."

"No, it's not. I like it," Mackenzie said.

"No you don't."

"Yes, I do."

Zoe looked over at Mackenzie with furrowed brows. "Not

what you said in Mrs. Henry's class."

"You don't know what I said."

"Yes, I do."

"No, you don't."

"Girls," Mary stated decisively. "If you're going to argue, then I'm sending you back to your rooms."

Instant silence. Lightning flashed. Thunder rumbled. Mackenzie softly sighed and curled her back against Mary.

Zoe held out her fist. "Can I put this under your pillow?"

"What's that?" Mary asked with curiosity saturating her words.

Zoe unfurled her fingers. "My tooth."

"Oh yeah." Mary did her best to keep her astonishment hidden. How had she managed to forget about that?

"I cleaned it too," Zoe informed proudly. "Do you think the tooth fairy will give me more money?"

"Maybe." Mary ran her hand over Zoe's head. "If anything, she'll appreciate what you did."

"So, can I put this under your pillow?" Zoe questioned in a decibel just above a whisper.

"Of course you can," Mary replied.

Zoe slid her hand toward the pillow, but abruptly stopped. "Will she know that I put it here instead of under the pillow in my room?"

"She will," Mary said. "She's good like that."

"Are you sure?"

"Yes, I am."

"But, what if she...?"

Mary rubbed Zoe's arm. "Trust me, she'll know. Now go to sleep."

Zoe tucked the tooth under the pillow and then wrapped her arms around her bear. "Good night, Mommy."

"Good night, sweetheart."

It was only a matter of minutes before sleep overtook Mackenzie. Zoe wasn't too far behind. Gentle, slumber-filled breaths rose upward from either side of Mary. Their warmth nuzzled against her. Rain pattered against the windows and echoed off the roof. Somewhere deep in the distance thunder moaned.

The kids were right; it was kind of scary not having power. There were candles though, and they helped. Mackenzie and Zoe only added to her level of comfort. It wasn't long before the heaviness of slumber weighed on Mary's eyelids. She lifted her phone to continue watching her show, but instead let it fall back on her lap. Became mesmerized by the way the candle-light danced across the ceiling. Her mind softened, left the conscious world behind only to drift into the realm of the Sandman. Before she knew it, she was asleep too.

THE ENTICING SCENT hung on the faint currents of air. Aryssa sniffed and let the delicate aroma swirl through her nose and into her lungs. Let it seduce her animalistic desires. There was something special about this one. She had to have it. Needed it to satiate her predatory lust.

Aryssa was getting close. The hairs on the back of her neck tingled with excitement. Her heart beat a little faster and her lungs filled quicker. Her thighs quivered ever so slightly as she crept down the hallway.

She cautiously peered around the door frame and into the bedroom. The light from the candles gently bounced off the walls and illuminated the air with a soft glow. Rain rhythmically tapped against the window. Flowed down a gutter. Lightning flashed. Thunder gently rumbled.

Aryssa took a deep breath and slowly exhaled to steady herself. She tiptoed across the floor toward the bed. Toward the little girl fast asleep clutching her fuzzy bear. The girl's mother and sister were deep in the throes of slumber too.

She crept closer, practically gliding over the hard wood. Didn't make a single sound. No creak of a board, pop of a joint or squeak from the soles of her shoes. This was one of her perfected talents—being absolutely silent when it was needed. And it was needed now.

Aryssa stood by the side of the bed. Save for the nearly imperceptible rise and fall of the little girl's chest, she wasn't moving and totally unaware that a person was standing over her. A quiet sigh. With a couple of bills in one hand, Aryssa slid her other beneath the pillow. The prize of her desire was somewhere under there; all she had to do was snatch it and leave. She reached a little farther, then a bit more. Barely nudged the little girl's head. Something smooth brushed across her fingertip. She curled her finger around it, pulled it out and stopped.

The distant creak of a floorboard. A beam of light danced off the wall outside the bedroom. A nearly imperceptible murmur of a voice. Who the hell was that?

Aryssa tucked the tooth in her palm and frantically looked for a place to hide. A dresser. Side tables. Out the window? Under the bed? How about the closet on the other side of the room? She swallowed her fear, quietly scampered around the bed and slipped between the partially open doors. Peered out through the slats, held her breath and waited.

A man in a dark knit cap with some kind of scarf over his face poked his head into the room. He disappeared behind the door frame, then reappeared and stepped out into the open. Within seconds another darkly dressed man appeared. This one was a little more portly than the other. The two figures silently crept to either side of the bed.

A sheen of nervous sweat glazed Aryssa's palms. Her lips tingled with fright. Who were these two men? What did they want? Were there more of them in the house?

The man on the far side of the bed looked up at the other. Pointed at the girl closest to him and then at her sister. A quick nod of agreement from the portly one closest to Aryssa.

The two men loomed sinisterly over the two sisters. Aryssa's heart thumped wildly in her ears. She bit her lower lip. Were they going to kidnap the girls? Hurt them in some obscene way? Aryssa blinked, hoping her lashes would slice the men to pieces. Nothing happened. What should she do?

The taller figure, who was nearest the girl with the fuzzy bear, held up his hand. His forefinger flicked upward. Then the middle. A third joined in and soon the fourth finger stood with the rest. His palm started to rotate. Thumb twitched.

Something inside Aryssa snapped. Before she could comprehend what was happening, every muscle in her body coiled then exploded, effectively propelling her out of the closet. She screamed and threw herself at the portly assailant.

Anguish rocketed from the man's throat. He stumbled forward, lost his balance and fell on one of the girls and her mother. Aryssa held onto him with both arms and used the momentum to roll to her side while at the same time pulling the assailant across her body and flinging him to the floor.

The man slid and then crashed into the dresser. Bottles filled with perfumes, lotions, nail polish, and who knows what else, tumbled and crashed onto the floor. Glass cracked. Others shattered. Liquid splattered. Several candles tipped over. Papers and a book ignited. Flames licked the drooling liquid then leapt to the floor and onto the assailant. The man screamed in pain as he violently beat at the flames spreading over his clothes.

MARY GASPED. ZOE screamed. Mackenzie howled with the shock of being abruptly awakened. The darkly dressed man standing over Zoe filled Mary's vision. The sudden surprise in his eyes quickly wrinkled into an expression of anger.

The dam to Mary's maternal instinct burst open, poured into her veins and flooded her limbs. She tossed the blanket upward, sprang from the bed and threw herself into the stranger.

She gave it everything she had. Forced the man to stagger backward and spin in a circle. He grunted. Still Mary held on tightly. Bit into the blanket that partially covered the stranger's head. She clamped down on what she thought was his ear. He yelped in pain and flailed his arms until he managed to somehow grab hold of Mary. She was no match to his domineering strength. He tipped sideways and easily flung her off him.

For a brief second, Mary was weightless. She crashed hard into the small table near the window. Searing pain pierced her hip and rifled up her side. She careened onto the floor. Her body convulsed. Air burst out of her lungs, forcing her to gasp for a breath. The edges of her vision darkened. Above her a flame snared the curtain and tufts of fire quickly climbed the volatile fabric.

The stranger bounced off the wall, staggered but managed to regain his balance. He shook the cloud of disorientation from his head. With outstretched arms he jumped toward a cowering Zoe.

Despite the intense pain, Mary rolled onto her feet and

crouched. With all the strength she could muster she sprang at the assailant before he could reach Zoe. She smashed into him and dug her nails into his flesh.

"Damn bitch!" he screamed. "Get off me!"

The stranger writhed. Grumbled. He got his arms around Mary and tried to rip her off. She clung as tightly as her strength would allow. Wasn't going to let go at any cost. A movement caught the corner of her eye. Who was that? She watched as a woman rolled across the bed and in one continuous motion stood and sent a kick into the man's groin.

His body convulsed with a pain-filled howl. The assailant stumbled backward and at the last possible moment he managed to turn just enough to place Mary between him and the wall.

Smash. The numbing pain blasted across Mary's back. She lost what little grip she had. The man snatched Mary, spun and threw her into the air.

She was weightless again. Arms and legs drifted in front of her as she flew backward. Things seemed to move in slow motion. She saw the woman. The darkly dressed man. Heard a scream. She struck something pliable that immediately shattered. Light twinkled off the shattered glass as she flew through the window and into the bushes.

Thud. A dull thump reverberated through her head. Pain fanned through her scalp, swirled into her brain and sent shooting stars zipping across her vision. She gasped before everything went black.

THE FIRE SPREAD and crackled with delight. Paint bubbled. Walls buckled. Smoke churned across the ceiling. The portly man screamed in pain as he desperately beat at the flames engulfing his body. He rolled across the floor, then crawled out of the room and into the hallway.

Aryssa wasted no time in lunging at the man she had just kicked. The last time her aim had been off ever so slightly and she struck his inner thigh. Aryssa stepped and aggressively cocked her leg just as he turned to face her.

This time she didn't miss the soft spot between his legs. The hollow gasp of pain shot out of his lungs. Eyes opened wide. Legs buckled. He staggered into the wall, but managed to stay upright.

Aryssa kicked again, but the assailant managed to snag her foot and fling her onto the bed. He lunged at her just as she recoiled off the mattress. She swung her foot upward and connected with the underside of his jaw.

The man grunted. Head snapped. Anguish spread across his face. Eyes glazed as he sank to the floor.

"Mommy!" a girl yelled.

The stranger grabbed the edge of the bed and slowly stood. Quickly turned his attention on the room. On the flames. To the disappearance of his partner. Finally on Aryssa, poised to defend herself. He grunted with frustration and darted out the bedroom.

Aryssa gasped for a breath. Then another. And another. Choked on the thickening smoke. The little girl with the bear coughed uncontrollably. The other screamed. "Mommy! Where's Mommy?"

There was no time to waste. The window was covered in flames. Aryssa grabbed each of the girls by the hand. "Come with me."

"But my mom," the girl with the bear cried out. "I want my mom."

Her sister with the dog began to cry.

Aryssa coughed. "Girls! Move it, now!" coughed again. "Or…or we die."

Their brows arched with fear. Tears dribbled down their cheeks. Aryssa yanked them off the bed. They were reluctant to follow, but Aryssa kept pulling. It didn't take long before they were all running out the bedroom door.

She led them into the smoke-filled hallway. Wood crackled. Drywall sagged. Flames filled nearly all the space between the walls. "Hold your breath!" Aryssa yelled.

Aryssa's legs trembled. She crouched and pulled the girls through the fire, but the end of the hallway was completely engulfed. Trapped. What to do? To her left she could just make out a door. Was it safe on the other side? There was no time to think; it was the only option. Aryssa thrust it open and dragged the girls with her.

A thick veil of smoke hung in the air. More poured through the door and stretched its dirty fingers across the ceiling. Flames circled the walls behind them. They all coughed and gasped for a clean breath.

Aryssa led the girls to the lone window at the far end of the room and flung it open. She sucked in the wave of fresh air. So did the two sisters. The flames fed on the fresh oxygen and burned brighter. Hotter. Alyssa grunted and kicked out the screen. She lifted the girl with the bear through the window, then her sister clutching the fuzzy dog. Finally she climbed through and staggered out into the rain.

"Where's my mommy?" the one with the fuzzy dog asked.

"Where is she?" questioned the other.

Aryssa coughed as she glanced back at the house. Flames poked through the windows, reaching their sinewy hands out into the open in search of something to grab onto. Something to feed upon. But the rain beat them back inside. "She's safe."

"Are you sure?"

"Yes." Aryssa did her best to hide her uncertainty. More coughing. She looked out into the street. Around the yard. Were more of those men lurking out here? Waiting to pounce? She had to get these girls somewhere safe. Had to assume their mother was out of harm's way somewhere outside the house. But where? Aryssa shook her head. This was not the time to try to figure it out.

"Look, girls." Aryssa coughed. "You have to trust me." She paused to look over her shoulder. Nothing stirred except for someone across the street talking on a phone and pointing toward the flames. "I'll get you to your mom, I promise. For now you need to come with me."

"When can I see…?"

"I'll find her." Aryssa placed her hand over her heart. "We've got to go."

"You're a stranger," the girl with the dog advised. "Mom said to never go with a stranger."

Aryssa sighed. "You're right. You shouldn't." Someone stepped out onto a porch. How would Aryssa explain what had just happened? Her presence in this part of the town? "But I'm also a friend who saved you and your mommy."

Whoosh! A ball of fire rolled out the nearby window. Somewhere glass shattered. The two girls gasped.

"It's not safe," Aryssa explained. "We've got to go." She grabbed the girls by the hand and nudged them into the shadows. Quickly led them down the street and away from the growing commotion surrounding the burning home.

13

THE DRIZZLE HAD to be the reason for the faint halo that circled the streetlights. Of course it blossomed around only the ones that actually worked. Charlie grunted to crack the quiet—break the near-somber stillness that made him shudder.

The soft rain had managed to dampen most of the city's vibrant undertones. Most, but not all. There was the distant sound of water flowing into a nearby drain. The squish of tires rolling over wet concrete. The plops of tiny raindrops diving into a puddle. The drips from an awning. Still, it was the thin layer of dew covering his shirt and skin that made him shiver. It didn't matter though. Charlie heard the noises, felt the moisture, but was in no mood to give it any of his attention.

There were other things occupying his mind. The fact that it was a slow night hadn't helped matters. He slid his hand into his pocket and fiddled with the lone coin. Solemnly bowed his head as he walked. Then there was Aryssa.

What had he done that made her skip out like that? Leave him staring at the melting ice in her Bloody Mary. How many times had the waitress come up to the table to ask if he wanted another beer? If he was ready to order food? If his friend would be back soon? The waitress had to have known. Knew that Aryssa had run out. Charlie could practically hear the whispers. The gossip that spread like wildfire among the workers. Even though he was tucked away near the back of the bar, he was still openly exposed to the embarrassment.

A balloon of frustration inflated and Charlie's internal thermostat spiked. The heat of anger billowed from under his collar. "Why!" He tightened his body to prevent his mushrooming annoyance from tearing him apart.

"Of all the lowdown things to do!" Charlie opened his mouth to scream, but at the last second swallowed everything that was ready to explode out of him.

The aggravation swirled back down his throat and became lost in the loops of his gut, leaving the apparition of melancholy to fill the void that remained. Charlie sighed. Shoulders stooped. Why had Aryssa agreed to meet him for lunch and then blown him off?

He stopped to look at the factory across the street. The chill of dread snaked around the bones of his spine. His fingers trembled. The hair along his arms and neck stood like terrified children standing outside a dilapidated and vine covered home.

The factory had been abandoned for as long as Charlie could remember. There were no lights. No movement. No sound. The crumbling façade was hidden by the shadows of darkness. It was the decaying ruin of a once-prosperous past. The gaunt arms of its smokestacks labored to reach upward only to be swallowed by the dismal night. Water towers buckled inward, emaciated from the want, or maybe the lack of anything to fill their stomachs. The place was nothing more than a gloomy entity silently dying from years of neglect. Slowly wasting away, bit by bit, mutating into the dust and grime below its rotting foundation. Still, something pulled Charlie toward it. Something inside begged for his attention.

What was it?

That familiar tingle mixed with drops of curiosity trickled through his veins. Tonight, for some reason, it was stronger. More pronounced. Charlie listened for some kind of noise. Watched for some semblance of life. Searched for a reason why he felt compelled to go over there. Instinctively he took a step toward the curb and...

"You're no good, you're no good, that place is no good!" a male sang.

That voice...it sounded so familiar. Charlie turned toward the singing. A solitary figure weaved amongst the cones of light cast by the street lights.

"Let me say it again...you're no good, you're no good, that place is no good." The figure spun in a circle. Wiggled his finger at the factory. "No good, I tell ya!" Slid sideways with his arms extended. Drew closer to Charlie.

"Johnny?" Charlie asked, assurance filling his tone. "Is that you?"

The figure stopped and let his arms fall to his sides. "Maybe." A pause. "Depends who's asking."

"It's me—Charlie."

"Charlie?" Johnny questioned guardedly. "Charlie the boat guy?"

"The one and only."

Johnny clapped his hands together. "Well, alright." His head bobbed as he walked toward Charlie. "Should've known that I'd see you this time of night."

"You're just as much of a night owl as I am," Charlie stated. "Looks like you're having a good time in this rain."

Johnny spun. "Feeling the groove deep inside." Brushed his hand down his torso. "A little Linda Ronstadt to help me get by that...that," his hand gestured wildly at the factory, "that no-good of a place."

Charlie nodded his agreement. "It is kind of scary."

"Kind of?" Johnny's smacked his thigh. "It's totally scary." A shadow of fear fell over his face. "Nothing good in there. Nothing." Shook his head. "Don't go near it. Not anymore."

"You've been in there?"

"Once." Johnny paused. "Maybe twice." Held up three fingers. "Okay, three or four." His body shuddered. "More. Had to have been more. Don't like it, though. Not at all."

Charlie shifted uneasily. He had purposefully avoided it. Suppressed the occasional lure to be an urban explorer. But why was he drawn to it in the first place? What was pulling him toward it? "Why don't you like it?"

"Things," Johnny answered vaguely. "Just things. There are...there are..." He ran his hand over his hair and gripped the back of his head. "You know, they want me to go in there. But I try not to. I really do. Make myself avoid that place. Go somewhere else."

"It must be tough," Charlie said somewhat softly. It looked like Johnny was falling into one of his chaotic moods.

"You've no idea the things they try and make me do. No idea." Johnny jabbed his arm toward the factory. "There are...there are...they want me to take them out. Take them..." He bowed his head. "They keep trying to make me do that." A grunt. "It's them...not me. But...but someone's got to get them out of there."

"Who, Johnny?" Charlie questioned. "Is someone in there?"

"Not just someone. Many someones."

Charlie glanced at the dilapidated building. Nothing stirred. That familiar chill returned. Were there people inside? Someone other than an occasional bum? "If someone's in there, shouldn't we get the cops?"

Johnny shook his head so uncontrollably that his torso shifted in unison. "No, no, no, no…" He suddenly stopped and looked right at Charlie. "They'll never find them. No, no, no. No one can." Tapped his cheek. "Unless you know how to look. But still…" he sighed heavily, "it's too much. They're watched by…by…by them. Can you see what I'm saying?" Johnny rocked side-to-side. "They want me to go and get them, but they're hard to find. I know…I know the way. You got to make it past the others if you can." He pointed at the far end of the factory. "That's if they don't see you first." A tense pause. "That's a whole other thing that I can't even speak of because…"

Charlie reached out to steady Johnny. "It's okay. You don't need to talk about it if you don't want to." He laid his hand on Johnny's shoulder. "It's my fault for bringing this up. I didn't want to make you…"

Johnny stiffened under the touch. He peered deep into Charlie's eyes, seemingly probing them. "Something happened to you. Something that…"

It was as if some kind of hand reached into Charlie. It wasn't cold. Wasn't warm, either. With the faintest of touch its fingers could sense events, emotions—the very currents that zipped along his nerves. Charlie shut his eyes, pulled his hand off Johnny's shoulder, stepped back and scowled. "What are you doing?"

Johnny held up his hands defensively. "Nothing, man. Nothing." He let his arms fall. "You're good people. Always good to me. Always. Don't want to mess that up."

The strange sensation evaporated like water on July asphalt. Charlie shivered. What had just happened? Was it nothing more than his imagination? "It's okay, Johnny,"

Charlie said apologetically.

Johnny was quiet for several seconds. "You know, there's a reason."

"A reason?"

"Yeah, a reason. She'll tell you." Johnny scratched his ear. "Got to ask, though."

"Her?"

Johnny strolled by Charlie. "You know who it is." Touched his chest. "I don't, but you do." Didn't stop walking. Didn't look back. "Got to ask her."

"What should I ask?"

"You know," Johnny answered. He pointed at the factory. Shook his hips. "You're no good. You're no good, that place is…"

Charlie continued to watch Johnny sing. Watched him grow smaller and smaller the farther down the street he went. Watched as the night finally swallowed him and digested the last bits of his voice. Charlie shrugged uneasily. Was Johnny talking about Aryssa? Did he know what had happened? Was he trying to tell him to talk to her?

His thoughts endlessly looped as he headed home. Lunch with Aryssa. Her sudden disappearance. The embarrassment when he paid the bill. His rollercoaster of emotions. Another slow night. Meeting Johnny. The factory. Johnny's cryptic message.

Charlie trudged up the stairs inside his apartment building. A lone drop of water broke loose from his rain soaked hair and trickled down his forehead. The wood groaned under the weight of his boots. Johnny's advice raced along the circular track in his mind. Johnny had to have been referring to Aryssa. But how did he know what had happened?

Charlie reached the landing at Aryssa's floor. Light slipped through the tiny crack under her door. She had to be home. Should he knock? Demand an explanation? His gut gurgled with irritation. She had left him sitting in that bar all alone. He deserved a reason.

Charlie slid over to the door and lifted his hand to knock. He let it hang in the air. It was late. Just because the light was on didn't necessarily mean she was home. Then again, she could be sleeping. Maybe it was better to come back in the afternoon when she would be awake?

He stepped backward, turned to leave, but stopped mid-spin. What was that? Some kind of distant sound drifted from underneath the door. Charlie strained his ears. Listened for any type of noise. Something stirred. Did he hear a voice? A chair scraped across the floor. Charlie stepped forward. Leaned in. Put his ear even closer.

Muffled voices. Someone was talking, but he couldn't understand what was being said. Someone else spoke. Was that a kid? Charlie rubbed his cheek inquisitively. Since when did Aryssa have children? What was going on in there?

Charlie moved closer and practically placed his ear against the door. Concentrated on the voices. Sure sounded like children. But at this time of night?

Click. The door swung open. Charlie jumped backward in shock. Aryssa still had her hand on the knob, her eyes wide with surprise. She gasped. "Charlie?"

14

ARYSSA SHUDDERED AND sucked in a startled breath. She lost her grip on the doorknob. "Charlie?" Her mind blanked. She had been waiting for him. Had been listening for the distinctive sound of his boots plodding up the steps. She thought she had heard them, but wasn't sure. Now here he was and everything that she had rehearsed suddenly disintegrated.

Charlie had jumped backward with surprise. His once-arched brows were now ironed straight with reservation. "Hey."

Aryssa kept her lungs filled with air, hoping to calm her nerves. She needed to talk to him privately. Needed him out of sight of her neighbors and inside her apartment. Without giving it much thought, she grabbed him by the arm and pulled.

Charlie halfheartedly jerked his arm free. "What are you doing?"

"Please." Aryssa paused. "I need..." She glanced up and down the stairwell. The hallway. At the other apartments. There was no one around, or so it seemed. "Will you just get in here?"

Charlie stood rooted outside her door. He looked past Aryssa and into the apartment. "What gives?"

Aryssa sighed. "I just...I...need your help."

"My help?" Charlie folded his arms over his chest. "You want my help, after what you did."

"I know it doesn't look good." Aryssa uneasily shifted her weight. "But if you'd just come in, I'll explain." Pouted her lips. "Things just sort of got out of hand…out of my control."

Charlie squinted. "Out of control? You went to the bathroom. How out-of-control could they have gotten?" He thumbed over his shoulder. "You blew me off."

"I know it looks that way." Aryssa bowed her head. "I'm sorry. I didn't mean for it to happen." Emotions welled up inside her. Flooded over her eyelids. She sniffled. "Can you please just…?" Swiped her finger under her eye. "I promise I'll explain."

Charlie slowly exhaled. Hesitated for several seconds. Nodded ever so slightly. "Okay, fine," he mumbled.

Aryssa stood sideways to let Charlie pass. Another glance out into the hallway and stairwell. Still no one. She sighed with relief as she quietly closed the door. How to explain…?

Charlie was standing in the entrance to the kitchen. Uncertainty froze his stance as soon as one of the girls spoke. "Hello, who are you?"

"Umm." Charlie apprehensively ran his hand over his hair. "Umm, I'm Charlie."

"Did you bring my mom?"

Aryssa scampered down the hallway to the kitchen. So much for easing into the explanation. She put her hand on Charlie's lower back and nudged him toward the kitchen table. "Why don't you have a seat?"

"Is he your friend?" Zoe asked without looking up from her drawing.

"Yes." Aryssa pulled out a chair. Motioned again for Charlie to sit.

"Is he your boyfriend?" Mackenzie teasingly elongated the last word, then giggled.

Charlie was slow to sit. Aryssa purposefully dodged Mackenzie's question. "So, how was your day?"

A cold, incredulous glaze varnished Charlie's eyes. "Really?"

"I mean work. How was work?" Aryssa tried to shatter her embarrassment with a shrug. "Would you like something to drink?"

"No, I'm fine," Charlie answered. He softly tapped the table with his finger. It rattled the bottles of liquor, half-drained hot sauce, salt-and-pepper shakers and glass candle holders. The nearly dead bamboo shoot in the cracked ceramic pot swayed precariously. "I never knew you had kids."

"Umm...well..." The hinges on the cupboard doors groaned, as if tenaciously adding to the awkwardness that permeated the room. "They're not exactly," she found a glass that looked cleaner than the others, "they're not really mine."

"So, you're their aunt?" Charlie questioned.

Aryssa dug a partially filled ice-cube tray out of the freezer. "Not exactly."

"Your friend's kids?"

"Kind of." Aryssa popped the last two cubes into the glass.

"When are we going to see Mom?" Zoe asked.

"You said it would be soon, a long time ago." Mackenzie laid her pen on the table. "Don't you have any crayons or something like that?"

"She already said she doesn't have any," Zoe advised.

"But she never looked."

"Yes, she did."

"No, she didn't." Mackenzie pointed at the drawer next to the sink. "What about that one?"

Zoe rolled her eyes. "She looked in there."

"How do you know? There's a whole bunch of drawers." Mackenzie gazed hopefully at Aryssa. "What about all of those?"

Aryssa clenched her fists. "I don't have any…" She took a deep breath to cool her frustration. Purposefully softened her voice. "I just don't have any crayons. I wish I did, but I don't.'

"It's okay," Mackenzie said with disappointment curdling her voice. "This pen will do."

Aryssa's heart crumpled. How could she have let herself get angry over a little girl asking for crayons? "I'm so sorry. I'll make sure that I buy some."

"You should," Mackenzie added. "They're fun to color with."

"They are," Zoe added. "Sometimes Mom colors with us too." She grabbed another piece of paper. "Will you draw with us?"

"I'm not good at it."

Zoe tapped her pen against her chin. "That's what Mom always says, but she still does it."

"She's good at stick figures," Mackenzie said.

"It's kind of late, don't you think?" Charlie leaned forward to see what the girls were drawing. "Shouldn't you be in bed?"

"We were," Mackenzie advised. "But, the fire woke us up."

"The fire?" Charlie asked. "There was a fire?"

"Yeah, our house," Zoe stated.

"You're house was on…?"

"Okay," Aryssa interrupted. Plopped the glass on the table. "Here's that water you wanted."

"But, I didn't ask for…" Charlie shifted in his seat. "Thanks." He spoke out of the corner of his mouth. "What's this about a fire?"

How to explain? Aryssa's thoughts tumbled. Tongue flopped like a fish out of water. She giggled nervously. "Well…you see, umm, there…" Maybe it was time to just get it out. She straightened her posture and solidified her voice. "Their house caught on fire and I helped get them out."

"You rescued them?"

Aryssa nodded her affirmation.

Charlie glanced at the girls, then back at Aryssa. "And their mother knows about this?"

"Yep," Mackenzie blurted. "She was there."

Charlie scratched his temple. "She was?"

"Mom stopped the robbers from getting us." Zoe gestured at Aryssa. "She helped, too."

"Kicked him right in the you-know-what," Mackenzie added.

Skepticism wrinkled Charlie's forehead. "A fire. Robbers." He started to stand. "And you were there for all of this?"

It was happening faster than Aryssa wanted. She gently nudged Charlie back down into the chair. Rubbed her arm to try to soothe her uneasiness. "I really need your help getting them back…"

"Why were you even there?" Charlie stared at the table. Apparently hadn't heard a single thing she just said.

Zoe stopped drawing and looked at Charlie. "Do you know my mom?"

Mackenzie stretched her arms across the table. "I don't think I've ever seen you before."

"I haven't either," Zoe confirmed.

Charlie didn't say a word.

"Are you and my mom friends?" Mackenzie questioned.

He still remained silent.

Aryssa tried to break the tension that gripped the air. "Okay girls, why don't we…"

Zoe reached for the bottle of bourbon in the middle of the table. "What's that?"

"You probably shouldn't touch that," Aryssa stated in her best motherly tone. "It's something adults drink."

Zoe scrunched her face. "Like alcohol?"

"Yes, sort of like that."

"Yuck." Zoe stuck out her tongue. "Mom drinks that stuff sometimes."

"I'm hungry," Mackenzie interjected. "Do you have anything to eat?" She fiddled with the bottles, as if hoping some kind of snack would jump out for her.

"I'll have to look, but…"

"You still haven't answered my question." Frustration stiffened Charlie's shoulders. "What's going on with you? First, this afternoon at the bar." He gestured at the girls. "Now this."

Aryssa's back stooped. She bent down next to Charlie and caressed his arm to try to relieve his irritation. "I really need your help." A pause. "I need to get them to someone before…"

"Before what?"

"Before…" The stress of the moment ballooned. Stretched her emotions even thinner. She sniffled. Hesitated. "Before someone finds out they're missing."

"As in someone like the cops?"

"Something like that." Aryssa kept her grip on his arm.

Charlie jerked the extremity free. Pushed the chair backward. "What in the hell are you getting me into?"

"Please, you don't understand," Aryssa pleaded. "I had to get them out of that house. The whole place was on fire." A pause. "Those men were trying to kidnap them, too." She put her hand on Charlie's shoulder to prevent him from standing. "I brought them here to keep them safe."

"From who?" Charlie questioned.

Aryssa shrugged. "I don't know, their faces were covered." Tipped her chin toward the girls. "They don't know either."

"What about their mother?"

"I don't think so." Aryssa shook her head.

"Where is she?"

"I don't know." Aryssa ran her hand through her hair. "One of them tossed her out the window." She looked at the girls. "Don't worry; I'm sure she's fine."

"Are you sure?"

"She's fine. Trust me."

Mackenzie absently nodded as she continued to pick over the bottles.

"Why is it taking so long for Mom to get here?" Zoe questioned impatiently.

"Soon honey. Very soon." Aryssa turned to Charlie. Lowered her voice to a near whisper. "You got to help me get them someplace safe. Somehow back to their mother."

"This can't be happening," Charlie grumbled. "How can I trust what you're telling me? Why were you even there in the first place?"

How was Aryssa supposed to answer that? Did she even understand it herself? Gathering rocks was something she'd always done. She took a deep breath and slowly exhaled. Opened her mouth to let the words spill out. Words she hoped wouldn't scare Charlie away. "I was…"

"What's in here?" Mackenzie held up the purple Crown Royal bag. Started to tip it sideways.

Aryssa's heart skipped a beat. She thrust her arm forward hoping it would stretch across the table and snatch the bag.

"Don't…"

Too late. Dozens of rocks spilled out of the purple bag, rained down on the hard surface and tumbled across the table.

Charlie's mouth fell open with astonishment.

Mackenzie's eyes widened. "Are those what I think they are?"

"Teeth! Look at all the teeth!" Zoe screamed.

15

CHARLIE'S THOUGHTS SPUN like a wheel; a bent rim on a just crashed bicycle that was lying broken on the side of the road. There was no logical reasoning that could slow the wheel and give Charlie some clarity as to what was happening. There was nothing that could provide some understanding about the fire. The kidnappers. The two girls. He gripped his temples with his thumb and forefinger. Why had Aryssa been in that house? What had really happened to those girls and their mother? He studied the teeth strewn across the table. Who was Aryssa, anyway?

Zoe ran her fingers over the enamel-covered bones. "Where'd you get all of these?"

"There's so many," Mackenzie added.

Aryssa backed into the kitchen counter and gripped its edge, her head bowed. The hair that fell over her face couldn't completely hide its red tint. She kept her lips pressed together and said nothing.

Silence froze Charlie's tongue. What was he supposed to say? An awkward hush soured the air. Seconds passed before he cleared his throat, hoping to churn up a few words. "There's a bunch of them, alright." He rubbed his eye. "How'd you…you know, get so many?"

Mackenzie gasped. "Zoe." She pointed at the teeth. Brows

arched with shock. "Zoe!"

"What?"

"What'd you do with your tooth?"

"Mom let me put it under her pillow."

"I knew it!" Mackenzie excitingly jabbed her finger in the direction of Aryssa. "Guess what, Zoe?"

"What?"

"She's got to be the tooth fairy."

Zoe glanced at the teeth, at Aryssa, then back at the teeth. She giggled happily. "Oh my gosh, are you really the tooth fairy?"

Mackenzie enthusiastically bounced up and down in her chair. "She has to be."

Aryssa held up her hand. "Hold on girls. I'm…"

"A real tooth fairy. I can't believe it." Zoe's smile widened. "Are you sure?"

"Why else would she be in our house when we're sleeping? Why else would she have all of these?" She picked up a tooth. "What does yours look like?"

"Kind of like a rectangle," Zoe answered. "It's clean, too. I brushed it a whole bunch of times." She faced Aryssa. "Is it true that you give extra money if it's cleaner?"

Aryssa held out her arm, but let it drop to her side. "It's…it's not like that," she mumbled.

Charlie's spinning thoughts shattered and slid across the surface of skepticism. The tooth fairy? He chuckled uneasily. "Kids. They can come up with the strangest things."

Aryssa's head bobbed slowly. "Yeah, they can."

"Umm…" Charlie shifted in his chair. Did he dare ask for an explanation? He couldn't help himself. "What do you do with these things?"

Aryssa shrugged. Didn't say anything for several long seconds. "It's kind of hard to explain."

"But you've got to do something with them."

Aryssa tipped her chin to acknowledge the question. She turned away from Charlie, grabbed a sponge then a plate from the sink.

It was clear she wasn't going to elaborate. Charlie decided on a different approach. "Where do they come from?" Was he really going to suggest that she was the tooth fairy? "I mean, do you get them from kids?"

"I'm not some creeper, if that's what you're implying."

Charlie held up his hands defensively. "Not at all." He paused. "I'm just trying to…"

"It's not like I'm stealing them, either." She started to scrub the plate. "I leave money."

Charlie sucked in a heavy breath of disbelief. Had he really heard what Aryssa just said? Did he believe her? "You…you actually take them from underneath some kid's pillow and leave money in its place?"

"Something like that."

Charlie glanced at all the teeth. They had to have come from all different kinds of children. "How is it that you've never gotten caught?"

"I don't…"

"Look!" Zoe held a tooth between her thumb and forefinger.

"Is that it?" Mackenzie asked excitedly.

"Yeah, I'm pretty sure."

"How can you tell?"

"I just know," Zoe answered.

"Oh my gosh." Mackenzie enthusiastically clapped her hands. "I can't wait to tell Mom that we know the tooth fairy."

"She'll never believe us."

"Yeah, she will." Mackenzie's brows crinkled. "I know it." A pause. "We can only tell her, though. No one else."

"It's got to be our secret." Zoe looked toward Aryssa. "Don't worry, we're not telling anyone. I promise."

"Me too," Mackenzie confirmed. "Except for Mom."

"Yeah, Mom," Zoe agreed.

"You might not want to tell her." Charlie chose his words carefully. Tried to make a line of reasoning that only a kid would understand. "Like you said, she may not believe you. She might even think that something bad happened and you're hiding it."

"Like what kind of bad?" Mackenzie questioned.

"Like you were kidnapped and hurt, and you're hiding it by saying you saw the tooth fairy," Charlie answered. "Adults will believe that before believing what you really saw."

"But, we did see the tooth fairy," Mackenzie stated.

"Why would we lie?" Zoe shifted in her chair. "Lying is bad. Mom told us to never lie."

"Lying is bad," Aryssa agreed. "But still, the tooth fairy? Would you believe your friend if she told you that?"

Mackenzie shrugged. "Maybe." She paused. "You never said that you weren't."

"Yeah, you never said that," Zoe agreed. She held up the tooth. "You even have this."

"But, I'm not..." The edges of Aryssa's voice rippled with doubt. She hesitated. Whispered to herself as if something from her past exposed itself. "Could it be true? Am I really...?"

Zoe set the tooth on the table, but kept it pinched between her fingers. "If you give me the money now, I promise even more not to tell anyone."

"Zoe!" Mackenzie yelled. "It's not nice to ask for money."

"Why not? She's the tooth fairy and she has my tooth."

"It doesn't matter. It's not polite. Mom would say the same thing, too."

Zoe braced her elbows on the table. "How do you know what Mom would say?"

"Because I know."

"Girls," Aryssa intruded firmly. "Please, stop arguing."

"See Zoe," Mackenzie whispered accusingly. "Look what you did."

"Me?" Zoe slid her arms off the table. "All I wanted was to put the money in this." She plopped her fuzzy bear on the table. "You're the one who had to make a big deal of it all."

Something tingled deep inside Charlie. The faint electric-like current circled his spine and zipped into his extremities. Somehow the charge grew stronger. More powerful. Numbed the tips of his fingers. Could it be coming from that bear? He studied it. It was nothing more than a toy. Still, there was something about it. Something that snared his attention and made his body tingle. "Where'd you get that?"

"I bought it," Zoe answered. "Mackenzie bought one too."

Mackenzie set her fuzzy dog onto the table. "See."

The current inside Charlie waned. In fact, his internal voltage meter practically read zero. What was it about the bear? "Your own money?"

"Yep," Zoe answered proudly.

"Me too," Mackenzie interjected.

"Where did you buy it?"

Zoe shrugged. "A gas station."

Aryssa perked up. "Which gas station?

"I don't know. A gas station," Zoe said. "Mom needed to get gas."

"I get that." Aryssa moved toward the table. "What did it

look like?"

"There were gas pumps," Zoe answered.

"We went inside the building with Mom." Mackenzie hugged her dog. "That's when we saw the worker putting these on the shelf."

"He wasn't very happy," Zoe informed.

"Not happy?" Charlie questioned.

"Yeah," Mackenzie said. "More like bored. Like he didn't want to be doing stuff." She petted her toy. "He pulled this out of the box and handed it to me."

"I got mine off the shelf," Zoe stated.

Mackenzie scratched her dog's ear. "He told Mom that she should put money in them for our college."

Charlie leaned forward. "Why would he say that?"

Mackenzie blinked absently. The weight of bewilderment drooped her cheeks. "Because they're banks."

Zoe eyed Mackenzie. "And that's why I wanted the money. So I can finally put some in it."

Charlie slid his hands closer to the bear. The vibration in his fingers intensified. "Are you sure that there's nothing inside it already?"

"Pretty sure." Zoe shook the bear. "It's a little heavier than Mackenzie's."

The tink of metal on metal was faint. Barely audible. The fragile sound was practically devoured by the apartment's stagnant air. Charlie did his best to make his tone seem as friendly as possible. "Can I hold it?"

Zoe pulled the bear into her chest and protectively wrapped her arms around it. "How do I know that you're not going to hurt it?"

"I won't. I promise." Charlie crisscrossed his finger over his heart.

"What is it, Charlie?" Aryssa asked curiously.

Charlie scratched his head. "I'm not sure. I…I just want to look at it."

"It's a fuzzy toy," Aryssa said dismissively. "What could possibly be…?"

"I don't know," Charlie responded. "There…there might be something inside it."

Aryssa tapped her chin as if debating how to respond. "It's okay, honey. I trust him."

Zoe clung to the bear. "You do?"

Aryssa nodded reassuringly. "I do. I promise he won't hurt it."

Zoe stared at the table, thinking about what she should do. She eventually nodded ever so slightly. Slowly pushed the bear toward Charlie.

Charlie gently grabbed it. The current was even more intense. It vibrated through his fingers, up his arms and sped along his nerves.

He turned the bear around. Spotted the slot on the top of its head. Charlie then flipped it upside-down, right side up and then back over again. He could feel a slight shift of something inside. Heard the faint but distinctive tink. Ran his fingers across the fuzz on the underside of the bear. Felt that tiny rubber notch buried beneath the fur. Was something really inside?

Charlie held the bear several inches above the table. Zoe and Mackenzie were clearly curious. So too was Aryssa who hovered over Charlie's shoulder. He picked at the notch until it broke free.

Cloth-wrapped disks poured onto the table like coins falling out of a slot machine. Mackenzie gasped. Zoe's mouth fell open.

"What the hell?" Aryssa spoke absentmindedly.

A jolt of shock caused Charlie's heart to skip a beat. Could it be? He grabbed one of the circular objects and unfolded the cloth.

The coin shimmered in the apartment's dull light. Charlie now understood why he had felt that sensation. He tossed the coin onto the pile of what he assumed were more wrapped coins. "I don't believe it."

16

THE POLISHED COIN shackled Aryssa's attention and left her mesmerized. She wanted to say something, anything, but somehow she couldn't string together any of her fleeting thoughts.

Mackenzie broke the lengthy silence. "How'd you know those were in there?"

Zoe grabbed one of the coins and spread open the cloth. The twinkle in her eye brightened even more. "They're so shiny."

Aryssa grabbed one, too. "What are these, Charlie?"

Charlie leaned back in his chair and stared blankly at the pile. "They're coins."

"I can see that," Aryssa stated the obvious. She peeled the cloth off the coin in her hand. Sucked in an awe-filled breath. "I've never seen anything like this." A pause. "How'd you know?"

Charlie shrugged. "I just did."

Aryssa flipped the coin over. It was noticeably thinner than a dime and nearly the size of a quarter. "What are they used for?"

"Payment."

"Payment?" Aryssa asked.

"Yeah, payment." Charlie ran his hand over his hair. "It's

how I get paid."

Aryssa cocked her head. "To use your boat."

"More for the ride."

"People pay you with these?" Mackenzie questioned with curiosity. "They must be worth a lot of money."

"Depends," Charlie said. "Some more than others."

Aryssa ran her finger over the strange markings on the coin. She held it up for Charlie to see. "What does that mean?"

Charlie squinted. "I have no idea. I think it's part of the Phoenician alphabet or something." He paused to watch Zoe unwrap another coin. "I do know that they're very old."

One the flip side of the coin Aryssa noticed the worn image of a female head. Her stoic stare made the coin look like something that belonged in a museum. "These have to be ancient."

"Most likely ancient Greece." Charlie reiterated.

"Really?" Mackenzie gasped. "We learned about that in school." She studied the coin she held in her fingers. "This must be like super old."

Were these things really ancient? "If people are giving these as payment, then where are they getting them from?" Aryssa gingerly held the coin. "It's not like you can pop into any store and buy them."

"No, you can't," Charlie responded. He looked down at the table as if he were trying to decide what he wanted to say next. "In all honesty, I don't know how people get them." He tapped his chin. "Maybe a pawn shop or a coin dealer. That's how I get my money."

"You sell these things?" Aryssa questioned.

"How else am I going to pay the rent, buy food or fix my boat?"

The warmth of embarrassment wafted off Aryssa's skin. "You've got a point." She tried to cool her body with a lengthy sigh. "I guess it's hard to believe that people pay you with these strange-looking coins so they can go on a simple boat ride."

Charlie folded his arms over his chest. "It's something more than a simple sightseeing tour."

Aryssa delicately ran her hand over Charlie's shoulder. "Sorry. I'm not trying to downplay what you do. It's just that they could pay you with, you know, regular money." She motioned toward the pile on the table. "Instead of those. It would make things a whole lot easier."

"It probably would," Charlie agreed. "But it's not how things are done." He slouched in his chair. "This is what's expected if I'm going to drop them off on the other side of the river. It's always been, and as far as I know, will always be like that."

"Drop them off?" Confusion clung to Aryssa's tone. "You mean they don't come back with you?"

"There's no coming back once they get over there," Charlie answered. "That's how things work."

Aryssa gazed at the coin. The strange markings. The face. The way the metal shimmered. There was something unique about it. She spun it in her fingers and they instantly grew warm. Tingled ever so slightly. A faint, nearly imperceptible, energy seemed buried deep within the metal object—an energy that spoke of those who had once possessed it. Energy that seemed to be fueled by a drop of their very soul.

It whispered of a long-forgotten history. Spoke about something so ancient that only a select few would understand. A secret shared by those who had been tasked to keep it, even though it had openly existed right under the nose of humanity.

For a brief moment she closed her eyes to listen. There was a voice. Distant. Cryptic. Words filtered through its cobwebbed larynx, but she couldn't make any sense of them. What was it saying?

Aryssa tried to connect the dots. Coins. Charlie's boat. The river. People being dropped off on the other side, to never come back. She couldn't pull any of it together. None of it made sense. The frigid chill of Death's hand fingered its way up her spine. She shivered. What the hell was going on?

Mackenzie yawned. "I'm tired. Can I lie down?"

Slumber's heaviness weighed on Zoe's lids. "I am, too. Can I have my bear?"

"Of course," Charlie answered in a tone filled with parental concern. He slid the animal across the table.

"It's late for both of you," Aryssa said. "Why don't you go over to the couch."

The two girls nodded their agreement.

Aryssa led them into the room off the kitchen. She fluffed one of the small pillows for Mackenzie and another for Zoe on the other side of the couch, then gave each of them one of the throws that were draped over the sofa. With their arms wrapped around their animal banks, they were both fast asleep within minutes.

Aryssa gazed longingly at Mackenzie and Zoe. A warm, maternal energy swirled outward from deep in her core. She desperately wanted to give each of them a hug, a kiss on the cheek, but instead held back. The girls weren't hers. In fact, she barely knew them. Still, she had been tasked, whether by fate or accident, with their protection. There was no way she was going to let anything happen to them.

She shut off a nearby lamp and took a seat at the kitchen table. Charlie had his finger on one of the coins and absentmindedly slid it in a circle. "What are you thinking about?"

Charlie thrust the coin across the table and watched it crash into the pile. "Those."

Aryssa sighed. She opened her mouth to say something about the coins, but hesitated. None of this made sense and it appeared to be bothering Charlie, too. She bit her lip with uncertainty. Did she dare explore this further? Before her mind could process a meaningful response, her tongue expressed its impatience. "I..." she paused, "I guess I don't understand why people give you these. I mean, who are these people?"

Charlie shrugged. "I don't know. It's not like I talk to them."

"Why not?" Aryssa cocked her head with doubt. "You're with them for the duration of the ride. How could you not talk to them?"

"It's not how things are done." Charlie braced his elbows on the table. "I don't ask their names and I really don't want to know about their day. My only task is to drop them off on the other side of the river."

"Where, though? Where do you drop them off?"

Charlie hesitated. His voice dropped several decibels, as if to express his reluctance to share the answer. "A cave." He traced his finger over the table. "There's an outlet tucked off the side of the river. Very easy to miss unless you know what you're looking for. I follow it for nearly a mile, then I maneuver through this network of caves."

"Caves?" Aryssa tapped her temple. "You drop them off in a cave?"

Charlie nodded his answer.

"Then what?" Aryssa paused. "I mean, what happens next?"

"They follow the dock that leads them to a path that takes them deeper into the cave."

"That's it?" Aryssa questioned. She needed more. "Where do they go?"

"They're following the path they've chosen," Charlie answered vaguely.

Aryssa frustratingly sighed. "I don't understand. It's like you're talking in riddles."

"Look, it's my job to get them there." Charlie gestured with his hand. "That's what I'm paid to do. Plain and simple. I'm not paid to make small talk, give advice or follow them into that place."

"But...but aren't you the least bit curious about where they're going?"

"Not at all," Charlie said firmly. "Maybe one day I will be, but not now." He sipped the water Aryssa had given him earlier. "They've lived out their time on this side of the river. When I take them across they move on."

"Move on?" A jolt of awareness startled Aryssa. "Are you saying that...?" Did she understand it correctly? "You're not taking people across the river, you're...you're taking their souls." A quick breath. "Is that why you're paid with those coins?"

Charlie slowly slid his hand over the top of his head. A long exhale. "Something like that." He was quiet for several seconds. Appeared to be finished answering questions. He motioned at the tooth lying on the table. "You have some explaining to do, too."

"Yeah, that." How was she going to explain it? "It's something I've done for as long as I can remember. If you ask me why, all I can say is that I don't know." She grabbed the bottle of bourbon and slid it close. Hungrily watched the tantalizing amber liquid slosh against the bottle's walls. Thought about taking a long gulp and letting the warmth numb her mind. A brief glance at the two sisters asleep on the couch. She resisted and pushed the bottle away. "Never been taught what to do. I've always just known." A pause. "It's why I dance. Easy money to get what I need. It makes me happy and I believe I make the kids happy, too." She looped the yellow cord of the Crown Royal bag around her finger. "I happen to put them in here, just like you put those coins in that bank."

"I don't know why they were crammed in there," Charlie stated. "I didn't do that."

"Then who…?" Aryssa sat up straight with alarm. Bits and pieces of the conversation she had overheard outside the dressing room peeked through the fog of her recollection.

Charlie curiously tilted his head.

"I think I may know who did."

"You do?"

Aryssa nodded. "Sammy and Ariek."

Charlie's brows crinkled. "Who?"

"Sammy and Ariek," Aryssa repeated. "Ariek owns the club and Sammy," she looked over at the sleeping sisters, "he owns a gas station. It could be the same one the girls were talking about."

"How can you be so sure?" Charlie questioned.

Aryssa dropped her voice to a near whisper. "I overheard them talking when I was taking a break." She tapped her forehead, as if she were trying to dislodge a piece of her memory. "I remember Sammy saying something about money in a toy bank." She closed her eyes in search of an image. "They argued over Ariek blaming Sammy for allowing them to be sold at his station. And Sammy hinted at something about his nephew being the one." She hesitated. "Then they went on and on about needing the money for some kind of shipment."

"A shipment of what?"

"I don't know," Aryssa responded. "They were worried, though. More like fearful for their lives." A moan of frustration. "I wish I knew what the hell they were talking about."

"Try not to think about it," Charlie advised. He kept quiet for a few seconds. "I wonder if these coins were the payment."

"Maybe." Aryssa shifted in her chair. Ripples of unease washed against her sensibility. Something wasn't right. She glanced at the girls, then back at Charlie. A jolt of realization zipped through her. She gasped.

"What is it?"

"Sammy said something about sending the *brothers* to take care of it." Aryssa gestured wildly toward the sisters. "I bet those were the two men who snuck into the house. They weren't trying to kidnap the girls; they were after the banks."

Charlie's voice became taut. Protective. "Did they see you?"

Aryssa slowly nodded. Dread swam through her veins. "I helped their mother fend them off." Held her head in her hands. "I'm to blame for that fire."

"You keep mentioning a fire." Charlie spoke with a cautious tone. "How are you to blame?"

"The candles," Aryssa answered simply. "They tipped over and that set it off."

"Did you purposefully tip them?"

"God, no." Aryssa grabbed her hair. "I threw one of those men into the dresser and things spilled. The other I...I..."

"In other words, those candles fell over because you were defending the girls." Charlie stood, stepped behind Aryssa and put his hands on her shoulders. "If it wasn't for you, things would've been a lot worse. You protected them and saved their lives."

Charlie's assuring touch was soothing. It calmed her anxiety. "They're still in danger, though. Those men could be searching for them and their mother as we speak." She sighed as Charlie began to rub her shoulders. "We've got to get them somewhere safe."

"Does anyone besides me know where you live?"

Aryssa shook her head. "Hardly anyone." She thought about it more. "For sure no one at work."

"If that's the case, then I think this place is as safe as any for now." Charlie gently grabbed her arms. "It's late; let them sleep. First thing in the morning we'll drop them off at the police station or the hospital. Maybe we can even find their mother."

"What happens if they think I kidnapped them?" Aryssa responded alarmingly.

"We'll make sure that you're not seen with them," Charlie responded reassuringly. "We'll work it out."

Aryssa exhaled with relief and nodded her agreement with the plan. "I'm glad that...that you believe me." She gestured toward a tooth on the table.

"It seems we both have some unique secrets," Charlie said.

Aryssa yawned. "That we do." The weight of exhaustion took residence in her. She could feel her lids droop. Motioned to the recliner next to the couch. "Will you please crash here until the morning?"

Charlie nodded his affirmation. "Of course."

Aryssa curled up in the other, more beat-up, leather recliner. "Thank you for doing this," she whispered.

Charlie didn't respond, but Aryssa knew. She could somehow feel the willingness and the kindness radiate from him. It made him all the more attractive. The jar holding her guilt tipped over and broke open. How could she have let herself sneak out of the bar like that? She resolved to find a way to make it up to him. For now, she closed her eyes and let slumber wash over her.

17

THE STENCH OF charred cloth and burned flesh dominated the office. Sammy rested his cell against his temple and placed his glass of Scotch under his nose, hoping it would devour that disgusting smell. It worked for a few seconds, but the power of alcohol was no match against its heavyweight opponent.

Ariek leaned forward, slid his elbows onto his desk and held his head in his hands. The two brothers were sitting side-by-side on the couch directly across from Sammy. Heads bowed. The taller one was purposefully resting his cold bottle of beer against his crotch.

Sammy swallowed his annoyance, but the burned odor still clung to his tongue. "Are you sure?"

The portly brother nodded. "Fairly certain." He gestured at his brother. "He got the better look."

"Has to be," the taller one said. "I know that face and that body." Tipped his chin toward Sammy. "Know you do, too."

Sammy waved the comment away. "I need you to be absolutely certain."

"She did punch out early," Ariek advised.

"Why?"

Ariek lifted his head and shrugged. "How the hell should I know?" He rubbed his eye. "She wanted to go home."

"That's not like her," Sammy said.

"She leaves when she wants," Ariek replied. "Yes, it was earlier than normal, but who am I to question it?" He waved his hand absentmindedly. "Who am I to question any of them?"

"Maybe you should be a little more firm with your workers." Sammy's words sizzled as if they had been thrown on a grill.

Laser beams of anger shot from Ariek's eyes. His brows furrowed. "I don't tell you how to run your damn business, so don't go telling me how to run mine."

The escalating tension billowed into every corner of the room and joined forces with the overbearing smoke-laden odor. No one said a word for fear of coagulating the already thick air. The portly brother fiddled with his fingers. The taller one tapped the beer bottle between his legs. Ariek folded his arms over his chest and leaned back in his chair. Sammy knew he had to break the tension. There were things that needed to be solved. He slowly exhaled to quell his own irritation.

"Okay, I get it. We're all frustrated," Sammy finally said. "We need to pull together and figure this out. If we don't, then we're all screwed."

Ariek took a second to respond. "Agreed."

The brothers nodded.

"Let's focus on what we know," Sammy said. "First of all, we know, without a doubt, that those girls have the banks."

"I saw…" The stocky one corrected himself. "I mean, we saw both of them. Especially that bear."

Sammy set his gaze on the brothers. "And without a doubt you saw her and were then beaten up…"

"She came out of nowhere," the portly brother interjected. "I had no idea she was even there."

The taller brother nodded. "She flew out of that closet just as we were about to snatch those things."

"Okay, I get it," Sammy did his best to subdue his annoyance. "I just want to know that you're absolutely sure it was her."

"One-hundred percent," the taller brother confirmed.

"But why?" Sammy questioned aloud. "Why was she there?"

The portly brother winced when he shrugged. Massaged his shoulder. "Don't know."

"We have to assume she wanted those banks," Ariek said. "But how does she know what's in them?"

"That's the million-dollar question," Sammy said somewhat contemplatively. "How would she know?"

"Maybe she doesn't," the taller brother commented.

Ariek cocked his head. "What do you mean by that?"

The taller brother rubbed his palms over his thighs. "Maybe she wasn't there for those banks. I mean, if she was able to hide in the closest, then she could've had them long before we got there." He kept his hands on his legs. "The way that mom and her attacked us makes me believe they were more concerned about the girls than those banks."

He had a point. Sammy tapped his chin. "Let's say that was true; it still doesn't explain why she was there or why she was hiding in the closet."

"I guess it doesn't," the taller brother agreed.

"It all points back to her," Ariek commented.

"That it does," Sammy said. "Not only do we have to assume that she knows what's in those banks, but that they're now in her possession." He bit his lower lip with uncertainty. "Do either of you know what happened to those sisters?"

The brothers looked at each other as if the other might have an answer. The portly one sheepishly shook his head.

Frustration gurgled in Sammy's throat. "Neither of you have any idea."

"The fire spread so fast," the taller brother said. "There was no way we could stick around to find out."

Were they telling the truth? "Nothing," Sammy said in an accusatory tone. "You've no idea what happened to the mom or her daughters, do you?"

The taller brother shook his head. "We were given short notice about this operation and we had to plan on the fly." His voice grew defiant. "We were told it was going to be simple. But guess what? It wasn't. We were attacked and I ended up throwing that mom through the window. Next thing I know, we're separated. The house was burning. That…that dancer took those two girls." A pause. "Everything fell apart before we could even regroup." He jabbed a finger at Sammy. "We had no choice but to double back and meet at our secondary spot. That's when we decided it was too risky to go back." A harsh pause. "So no, we have no idea what happened to anyone or those damn banks, for that matter."

Ariek huffed, "What are we supposed to do now? Poke around the police stations? See if they're camped out at the hospital? Wander around to the hotels and ask? None of this is going to work."

Sammy swung his hands to bat the words away. "If we start our search with anyone, it needs to be with Aryssa. She must have some connection with that family and those banks." He shook his head to erase his doubt. "It's all got to start with her."

Ariek aggressively nodded his understanding. "It could be days before she comes back to work. We need them now. Before…before…you know what I mean."

"Enough. I don't need the added stress right now." He

glared at the brothers to drive his point home. "We don't have the time to wait it out." Turned to face Ariek. "Don't you have some kind of an employee file on her?"

"Just the basic stuff," Ariek answered without moving from his seat.

Sammy sighed heavily. "Can't you get it?" He gestured harshly. "I need to know where she lives."

"You don't know?" The portly brother asked with surprise. "After everything you've been through?"

"No, I don't." Sammy scoffed. "If I did, do you think I'd be sitting here asking?" He smacked his hand on the chair's armrest. "I need that file."

Ariek turned to the file cabinet behind him and opened the middle drawer. His fingers walked across the rows of files until he came on Aryssa's. He opened the manila folder. Flipped through some pages. "I'm afraid it doesn't have what you want."

"All I need is her address," Sammy said bitterly. "You know, where she lives."

"Only a P.O. box. No address." Ariek slid the folder across his desk toward Sammy.

Sammy stared in disbelief at a head shot of Aryssa. Flipped a page to her application. Then another. "This is useless." A grunt. "You're her employer. Why wouldn't you have more?"

"I have what's required." Ariek reached across the desk and grabbed the file. "Besides, dancers are considered private contractors. I don't directly pay them any wages or provide them any benefits." He cleared his throat. "That's all on them."

"You're kidding me!" Sammy retorted.

"Nope." Ariek laid the file in front of him. "You know money flows through here like water. I've kept things to the bare minimum for everyone's protection."

"I can't believe this," Sammy muttered.

Ariek sighed. "It's all I have." His cheeks had become red with frustration. "I wish I had more, but I don't. It's a don't ask-don't tell policy." He pointed at the phone in Sammy's hand. "You have her number."

"I was hoping to use it as a last resort." Sammy tapped the cell against his chin. Was this really his last option? How many times had he tried getting Aryssa to tell him where she lived? Would she give it up if he tried again? "You're the one who told me to let her go."

"Unless you've got a better idea, that's not going to work," Ariek said. "Or we wait until she shows up for her next shift."

Waiting wasn't an option either. Sammy sighed. What would he say if he did call? "There's got to be another way. She's turned me down all the other times I've asked."

"Maybe this time you'll get lucky," Ariek said.

"You've swooned her before," the taller brother said. "You should be able to do it again."

"Even a hint will help us," the portly brother stated. "Anything. You've got to try."

Maybe what they were saying was right. He had to at least try. Sammy tipped his chin with understanding. "I'll be right back."

He walked into the hallway outside the office. Things were much quieter now that the club was winding down for the night. Sammy opened his cell, found Aryssa's number and tapped call.

The phone rang. It rang again. And again. He was about to hang up when a jostling noise echoed through the speaker.

"Hello," Aryssa answered in a voice weighed with sleep.

"Hey Aryssa, how's it going?"

"Umm..."

18

IT HAD ONLY been a couple of minutes, maybe a little longer. Aryssa couldn't tell, but the conversation had gone on long enough. She abruptly ended the call and let her phone fall into her lap. The heat of dread spread through her body, leaving a razor-thin layer of sweat glazing her skin. "He knows," she blurted to no one in particular.

Charlie stirred. He opened his eyes and swiped his hand across the corner of his mouth. "You say something?"

"He knows," Aryssa repeated. "He knows about…"

"Who knows?" Charlie exhaled sharply, as if his lips were a valve allowing the compressed air of sleep to escape his lungs.

"Sammy," Aryssa answered.

"Sammy?"

"You know, Sammy." Aryssa snapped her fingers as a way to force her mind to clarify itself. "He…he owns the station."

Charlie rubbed his eyes. "Station?"

Aryssa's mind spun and blindly reached for a solid thought in which to anchor itself. "Yeah, the station. The gas station." She pointed at Mackenzie and Zoe sleeping on the couch. "Where those animals came from."

"You mean the banks?"

"Yes," Aryssa nodded quickly. "He knows." She frantically

looked around the room. Was the door locked? Windows shut? Could he be hiding in the closet? "Sammy." Hesitated as if speaking his name would invoke his presence. "He asked about them."

Charlie leaned forward and clutched Aryssa's hand. "Take a deep breath and slow down."

Aryssa did her best to steadily exhale. It was Charlie's touch that was reassuring. Comforting. The very warmth of his hand began to break apart the infection of dread.

"Tell me what happened." Charlie said.

Aryssa sighed. "Sammy called and started asking me a bunch of questions." She paused to lick her lips. "At first it all seemed harmless. He wanted to know why I had left the club early and what I had been doing all night. Things like that."

"Why would he be calling you this late?" Charlie questioned.

"He does that sometimes," Aryssa answered. "He's usually looking for a little…a little…you know."

Even though Charlie's expression remained stoic, there was a brief flicker of hurt that dulled the shine in his eyes. "Just like that? He calls and expects to get a piece?"

"He can call all he wants," Aryssa said. "He's not getting any, no matter how hard he tries." She cleared her throat. "That's what I thought he wanted, but it didn't take long for things to change."

Charlie rubbed his temple. "He started asking about the banks?"

"Not directly," Aryssa said. "It was more about what I had been doing. What shows I had been watching. What I had for dinner." She rubbed the back of her neck. "I thought it kind of strange, because he rarely asks me things like that."

"Why didn't you hang up?"

"I don't know." Aryssa shrugged. "I guess I didn't want to sound like I knew things."

"How'd he know, though?" Charlie questioned. "What'd he say to you?"

Aryssa bowed her head and grabbed her hair. "He asked me if I had watched the news and heard about the fire."

Charlie motioned toward the sleeping sisters. "You mean...?"

Aryssa nodded. "I tried to play dumb, but he kept pressing." She shifted in her chair. "He said the mother was in the hospital and there was some kind of reward for finding the missing kids." Her voice filled with worry. "What if the cops think I kidnapped them and now there's a huge manhunt?"

"I don't..." Charlie stared at the floor, lost in thought. "I don't think that's happening right now. Seems awfully fast for things to have progressed to that level. He could've been yanking your chain to see how you'd react."

"Well, he yanked pretty hard."

Charlie's head bobbed ever so slightly. "So it seems."

"Trust me, he made it sound convincing," Aryssa said, her voice coated with hysteria. "I don't know what to believe." She pressed her hands together. "I've got to get them back to their mother. You and I both know that someone's looking for them as we speak. It's only a matter of time before..."

Charlie gently squeezed Aryssa's hand. "You need to calm down," he said in a firm voice. "From what you've told me, no one knows that you have them. It's not like the police are going to come charging through your door right this very moment."

Despite the firmer grip, his touch was still soothing. "What should I do? I can't keep them here forever."

"No, you can't," Charlie said reassuringly. "Let's take it

one step at a time." He glanced toward the apartment door. "Does Sammy know where you live?"

Aryssa shook her head. "No way. He's asked me hundreds of times, but I've never told him."

"Your boss?"

"Ariek." Aryssa slashed her hand through the air dismissively. "Nope. No way." Shook her head. "I try to remain as private as possible."

"What about anyone at the club? Friends? Coworkers? Maybe a customer?"

"I don't remember telling anyone," Aryssa said. "I might have let it slip out, but I'm pretty sure that I haven't."

Charlie gestured toward the couch. "What's making him believe that you have them?"

Aryssa sighed. "I wish I knew."

Charlie quietly tapped his finger on the table. His thoughts seemed to drift away for a bit. "You said there were two men that snuck into that room?"

"Yeah," Aryssa answered.

"And you couldn't see their faces?"

"They both had covered their faces with some kind of scarf."

"But they could see you?"

Aryssa nodded. Her jaw slackened from the sudden realization. "Oh my…"

"You think they know you from the club?"

"They must," Aryssa confirmed. "How else would they know?"

"More like, how else would Sammy know?"

The puzzle pieces began to fit together. That conversation outside the dressing room emerged from her memory. Sammy and Ariek talking about the banks, the shipment and the need for money for some payoff. "Those two had to be the ones Sammy hired to 'take care of things.'" She compressed her frustration into her fists. "They must've recognized me and then told Sammy."

"And he called you to try to confirm it," Charlie said. "Did he say anything specific about the banks or those coins?"

"Sort of," Aryssa answered. "He mentioned the police were looking for some of the girls' personal things. Stuff like clothes and things they might've taken to bed." She paused. "Like a teddy bear or a blanket." The balloon of anxiety began to inflate in her gut. "That's when he said he wanted to pick me up."

"Come over here and get you?"

"No, not here," Aryssa said. "Somewhere of my choosing."

"That was a slick attempt to deceive you." Charlie rubbed his cheek. "He knows that you're not going to tell him where you live."

"I'm not." Aryssa folded her arms against her stomach. "He wanted to share the reward money with me." Aryssa waved her hand. "Said he knew the neighborhood where those girls went missing." Bowed her head and mumbled. "Kept saying something about getting his face on the news would help his business."

Charlie slowly exhaled. "Definitely yanking your chain."

Aryssa massaged her temples to pacify her sudden headache. "Well, he thought he could find them before the cops did." A nervous tremor rippled across her hands. "You know what else he told me?"

Charlie tipped his chin as a way of encouraging her to continue.

"Said if the cops figured out who had them, that person would go to jail for the rest of their life." She shivered anxiously. "I can't go to jail."

"You're not going to jail," Charlie affirmed in a calm tone.

"How do you know?"

"Because…" Charlie hesitated. "You and I both know that he was lying to you."

"Well, it worked," Aryssa responded. "He said that whatever belongings the kidnappers had would be used as evidence." She tented her fingers over her heart. "I kind of froze and then I hung up."

Charlie sighed. "I'm surprised he hasn't called you back."

Aryssa held up her phone. "Three times. I turned off the ringer so I wouldn't hear it."

"That's smart of you," Charlie said. "I don't think he's going to stop, though."

"He won't, and neither will the cops," Aryssa said with alarm. "What happens if he tells them?"

"He won't," Charlie stated.

"He could. Then the next thing you…"

"Think about it," Charlie interrupted. "If he wants those banks, there's no way he wants the police involved." He paused. "He wants you to believe he will call the police, but I know for a fact he's not saying a thing to them. Trust me on this."

Aryssa smiled. What Charlie had said made sense. Still, there was a part of her that clung to the fear of being arrested. Clung to the chance that Sammy and his friends could find her and the two girls. Find the banks and the coins. "What should we do?"

Charlie turned toward Mackenzie and Zoe. "Let them sleep a little longer. They need it." He rubbed his brows with his forefinger and thumb. "Just before most of the world starts waking up, we could take them…."

"Where can we possibly take them?" Aryssa asked with worry coating her voice. "I'm not going anywhere near a police station."

"It would be the easiest."

"No way," Aryssa stated sharply. "I'm not taking that chance."

"Well…" Charlie paused. "We could take them to the hospital. I'm guessing that their mom was taken to the emergency room—most likely the one closest to her home."

"What happens if she's not there? Then what?"

Charlie yawned. "It shouldn't be that big of a deal if she isn't."

"Not a big deal? We can't just walk in there and find out." Aryssa uneasily ran her fingers through her hair. "Cops tend to notice kids. Especially ones that are missing."

"It'll be okay," Charlie said reassuringly. "We'll just show the girls where they need to go."

"You mean abandon them?"

"We're not going to abandon them." Charlie's face scrunched with exasperation. "We point them toward hospital security. The girls tell them who they are and before anyone can figure out what's going on, we're long gone."

Aryssa sighed. "I don't know about this."

"Would you rather try to explain things in person?"

"You've got a point. "Aryssa glanced at the pile of coins. "What about those?"

"I've been thinking about that," Charlie said. "Just in case something happens, I think it best that we keep them. When this finally blows over, we can give some back to the girls."

Aryssa slid back into the recliner and let the footrest lift her feet. "I'm good with that, as long as they get to keep a few." She fluffed the pillow behind her head. "I just hope you're right about all of this."

19

SAMMY GRUMBLED. TAPPED redial. Listened as the phone rang and rang and rang once more until it finally went to Aryssa's voicemail, yet again.

"Damn it," Sammy mumbled. He paced back and forth in the hallway as he mulled over what to do next. Call again? Go to the cops? Shook his head to the contrary. Drive around and try to find her? If that wasn't like looking for a black cat in a coal cellar. What about cancelling the shipment until this blows over? The Network would never go for...

"No luck?" Ariek was standing in the doorway to his office.

"I had her," Sammy said proudly. "She was about to tell me."

"Tell you what, exactly?"

"Where those kids and the banks are." Sammy glanced at his phone to make sure he hadn't missed a call. The screen was blank. "That is, until she suddenly freaked out and hung up." He pressed redial and put the phone to his ear.

"Whoa, whoa, whoa." Ariek reached for Sammy's cell. "What are you doing?" he asked in a tone filled with alarm.

"What does it look like?" Sammy said condescendingly. "She's got to pick up."

"Not if she knows what you're trying to do," Ariek replied sternly.

The call clicked to voicemail. Sammy grunted. He ground frustration in his clenched teeth. "This is bullshit."

"Yeah, it is," Ariek confirmed. "But we've got to come up with a better plan."

"Like what?"

"I don't know yet." Ariek answered. He gestured at Sammy's phone. "You've proven what we had expected. She knows about all of it." A pause. "The more you try to call, the more desperate it makes you look. And that just gives her more of a reason not to answer."

Despair took Sammy's finger and nudged it toward redial. What Ariek had said made sense, but it wasn't solving the issue at this very moment. Sammy needed to do something, anything, but be patient. "There's too much at stake to do nothing."

"We've got to be smart about this," Ariek advised. He held his office door open. "Put your phone away and get in here."

There was no way Sammy was going to slip his cell into his pocket. He instead gripped it tightly and held it up for Ariek to see. "Just in case she calls."

"I wish she would," Ariek said. "It would make things so much easier. Just don't call *her*."

"I won't," Sammy said as if he had just been scorned by a parent. He despised being talked to like that. A sigh. It was the right thing to do, though. He took a deep breath and forced himself to step across the threshold into the office.

Ariek quietly shut the door. The two brothers hadn't moved from their spots on the couch. That damn burnt odor still permeated the air. Ariek's head was bowed, making it appear as if he were deep in thought. He slowly walked to his desk, sat in his chair and took a swig from his drink.

Ice cubes rattled against glass. It was late. The taller brother yawned. Exhaustion clung heavily to the mood inside the office. Sammy shifted uneasily in his chair. After a minute or two, Ariek shook away his thoughts and glanced at the group. "I have an idea."

20

ARYSSA LOWERED HER head and cocked it sideways, away from the street. She buried her face deeper into the hood of her sweatshirt. The oncoming headlights grew brighter. The sound of rubber spinning over concrete became louder. The car wasn't slowing down; the driver must not have seen her or maybe he didn't care. Either way, it passed by and disappeared into the distance. Aryssa sighed with relief and lifted her gaze.

Streetlights dotted the sidewalk that led the two or three blocks to the hospital. Traffic lights were blinking their cautionary yellow. She could just make out the glowing red sign that pointed toward the emergency room. Zoe and Mackenzie were huddled close to her side, their arms wrapped snugly around their animal banks. Slumber dulled the sheen in their eyes and weighed heavily on their cheeks.

"Why do we have to be up so early?" Mackenzie questioned.

"Yeah," Zoe chimed in. "It's still dark out."

Aryssa gestured to the sky, which had lightened to a shade below midnight blue. "It'll be daylight soon enough."

"But it's not now," Zoe said.

Aryssa gently rubbed Zoe's shoulder. "It's better this way."

"No, it's not," Zoe countered.

A wave of guilt washed over Aryssa. She had struggled with the thought of waking them so early. Now, she forced them to walk down the street before the sun had even peeked over the horizon. They should be in bed, preferably their own.

"Are you sure Mom is going to be there?" Mackenzie asked.

Aryssa was slow to answer. "You have to trust me on that." She looked at each girl in order to give them a sense of reassurance. "Do you remember what I told you to do?"

Mackenzie stared blankly at Aryssa. Zoe yawned and then picked at her bear's fur. Neither girl uttered a sound.

"Come on, you two," Aryssa commanded. "Help me out. What are you going to do once you get inside?"

Mackenzie rubbed her cheek. "Why couldn't Charlie come with us too?"

"He's watching from the car."

"He could've driven us to the front door and then we all could've gone in together."

Aryssa quietly sighed. "It's too risky to pull the car up in front of the hospital. It's just better if I walk you most of the way.

"No, it's not," Zoe said. "If you've walked us this far, you should be able go all the way."

Aryssa wrapped her arms around each of the girls and pulled them close. "I don't think the police would understand why I brought you. They would end up asking way too many questions."

Mackenzie nestled against Aryssa. "What kind of questions?"

"Oh, you know." Aryssa's mind blanked. "Umm, stuff like who am I? How do I know you? Why are you with me?" A pause. "Kind of makes me look suspicious."

"But you're not. You're the tooth fairy," Zoe said. "Everyone likes the tooth fairy."

"It's not that easy." Aryssa kneeled next to her. "Let's stick to the plan, okay?" A pause. "Who are you going to talk to once you go inside?"

"The security people." Mackenzie smiled with satisfaction.

"That's right," Aryssa answered. "Who else?"

"A nurse," Zoe said.

"Good girl." Aryssa caressed the arms of both girls. "And what are you going to tell them?"

"That we're looking for our mom, Mary," Mackenzie said. "She was in a house fire."

"Very good." Aryssa could feel her cheeks scrunch into a smile. "And if your mom isn't in there, will the security people help you find her?"

"That's what you told us," Mackenzie said.

"I did." Aryssa looked down the sidewalk toward the hospital. Someone stepped out from the other side of the hospital sign and walked across the street. Another car passed them on the opposite side of the road. Nothing else was moving. It all appeared safe and sound. Maybe this was going to be easier than she'd thought.

Aryssa gave her surroundings one last scan. As far as she could tell there were no security cameras scrutinizing her movements. No one peeking from the side of a building or a nearby window. A couple of blocks behind her Charlie was watching from inside his car. Aryssa quickly waved and then made sure the hood was covering her head. "Okay, ladies. Let's go."

"If you say so," Zoe responded with a slight scoff in her tone.

Aryssa ignored it and nudged them forward. "Aren't you

excited to see your mom?"

"I am," Mackenzie answered.

"What about you, Zoe?" Aryssa asked in her best chipper voice.

"Of course I am," Zoe said. She was quiet for a few seconds. "But I like you, too."

"Will we see you again?" Mackenzie questioned sincerely. "And it doesn't count when we lose a tooth."

Admiration melted Aryssa's heart. "Of course you will." She stopped at the street corner and glanced left, then right. "And it won't be because of a tooth."

"Promise?" Mackenzie held Aryssa's hand as they crossed the street.

"I promise," Aryssa happily answered. She stepped up onto the curb and continued to lead the two sisters down the sidewalk.

"You need to swear on it," Zoe stated.

Aryssa bit her lip with uncertainty. "Swear on it?"

"Yeah," Zoe said. "Pinky swear."

Confusion coated Aryssa's tongue. "How do I do that?"

Zoe held up her hand and extended her pinky finger toward Aryssa. "Lock yours with mine and say you promise."

Aryssa wrapped her fifth digit around Zoe's smaller one. "I promise I'll visit you."

Zoe gripped tighter. "And it won't be because of a tooth."

Aryssa nodded. "I promise to visit and it won't be because of a tooth."

Zoe smiled and unclasped her finger. "Now you're bound by your promise."

"You have to do mine." Mackenzie held up her hand.

"Okay." Aryssa started to extend her finger when a pair of headlights filled her vision.

A dark SUV raced up onto the sidewalk. Tires fought to grab the concrete as the car screeched to a stop. The passenger door flung open and a man dressed in black jumped out.

Mackenzie and Zoe screamed with fear.

Panic flooded Aryssa's veins. It flowed into her arms and legs. She desperately grabbed the two sisters and pulled them behind her.

A black bandana covered a chunk of the man's face. Was this the man from the…? He ran right toward Aryssa. Laser-like beams of anger shot from his pupils.

Aryssa backpedaled as quickly as she could. She tried to create some distance between herself and the attacker. Tried to find a moment to regroup and think. It was all happening too fast.

The man was practically on top of her in no time. There was nowhere to run. She had no choice but to stand her ground. Aryssa shoved Mackenzie and Zoe farther behind her. Set her feet underneath her and lifted her fists to her face.

"You damn bitch!" the man grunted. His arm cocked, fist clenched. It shot forward in a blur of movement.

Thwack! The punch caught her above the left eye. Thrust her head backward. Her brain smashed against the wall of her skull and sent static spilling across her vision. Her legs buckled. Balance teetered. She slumped to her knees and grabbed the sides of her head to try to steady the wobble. It wasn't helping. A wave of darkness smashed against Aryssa and caused her to fall forward.

"Leave me alone!" One of the girls yelled.

"Help!" the other screamed.

"You're coming with me, now!" The man demanded in a voice that rumbled through his clenched teeth.

Aryssa fought to push herself up. Her arms felt as if they

were made of melted plastic. She struggled to get her feet underneath her, but her strength faltered. She collapsed back toward the ground.

"No!"

"Get in there."

The rustle of unwilling bodies. The screaming. The sobbing. A plea. Aryssa needed to save Mackenzie and Zoe. She frantically tried to get up. Roll to her side. Her equilibrium wavered. Stability betrayed her.

A car door slammed. Then another. An engine revved. Tires squealed.

What had just happened?

CHARLIE WATCHED ARYSSA, Mackenzie and Zoe stop at the street corner. He purposefully mimicked Aryssa's movements. Looked left when she looked left. Then right when she did. As far as he could tell, the streets looked perfectly harmless. Quiet and unthreatening. Aryssa must have felt the same, because she started to lead the girls across the street.

Static trampled over the song on the radio. Charlie grunted his annoyance and fiddled with the dial. It took a few seconds to retune the station, except the music blared from the speakers. What's wrong with this damn thing? He reached for the volume, but something rerouted his attention, forced him to look up and...

"What the..."

A dark SUV jumped the curb and skidded to a stop right in front of Aryssa. Someone dressed in black clothing leapt out the passenger door, ran up and punched her.

Charlie stomped the gas pedal. Car wheels spun mercilessly. The scream of the engine filled the interior and clashed with the yelling that filled his head.

Mackenzie and Zoe were thrown into the back of the SUV. The figure dressed in black slammed the door and jumped into the passenger seat. How was Charlie going to save them now?

He gripped the steering wheel tightly. Aimed his car right for the SUV. The speedometer quickly accelerated. The distance closed fast, but the larger vehicle wasn't backing down either. It was a game of chicken. Would the SUV swerve out of the way? Would Charlie? What would happen if they both turned the same way?

Eighty yards was sliced to forty, which was chopped to twenty in a matter of seconds. The SUV wasn't letting up. Neither was Charlie.

Charlie's focus narrowed. Heart thumped wildly in his chest. His car was no match against that mammoth SUV. He chomped down on his teeth and clamped his jaw. At the last second he slammed the brakes and swung the back end of his car to try to block as much of the road as possible.

Bam! The SUV slammed into the back of Charlie's car. Metal crunched. Glass shattered. Tires screeched in agony. Pandemonium crammed itself inside the car. Charlie was thrust sideways as everything around him spun uncontrollably. The car finally came to rest somewhere in the middle of the street. All went quiet save for the screaming in his head and the music blasting from the radio.

Charlie rubbed his forehead. All sense of direction had been decimated. He glanced over his shoulder. Out the windows to his left, then right. Nothing made sense. He happened to catch the SUV's taillights shrinking smaller and smaller the farther it raced down the road.

"Shit!" Charlie shouted. He caught a glimpse of movement

out of the corner of his eye.

Aryssa stumbled toward the car. She braced her head with one hand and reached forward with the other. "Charlie."

Charlie climbed out of the driver's door. The world rocked back and forth as if he were on a boat in a stormy sea. It took him a moment to find his voice. "Are you alright?"

Aryssa moaned with pain. "They got them!" She collapsed into Charlie's arms. "I couldn't stop…"

Charlie firmly held Aryssa and led her to the passenger door. "Get in."

"What are we going to do?" Aryssa began to sob. "This can't be happening."

Charlie braced his hand on the hood as he staggered back around the car and slid into the driver's seat. Turned the ignition. It cranked, but the engine refused to respond. "Damn it."

Aryssa rested her forehead against the dash. She sniffled. "It's my fault."

Charlie turned the key again. "Not the time to place blame." The starter whined. "There are more important things to worry about."

Aryssa rubbed her temple. She glanced toward the back of the car and then at Charlie. "Are you okay?"

"Yeah," Charlie answered. "This car is screwed." He turned the key again. Miraculously the engine stuttered to life. He shifted into Drive and the car stammered forward. Plastic crunched under the weight of the tires. "Let's get out of here."

"Where'd they go?" Desperation coated Aryssa's voice.

"I don't know."

Aryssa grabbed her head. "We've got to get them back."

"I know," Charlie simply answered. "I know." He looked into the rearview mirror. The street was empty. A sigh. Where were they taking Mackenzie and Zoe? What was going to happen to them? Charlie rubbed his shoulder uneasily. What could he possibly do now?

21

SAMMY ANGRILY TOSSED the head he'd torn from the bear bank across the table. Tattered cloth entrails wavered from its neck. Bits of stuffing swirled through the air and quietly landed as if they were too frightened to disturb the tension in the room.

"Nothing!" Sammy thrust his fist forward, making it the dot to an exclamation point. A scorn-filled glance around the table. "Do any of you see anything that resembles a coin?"

No one said a word. The silence stoked the flames to his frustration even more.

"Well, do you?"

The taller brother furrowed his brows. "Of course we don't."

"That's because there's nothing to see." Sammy sharply gestured toward the two sisters sleeping side by side on the floor mattress. "But I do see them." Repeatedly tapped his knuckles against his forehead. "What were you thinking?"

"They came out of nowhere. It wasn't like we had time to analyze the situation," the portly brother said. "We had to make a quick decision."

"You've been making a lot of those lately," Sammy commented with a hint of condescension. "It's not what I'm paying you to do."

"I haven't seen any money yet," the portly brother stated.

"That's because you haven't produced anything," Sammy fired back. A nod at the kids. "Except that."

The taller brother postured. Stepped toward Sammy. "Maybe, just maybe, there was never any money after all." A tense pause. "Maybe you're the one wasting our time and sending us on a wild-goose chase."

"I know where I kept my money," Sammy said defensively. "Why the hell would I turn into a snitch?"

"I don't know. You tell me." The taller brother took another step. "Maybe you're trying to set us up. Sell us out. That car did come out of nowhere. No one said anything about this dancer friend of yours having someone helping her."

"I had no idea." Sammy postured. Wasn't going to back down. "You better choose your words carefully, especially if you're going to accuse me of lying."

"And what are you going to do about it?" The taller brother took a step toward Sammy. "Me and my brother have been the ones who've put our necks on the line." He tipped his chin curtly. "While all you've done is bitch and moan about…"

"Enough!" Ariek slammed his fist against the table. "All this arguing isn't helping solve the issue at hand."

The taller brother faced Ariek. Anger wrinkled his forehead. "It was your idea to have us watch the hospital." His voice became more pressured. "We did what we had to do." Jabbed a finger toward Sammy. "I don't need this…this piece of crap telling me all the things that I've done wrong."

Sammy puffed his chest. "We wouldn't be in this mess if you hadn't…"

"Sammy!" Ariek fired off.

"I'm not going to let this two-bit criminal try to blame

me…"

"Both of you need to chill the hell out!" Ariek's face was the color of a fire-roasted chili pepper. "Yes, it was my idea that started this ball rolling. And I take responsibility for it." A pause. "However, we need to tackle the situation before us. Not the one that got us into this mess." He glanced at each of the men standing around the table. "Like it or not, we're in this together. And we better figure a way out, or we're all as good as dead."

Voices went dormant behind sealed lips. Sammy slowly rocked back and forth on the balls of his feet. The silence was an annoying drip splattering against his patience. He couldn't hold back. "What are we going to do with them?"

Ariek shrugged. "Haven't figured that out just yet."

The portly brother slid his finger across his throat. "It's the quickest."

"No way," Sammy said in a voice wrinkled with shock. "Which of you has the guts to kill two little girls?" A pause. "I sure don't."

"They've seen our faces," the portly brother argued. "There's no other way."

"A bit harsh," the taller brother stated, "but I've got to agree. There aren't many options."

Ariek shook his head. "Look at them." He swung his attention toward the two girls. "It's the middle of the afternoon and they're sound asleep. You've pumped them so full of drugs that they're not going to remember a damn thing."

A faint smile thinned the taller brother's lips. "Had to shut them up somehow."

"It's a blessing in disguise," Ariek commented. "But I have to agree with Sammy. There's no way that I could live with myself if we killed them."

"You can be disgusted with the results, but something has to be done. And sometimes you've got to get your hands dirty," the taller brother said. "What worries me right now is that the entire police force is searching for them as we speak. And the longer they remain in our possession, the greater the chance they'll be found." He tapped his chest. "I'm not going down for something that could've been fixed in the first place."

"Well, I don't want the blood of two kids on my hands," Sammy said firmly. "There's got to be a better way."

"You could sell them." The portly brother suggested. "You've been worried about not having enough for that shipment."

"Into the trade?" Ariek questioned with curiosity staining his tone.

The portly brother nodded. "Why not?"

Ariek rubbed his chin, as if encouraging his prudence. "It would rid us of the problem." He looked right at Sammy. "Give us a chance to pay off our debt, too."

Sammy nodded his agreement. "Young and innocent. I'm sure they'd fetch a damn good price."

Ariek chuckled. "And if something happens to them, we'll never know."

"Ignorance is bliss," Sammy commented.

"After a few days, you won't even remember them," the taller brother said encouragingly. "I'll just keep them stoned until they wake up someplace far from here."

"In a land far, far away," Sammy added.

Ariek slid his hands into his pockets. "While I love this idea, I think we can do better."

"Better?" Sammy questioned with curiosity. "They help us with the payment and we get rid of them. How can that get any better?"

Ariek face scrunched as if he'd swallowed something bitter. "By dealing a final blow to the source of our problem."

Sammy folded his arms over his chest. "You want to take out the Network?"

"No," Ariek answered bluntly. "You must have a death wish to think we can do that." He pointed at the torn bear head. "I'm talking about Aryssa."

Sammy's thoughts came together. He tapped the table with certainty. Glanced at the sleeping sisters, then at the shredded bank. The coins—Aryssa had to have them in her possession. Was there any other logical explanation? "I think I understand what you mean."

"See how calmness makes you see things more clearly." Ariek sighed. "She's got to have them."

Sammy clenched his teeth. He hated when Ariek tried to impart some kind of wisdom on his behalf. His breath smoldered. That argument with the taller brother had only added to the storm cloud covering his judgment. He slowly exhaled and did his best to let the tension escape from his throat. Took a moment before he quietly nodded. "Are you suggesting we use them as bait?"

"The girls for the coins," Ariek concurred. "It means that you're going to have to make another phone call."

Sammy pulled his cell from his pocket and gripped it tightly. "If we do this, what's preventing Aryssa from going to the cops?"

"Once the exchange occurs, we call them before she does," Ariek answered. "Make it look like she's the kidnapper."

"Too risky," the portly brother said. "She'll be given the chance to tell her side of the story and the cops will eventually figure it out that she isn't the one. They'll then come after us." He sat in a nearby chair. "I say we off her once the money exchanges hands."

"That's if she has it," the taller brother commented rudely.

Sammy contained his ire. "I know she has it."

"If you say so," the taller brother said.

Sammy grumbled. Swallowed the words that were ready to spew out his mouth. "Killing her is a bit extreme, especially in front of those kids."

"Why does it matter?" the portly brother asked with a shrug. "They'll be too stoned to remember."

"We could off them all," the taller brother said.

Ariek leaned over the table. "That's just creating an unnecessary bloodbath." A pause. "No one has made mention of that person helping her."

The portly brother punched a fist into his open hand. "I say kill him, too."

Sammy held out his hand to stop the flow of escalating ideas. It was time to make a command decision. "This is what we're going to do." He took a brief survey of the mattresses on the floor. The bathroom in the corner. The showers. The makeup counter with its several mirrors and chairs. The hooks embedded in the walls and floor. And finally the box of chains and leather restraints.

"I'm going to call Aryssa and convince her to exchange the coins for the girls." Sammy looked toward the taller brother. "Don't worry, if she says she doesn't have them or doesn't know where they are..." he smiled sinisterly and briefly stared at the sisters. "Let's just say that I'm going to effectively encourage her to give me what I want." Held up his finger to snuff any comments. "And when we make the trade, this is what we're going to do."

22

ARYSSA HASTILY SCAMPERED up the flight of steps, darted down the hall and then pounded on the door with the side of her fist. "Charlie!" She sharply exhaled to try to quell her anxiety. "Charlie, are you home?"

He didn't answer. Panic frayed the ends of Aryssa's nerves. Numbness trickled down her legs. She tightened her thighs to prevent the almost inevitable slump to the floor. Bit her lip to keep it from trembling. Tried to rein in her jumbled thoughts. Why hadn't she been more aware of her surroundings? How could she have let herself get beaten like that? Where had they taken Mackenzie and Zoe? Were they okay? Would the coins really get them...?

Aryssa pounded again. "Charlie, please answer." She lifted her fist and was about to descend on the door. *Click.* The lock. *Clunk.* The deadbolt.

Charlie swung open his apartment door. Slumber weighed heavily on his lids. He rubbed his temple. "What's going on?"

Aryssa held up her phone. "He called."

"Sammy?"

"He wants the coins for the girls." Aryssa hastily slid past Charlie.

Charlie sighed. "A one-for-one exchange?"

The door clicked shut behind Aryssa. She nodded. "If I

don't do it, he'll kill them." She sniffled. "I...I can't have that on my conscience for the rest of my life. Especially after I screwed everything up."

"It wasn't you," Charlie said reassuringly. "We've been over this. It was both of us."

Aryssa lowered her head. "I can't help but feel..."

Charlie rubbed Aryssa's shoulder. "What else did he want?"

"To meet him at ten o'clock in the alley behind the ..." Aryssa hesitated. The place had already created friction between herself and Charlie. Was it another unintentional reminder of all she had done? She let the name slip slowly past her parched lips. "The Penn."

"Umm." Charlie seemed to reel backward from the words. "Really...he really wants that...?"

Aryssa nodded her affirmation. Time was of the essence. She needed to put that past behind her. "We've got less than two hours."

Charlie scratched his cheek. "Maybe we should get the police involved. I mean, this has taken us deeper and deeper into..."

Aryssa waved her hand to cut Charlie off. "No cops. He said no cops." She shivered. "If there's even a hint of them...then the deal's off. He'll kill them."

"The cops could hide themselves. You know, like watching from the rooftops."

"No. I'm not taking that chance," Aryssa said firmly. "Let's just give him the coins, get the girls and get them safely to their mother." A sharp inhale. "Then we can put this whole thing behind us."

Charlie leaned against the wall. "I don't like the sound of any of this. Why does he want those coins so badly?"

"I don't know," Aryssa responded bluntly. "And I don't care." She gestured out the door. "Those girls are more important than some damn coins."

Charlie sighed. He bowed his head and lost himself in his thoughts for several long seconds. "That money is replaceable. Those girls aren't."

"I don't see any other choice but to give it to him."

"Neither do I." Charlie bowed his head. "This time we're not letting them get the better of us."

A BREEZED STROLLED down the alley and gently flicked Aryssa's hair. It whisked away a few drops of humidity's perspiration, but there was still a large part that clung to the air the way dirt clings to sweaty skin. Aryssa took a deep breath to try to suppress her ballooning apprehension. She coughed. "What's taking them so long?"

"I don't know," Charlie said in a tense tone.

"It's almost twenty after," Aryssa said. "They should've been here by now."

"They will."

"How do you know?" Aryssa did her best to shore up her resolve, but the entire situation had already taken a bite out of the foundation of her fortitude.

"He's the one that called you, didn't he?"

"He could be playing us." Aryssa glanced over her shoulder to her right, then her left. "He could be watching us right now and planning a way to rob us."

Charlie peered into the alley's darkness. "I bet they're not even sure that we have them." He sighed. "This all started when they tried to steal those banks. It shows me that they want those coins and they want them bad."

"Is there a point to what you're saying?"

"Yeah. They'll be here."

Silence built a wall between Aryssa and Charlie. It crumbled after a couple of minutes when a pair of headlights lit up the other end of the alley. A dark SUV slowly made its way between the buildings, past the several Dumpsters that stood stoically against soot-stained walls and garbage cans stuffed with burgeoning plastic bags. It slowed to a stop some sixty feet away.

Aryssa's heart thumped wildly against her ribs. She tightly gripped the toiletry bag with palms glazed in sweat. Stood perfectly still, almost defiantly, in the headlights. Charlie muttered something, but she refused to turn away from the car. Refused to move her lips to ask what he had said. Refused to display any sign of weakness.

The two front doors swung open in unison. A man in dark clothes stepped out of the driver's side and slid himself to the far edge of the door. Sammy stepped out of the other. He kept it open as he walked to the front of the car and then leaned against the hood. Folded his arms across his chest.

"Aryssa, Aryssa, Aryssa," Sammy repeated in a tone overflowing with disappointment. "I had hoped it wouldn't come to this."

"Don't put the blame on me. You're the one who put this in motion," Aryssa said firmly.

Sammy seemed to sway from the impact of Aryssa's accusation. He stiffened with anger, but just as quickly the edges of his posture softened. "More like fate had her hand in this." A pause. "She can lead in some strange ways." He sliced his hand in front of him. "Suffice it to say that this will be the end of her influence in this matter."

"The end will be when the girls are home safely," Aryssa

stated.

"And the coins are in my possession," Sammy retorted.

"So where are they?"

Sammy smiled. "In due time. There are details that need to be worked out."

"Like what?"

Sammy pointed at Charlie. "Like, who's that?"

"A friend," Aryssa responded. "And who's that?" She gestured at the man standing by the driver's door.

"A business associate."

Aryssa tipped her chin at what looked like the more portly of the two intruders from the house fire. "We've meet, haven't we?"

"Twice," the portly intruder fired back. "It was brief, to say the least."

Aryssa smiled curtly. "Third time can be the charm."

"It could, but we'll see."

Charlie reshuffled his stance but remained standing tall and unmoving. Aryssa's patience was nipped by her apprehension. She wanted this done and over with. "Enough with the games, Sammy. Let's finish this so we can all be on our way."

Sammy took a few seconds to respond. "As you wish." He popped himself off the hood. "Why don't you toss those coins over here?"

"No way," Aryssa responded. "Show me the girls first."

"See what I mean by details?" He tapped his chin. "For the moment, I'll oblige your hastiness." He pointed at the portly man and then swept his hand toward the back of the car.

The man reached into the back seat and pulled out two small figures. He shoved them toward the front of the car. Gripped each of them by the nape of their neck and held them upright as if they were on display.

Aryssa did her best to keep shock from spreading over her expression. Mackenzie and Zoe swayed like saplings in a strong breeze. Their eyes were barely open. Zoe's head slumped forward. Mackenzie's shoulders slouched.

"There they are," Sammy said. "Now toss that bag over here and then I'll send them to you."

Shouldn't Sammy be the one to make the first move? Aryssa opened her mouth to demand another way. Something more favorable. Instead she sealed her lips shut. All she wanted was the girls safely in her possession. Get them out of here and put all of this behind her.

Aryssa squeezed the bag. "Fine." With an underhanded motion she tossed it and watched it slowly spin through its high arc. It landed with a thud some twenty feet from Sammy.

"A little short," Sammy said.

"Close enough," Aryssa responded. "Send them over."

"Not so fast." Sammy pointed at the bag. "How do I know the coins are in there?"

"They're all there," Charlie said reassuringly. "We're not like that."

"So you say," Sammy replied. "I need to see for myself."

"Open it," Aryssa suggested. "It's all there."

Sammy shook his head. "Again, such difficulties could have been avoided if you would've shown a little patience from the beginning." He paused. "There could be something very unpleasant waiting for me inside that bag. Some kind of trap. Maybe even a bomb."

"When would we have had time to put that together?" Charlie questioned.

Sammy shrugged "How do I know that you didn't?" He sighed. "For the sake of saving time, this is what's going to happen." A gesture toward Aryssa. "You bring that bag over here and show me that it's legit. Once I see that it is, I'll let you take the girls back with you."

"It's a bag full of coins," Charlie said with a faint growl. "Just open it."

Sammy tipped his chin toward Aryssa. "If you don't do it, then this entire exchange is off. It's your call."

Aryssa clicked her tongue with uncertainty. She glanced at the bag, then at Mackenzie and Zoe. What would happen to them if she didn't go over there? A sigh. "Fine." She stepped forward.

Charlie thrust out his arm to try to stop Aryssa. "Wait a second. I don't…"

"This needs to be over with." Aryssa walked over to the bag, picked it up, then stopped a few feet short of Sammy. Shoving her apprehension aside, she opened it to expose the coins. "See. No traps. It's all here."

Sammy's eyes sparkled. "Very good." He pointed a few steps ahead of Aryssa's feet. "Set it down right there and I'll give you the girls."

Aryssa walked a couple of steps, crouched into the cocoon of headlights and set the bag on the ground. Sammy remained perfectly still. So did the man holding Mackenzie and Zoe. She was about to stand when a movement zipped into her periphery.

Someone sprang through the beams of light and pounced on Aryssa. She screamed as the venom of panic rushed through her veins. She tried to spring backward, but the darkly dressed figure was too quick. Before she knew it, some kind of bag was thrust over her head.

A gun cocked. "Don't do it," Sammy demanded authoritatively.

Who was Sammy talking to? The man on top of her wasn't letting up. She tried to squirm from his grasp. Kick. Punch. Rip that bag from her head. But the man overpowered her and kept her pinned to the ground as if she were caught in a vice.

"Let her go!" Charlie yelled. "This wasn't part of…"

"Don't be a hero," Sammy demanded. "It'll only get you killed."

Aryssa screamed in pain as something sharp sank into her thigh. She fought for a breath. Then another. Tried to wrangle out from under the oppressive weight. A strange, acrid odor was somehow woven into the bag's fabric. It filled her lungs and swirled into her chest. Her heart thumped wildly. Thoughts went numb. What in the hell was happening?

The strength evaporated from her limbs. She struggled to expand her chest and fill her lungs with air. The metallic colors of an oil slick swirled across her vision. Was this it? Was she dying?

Aryssa gave one last thrust of her hips. Pushed with her arms. Tried to force the scream out of her lungs, but it didn't have enough energy to pass her lips. It fell back down her throat, just like her awareness slipped into the abyss of unconsciousness. It sank deeper and deeper into the liquid void until the last bits of her resolve drowned in the blackness.

23

CHARLIE SCREAMED THROUGH a clenched jaw. He sprang forward to throw himself into the fray. Knock some heads. Rescue Aryssa. He had made it two or maybe even three steps before Sammy pulled a gun and racked the chamber. "Don't do it," Sammy commanded.

Charlie ground to a halt. Froze where he stood and raised his arms. "Let her go."

Some thirty or so feet of empty blacktop stood between Charlie and that gun. How far could he make it before Sammy fired his first round? How quickly could he cover the distance if he zigzagged to avoid the bullet?

"Don't be a hero," Sammy demanded. "It'll only get you killed."

Anger swelled inside Charlie. It flooded his legs. His arms. He was ready to explode forward, except that gun kept him rooted. Forced him to quash every impulse that urged his desire to brawl. He could only watch helplessly as the fight in Aryssa dwindled. Her efforts to punch and kick her way free became weaker. Less frequent. It didn't take long before there were none at all.

"If I were you, I'd forget any of this ever happened," Sammy advised. "This isn't your fight."

Charlie opened his mouth to challenge Sammy, but chose

to let silence quell his response. He squeezed his fists and tried to crush his frustration into his palms.

Sammy smiled. "You want to do something so badly, don't you?" A gesture toward Charlie's hands. "Let me be perfectly clear. If you try to rescue her or think you can get the police involved, then wipe that thought from your mind. The moment I sense something foul, people will die. Do you understand me?"

"Perfectly," Charlie said in a voice as taut as a steel cable.

He desperately wanted to say more. Fling his words as if they were darts filled with the poison of instigation. Somehow taunt Sammy and those other men into a fight. Could he take all three of them? Would Sammy use his gun? He glanced at Mackenzie and Zoe, to Aryssa then back to the weapon. Charlie was stuck. There was nothing he could do except seal his lips and keep his voice buried in his throat.

Sammy perked up at the sound of sirens echoing in the distance. Tipped his head at the man atop of Aryssa. "Get her in the car."

Without saying a word, the man slipped his arms underneath Aryssa's armpits and dragged her limp body toward the back of the SUV.

Charlie could only glare at Sammy. Those sirens were growing louder. Was some kind of emergency happening close by? Had someone witnessed what was happening here and called the cops?

Aryssa was crammed into the backseat by the darkly dressed man. When he was finished, he waited by the door. "Let's get out of here," he said.

"Not just yet," Sammy responded. He slowly shuffled toward the passenger door, all the while keeping his weapon fixed on Charlie.

Charlie kept his focus on the gun. Remained perfectly still. Why was Sammy taking his time getting into the car? Was he waiting for those sirens to get closer?

"You've got a choice," Sammy advised. "Save the girls or get busted by the cops." He let the options hang precariously in the air. "Of course you can choose to try to save Aryssa," waved his hand in dismissal, "but you and I know where that'll get you."

What did Sammy mean by getting busted by the cops? Those sirens were getting louder. Closer. Where they coming for him?

Sammy gestured toward the man holding Mackenzie and Zoe. "Now!" Sammy lifted his gun and pointed it right at Charlie's head. Kept it there for a few heartbeats. At the last moment he swung it upward.

Bang! The gun went off. The sisters cowered. One of them shrieked with fright. Charlie dropped to the ground.

He lifted his head when he heard the car doors slam shut. The engine revved and quickly backed out of the alley. One of the girls stumbled toward a cinder-block building. The other staggered haphazardly toward a Dumpster. Something was wrong with them, but what?

The screaming sirens reverberated down the alley. It would be only a matter of a minute, if that, before the cops were actually surrounding him.

Dread coiled around Charlie's limbs. He pushed himself onto his feet and ran his hand over his head. What was he going to do? Stay with the two girls? Explain himself to the police? Would they believe his story? He needed to do something and it needed to be done now.

Charlie sprinted over to Mackenzie, who was the closest to him. Grabbed her by the arm and spun her around to face him. His jaw dropped in shock.

Mackenzie's expression was as blank as a sheet of paper. Eyes glazed. Cheeks plum red. Had she been slapped? Was her lip swollen too? Charlie shook her by the shoulders. "Can you hear me? Are you okay?"

Mackenzie's mouth hung open. She mumbled something, but Charlie couldn't make out the words. There was no time to figure it out. Blue-and-red lights were flickering off the buildings. He pulled Mackenzie across the alley and caught up to her sister.

Zoe had the same blank look and glazed sheen swirling on the surface of her eyes. Had they been drugged? Physically harmed? Would Charlie be blamed for it? Is this what Sammy had meant by being busted by the police?

Charlie took a deep breath to try to calm himself. There were too many questions. Too much explaining. He forced the girls to sit on the ground, their bodies slumped against each other. Heads sagged. Shoulders drooped. He ducked behind a Dumpster and felt his way along the walls of the darkened alley. Behind him cars screeched to a stop. Doors swung open. Footsteps pounded pavement.

"I have something over here!" a cop yelled.

"Is it them?"

"I think so."

"Spread out!" Someone commanded authoritatively. "Lock this area down!"

Charlie didn't stop. Didn't look behind him. He dashed along the walls, slipped behind several Dumpsters and darted past numerous garbage cans. Slithered across the trunk of a parked car. He came to the alley's entrance and momentarily stopped. Would someone see him dashing out into the open? Was another cop waiting on the street? He knew he couldn't stay here. He had to get away and that meant stepping out into the public.

He straightened his shoulders and did his best to appear as nonchalant as possible. Charlie slid his hands into his pockets and walked out onto the sidewalk. Strolled behind a couple holding hands. Made sure his focus remained forward, all the while keeping a casual pace. So far so good. Could he keep it up? Would he be able to get away without being spotted?

24

SOME KIND OF wire dug into Aryssa's shoulder. The searing pain from the kink in her neck spread like a brush fire down her back. Limbs felt as if they were filled with concrete. A thick paste of confusion oozed through her head and rhythmically lapped against her skull, sending a dull ache pulsing through the bone's matrix.

Footsteps stepped heavily across the hard floor. Someone sniffled. Someone else coughed. A shuffle of a body turning on a couch or maybe a bed. Clunk of a plastic bottle onto a table. The faint laughter of some sitcom echoed from a distant television. Aryssa quietly groaned. Where was she? What had happened to her?

Bits and pieces of the past day or two paddled along the choppy waters of her memory. The alley. A car's headlights. Tossing the bag of coins. Being tackled by a dark figure. The bag thrust over her head. That needle jammed into her thigh.

A jolt of panic ran across her nerves and jarred Aryssa awake. She slowly opened her eyes to scuffed drywall in the corner of a room. A dank and dreary room in what seemed to be a basement. A yellow light filtered through the tiny windows near the ceiling, making it the only warm thing that dared to take up residence in the place.

Aryssa slowly lifted her head off the stained mattress she

was lying on. Wiped a string of drool from the corner of her mouth. Tried to moisturize her overly dry lips with a lick from her parched tongue. How long had she been lying here?

Several empty mattresses were scattered about. She counted nine women occupying the others. Four of the women appeared to be sleeping. Two were lying on their stomach. Another had her back against the wall and listlessly picked at her nails. The other two were sitting upright with heads sagged on the hopelessly dried and frayed vines of their necks.

Aryssa moaned with agony as she slowly rolled herself upright. She grabbed her head to try to steady the teetering room. Fought back the nausea that churned like a lava lake in the pit of her gut. What in the hell had been in that needle?

A blonde haired woman on a nearby mattress looked at Aryssa. A satin sheen dulled her blue eyes. She half smiled, then let her head droop between her legs.

Aryssa rubbed her throbbing temple. "Hey," she said quietly.

The blonde woman briefly looked up.

"Are you...?" Aryssa waited for the pain to pass. "Are you okay?"

The woman quickly nodded. Held her finger to her lips and tipped her head toward the far side of the room.

"What's going on?" Aryssa questioned.

The blonde motioned with her hand to keep quiet. "No loud speak," she whispered in a voice heavily laden with what sounded like an Eastern European accent.

"I'm Aryssa," she said, hoping to ease the tension that filled the space between them.

The blonde hesitated. "Kamelia." She wiped the corner of her mouth. "Call me Kami."

Aryssa glanced toward the area of the room where Kami

had recently focused her attention. A long table, chairs and mirrors—nearly identical to the setup at the club. "What's all that for?"

"Us," Kami said simply.

"Us?"

Kami nodded. "Make me and you pretty."

Aryssa rubbed her eye. "Pretty for whom?"

"Anyone who wants to pay money."

Was Aryssa hearing Kami correctly? Anyone who wants it? Pays for it? She took note of the others inside the room. All women. All young. All good-looking. Was this some sort of prostitution ring? Was she now a part of it? "You mean those who want sex?"

"Sex, yes." Kami nodded.

The answer was a shock wave that crashed into Aryssa. "How do you know?"

Kami ran her hand through her blonde hair. "I know, I just..." her voice trailed off into silence.

Aryssa sighed. She desperately wanted to reach out and hold Kami's hand. Wrap her arm around her as a gesture of reassurance. Provide some form of protection. She instead held back in fear. In fear of someone barging into the room and physically reprimanding the comforting gesture. "How...how long have you been doing this?"

Kami shrugged. "I don't know. Many months." She sniffled. "Long time."

"You've been here all this time?"

No," Kami answered. "Many places. They move me all over."

"Who moves you?"

"Them." Kami briefly gestured at the far end of the room. "Always moving. Always make me do it for the money." She paused. "Money they keep for themselves."

"You mean you sleep with men for money, but they keep all of it?"

"No sleep." Kami waved her hand in negation. "There's no sleeping. Only after do I get to sleep…only if they tell me."

"No, no, no," Aryssa repeated. "By sleeping I mean…" She paused to clarify what she wanted to say. "I mean sex with men."

"You mean sexual relations, no?"

"Yes," Aryssa confirmed. "Sexual relations for money."

"Every day." Kami ran her finger under her lid to stop the tear from dribbling down her cheek. "Sometimes many a day."

"More than two?" Aryssa questioned with disbelief.

"Sometimes four or five."

"That's just not…" Aryssa cringed. "It's got to be painful."

"I do what they tell me."

"And you don't get any money?" Aryssa did her best to temper the rage that burned deep inside her.

"No." Kami shook her head violently. "I told you. I get no money." She held her thumb and forefinger close together. "Sometimes only a little. They keep because I owe money for passport."

"How much do you owe?"

Kami shrugged. "They no tell me." She scoffed her displeasure. "Many months. Always say many more months."

Aryssa leaned forward and lowered her voice. "Don't do it anymore."

Kami's eyes widened with fright. "You no understand. They will kill my mother. Make my sister do this." She wrapped her arms around herself. "They know where they live. Show me pictures to prove it." A lengthy pause. "Weeks ago someone try to quit. Try to walk out." Worry glazed her tone. "You know what happen to her?"

Aryssa silently shook her head.

"They took her in room and beat her." Kami shivered. "Beat her until she cry no more." An uneasy silence lasted several heartbeats. "Never see her again."

Dread tingled along Aryssa's skin. Her body went numb with fright. She pulled her knees into her chest. Was this her fate, too? Gestured at the other women in the room. "Do you know them?"

"No," Kami answered. "Never see them before." Took a deep breath. "We come in the night. I get here first. They come later. Could be first time…I don't know."

The woman, who had tattoos running the length of her arm, shuffled her body across her mattress. Aryssa smiled at her. "Where did you come…?"

A large man burst through one of the doors near the far corner of the room. Aryssa recognized him as one of the bouncers from the club. Couldn't pull his name from the files of her memory. Did it matter? He strode to the middle of the room. "You all are going to a party tonight," he said in his thick voice. "You're expected to dress like you're going out. You know, like clubbing. Do you understand what I'm telling you?" He glared at each of the girls. When he reached Aryssa, his eyes grew cold. "That means each and every one of you. We leave in a couple of hours."

"Clothes. We need clothes," said a short-haired brunette who looked like she might be a few months past her twentieth birthday.

The bouncer pointed to the closet. "Dresses and shoes are in there." Chopped his hand downward. "No flats. Everyone must wear heels. Panties and bras are in that dresser. Makeup is on the table." Gestured at a filth-stained door, adding, "Showers are in there. Make yourselves extra clean. And I mean *extra* clean." He jabbed his thick finger at the women. "You're going to the Cad. If you don't know the place, you will." He articulated his words to weigh them with significance. "There'll be important people where you're going. Don't screw it up by being unkempt. They're expecting a lot and paying for it."

"Am I getting some of it?" asked the young woman who looked like she might be a teenager.

"Some of what?" the bouncer retorted bluntly.

"Money," the teen said, somewhat defiantly. "If they're paying more, I deserve more."

The bouncer folded his arms over his chest. "That's not how this works."

"Some of us have traveled through the night." The woman stifled her yawn behind closed lips. "I, for one, could use a night off." She gestured around the room. "I'm sure they could use some rest, too."

"Did you not hear what I just said?" the bouncer questioned sarcastically.

The young woman ran her hand through her hair. "I heard you loud and clear. It's just that we were made to stay awake. We've barely rested and now you want us to ready ourselves for some important people."

The bouncer's brows furrowed. "And your point?"

"You want us to do all these extra things and yet we see none of the rewards."

"And you won't if you keep running your mouth."

The teen stood up off her mattress. "None of this is what you promised."

The bouncer's eyes narrowed. "Take it up with customer

complaints. Until then, you will get ready for tonight's festivities."

The teen cocked her hip. "No. I want what I work for."

"Or what?"

"I won't go to this party of yours."

"Oh, really?"

The teen nodded. "Yes, really."

Anxiety plunged its chilled hand into Aryssa's chest and squeezed her lungs. Nothing good was coming out of that argument. She started to lift her arm to prevent the teen from saying anything else, but Kami nudged it down. "Don't. It will be bad for you, too."

The bouncer stepped close to the teen. Pointed at the showers. "Get your ass in there and get ready."

"No, not until I get some guarantees," the teen said with determination.

"The only guarantee is the one that says you will do as I say!" The bouncer grabbed her by the arm and thrust her toward the filthy door.

"Let go!" The teen tried to wrangle her arm free. "Let go of me!"

"Not until you do as I say" The bouncer forcefully pulled her across the room.

"Get off of me." The teen dug her heels into the floor. She staggered against the overbearing strength of the bouncer. "I'm not doing a damn…" She raised her hand. *Slap!*

The bouncer touched his cheek. His stunned look morphed into anger. Face reddened like a demon. Lips snarled. "You bitch!" His fist became a battering ram.

Bam! The teen's head snapped sideways. Agony burst from her lungs. She flew through the air and tumbled across the floor.

Several of the women gaped in horror. One screamed. Another gasped with fright.

"Don't you ever, and I mean ever, do that again!" the bouncer commanded. "That goes for each and every one of you."

The teen landed a short distance from Aryssa's feet. Aryssa started to reach out to her, but hesitated. The teen struggled for a breath. Torso heaved. Bloody drool dangled from her lip.

Two other large men entered the room. Neither of them looked familiar to Aryssa.

"What the hell happened?" the one wearing a dark shirt questioned.

"Wouldn't do what I told her," the bouncer stated. "She had to pay the price for her disrespect."

The other man walked over to the teen. "Oh man, you really messed her up." A gesture toward her face. "Damn, that lip is all jacked up. She can't go out looking like that."

The teen tried to shake it off. Grunted several times to try to ease the pain. More drool oozed from her mouth. She spat a wad of bloody mucous onto the floor.

"Not my fault," the bouncer reiterated. His voice grew firmer. "The rest of you will have to work harder to fill in for her." Huffed his irritation. "This is what you get for disobeying what you're told to do. Remember that for the next time."

Filaments of fear bound every woman in the room. Kami cowed. Several others buried their heads into their knees. Someone pouted. Aryssa tightened her arms and legs to prevent them from trembling.

The bouncer thrust his arm toward the teen. "Tie that bitch up."

The other two men nodded their understanding, dragged the teen by her arms and threw her onto a mattress. Handcuffs were shackled to her wrists. The head bouncer flung a thick chain that hit the ground with a serpentine thunk.

Aryssa looked away. Stared at her feet as the two men chained the teen to the hooks embedded into the wall and floor. There was something near the tips of her shoes. Something that caught Aryssa's eye. Something in the teen's bloody ball of spit. Something white. Could it be…?

There was no time for second-guessing. No time to get queasy over a wad of bloody phlegm. She quietly leaned forward and pulled the tooth toward her. Tucked it under the edge of her mattress.

The men snapped the locks around the young woman's ankles. "She isn't going anywhere," the one in the black shirt said.

"Serves her right." The bouncer kicked the edge of her mattress. "The rest of you get yourselves ready."

"You heard him." The black-shirted man clapped. "Get a move on."

One by one the women began to make their way to the closet. Some toward the showers. Aryssa studied the chairs at the makeup counter—more particularly their metal legs. Could she use it to crush the tooth? Would the one tooth be enough?

25

"MOMMY!" MACKENZIE BURST over the threshold and sprinted across the room.

"Mom!" Zoe wasn't too far behind.

The lightning of euphoria zipped through Mary. Her heart overflowed with gratitude. With love. They were alive. Safe. "My babies!" she said with joy.

The two girls ran to either side of the bed. A nearby nurse reached out. "Go easy on your mom."

Mackenzie was oblivious to the warning. She hopped onto the bed and threw her arms around Mary. "Mommy!"

Zoe was a little more cautious. She gently laid her head against Mary's shoulder.

Mary flinched from the pain. Clenched her teeth. She fought back the tender ache that sent pins and needles churning down her extremity before she gingerly caressed Zoe's arm.

"Are you okay?" Mackenzie questioned with concern.

"I'm better now that you and Zoe are here."

Mackenzie tapped the plastic collar. "What's this for?"

"It protects my neck."

"Why?" Zoe ran her fingers across it. "What's wrong with your neck?"

Mary hesitated. Did she want to bring up everything that

had happened, so quickly?

"What happened to it, Mommy?" Mackenzie's brows arched with fright.

"I hurt it during…during…you know, during the fire."

Mackenzie gasped. "Can you move your arms and legs?"

"Of course I can," Mary said reassuringly.

"Are you sure?" Mackenzie dared not move. "I heard that you can't move your arms and legs if you hurt your neck."

"She can move them," Zoe commented.

"How do you know?" Mackenzie glared at Zoe. "She could be stuck this way for the rest of her life."

"No, she couldn't."

"Yes, she could," Mackenzie countered. "I heard it."

"Where?"

"I just heard it and I know it's true."

Zoe pinched Mary's arm. "Can you feel that?"

"Ouch." Mary recoiled. "Yes." She fluttered her legs. Lifted the arm that had just been pinched. She tried to reposition her other arm, but the sling prevented any movement. Instead, she wiggled her fingers. "See, they all work."

"Oh," Mackenzie responded with relief. "Why didn't you say so?"

Smiles creased the faces of the doctors, nurses and police officers standing in the room.

"I tried, but…" Mary sighed. For once their argument was joyful music to her ears. She could feel her lips curl from her smile. "I'm so happy to see you both. I love you so much."

"I love you too, Mommy," Mackenzie said.

"Me too," Zoe chimed.

Mary studied Mackenzie's complexion with motherly concern. Then Zoe's cheeks and eyes. "What happened to your faces?"

Mackenzie shrugged. "I don't know."

"You don't know?"

"I don't remember," Mackenzie answered. "It's kind of fuzzy."

"Yeah," Zoe agreed. "It's like a dream. Especially everything that happened after we left her house."

Was this the right time to delve into it? Mary looked over at the detective. Cocked her head in uncertainty. The detective readily tipped his chin to express his approval.

A snippet of the conversation she had with him before the girls entered the room echoed in Mary's mind.

"Are you sure this is the right time to bring it up?" Mary had asked with concern. "I mean, I don't want to traumatize them any more than they might already be."

"That's a concern," the detective had answered. "But the doctors have assured me that they've recovered with amazing speed."

A doctor wearing light-blue scrubs had laid his hand on the head of Mary's bed. "Kids are resilient. Yours are amazing."

Mary had grinned with gratitude. "And you think they'll be okay reliving those memories?"

The doctor had nodded. "I do. They've shown a willingness to talk, but what they're saying is kind of confusing."

"Confusing?" Mary had asked.

"It's my experience that the sooner you can get someone talking, the less clouded the details will be. Unfortunately, we're a couple of days behind the ball, so if we allow Mackenzie and Zoe to..."

Mary shook away the memory. "Whose house?" she asked Zoe.

Zoe rubbed her cheek. "Umm, I don't remember." She

glanced at Mackenzie. Uncertainty arched her brows. "Do you know her name?"

Mackenzie opened her mouth and held up a finger. Her arm dropped to her side. "I...I don't remember."

Mary cautiously spoke. "Was this the same woman who helped me fight off that man?"

"Yep." The shimmer in Zoe's eyes brightened. "She's the one who got us out of the house."

Mackenzie nodded enthusiastically. "It's true." She rolled onto her knees. "She took us to her home."

"Her home?" Mary blinked. "Do you know her?"

"Of course, Mommy," Mackenzie answered. "Everyone knows her."

"But, I don't think that I do."

"Yes, you do," Zoe said.

"I do? Are you sure?" Mary asked doubtfully.

"Very," Zoe countered. "She's the tooth fairy."

"Yeah, Mommy, the tooth fairy." Mackenzie bobbed up and down on the bed.

Mary bit her lip with uncertainty. "The tooth fairy?"

"Yes, the tooth fairy." Mackenzie confirmed again.

"Umm..." Mary paused. Had those drugs messed with their memory? Had Mackenzie and Zoe been brainwashed? The detective used a hand gesture to encourage Mary to continue. "How do you know she was the tooth fairy?"

Zoe pointed to the gap in her mouth. "She had my tooth." Closed her lips and licked them. "She had a whole bunch of them in a purple bag."

Repulsion trembled through Mary. "An entire bag of teeth?"

"Yep," Mackenzie confirmed.

"What was she doing with so many?"

Zoe shrugged. "I don't know; she's the tooth fairy."

"What else is the tooth fairy supposed to have?" Mackenzie leaned to her side. "That's why she's the tooth fairy."

Mary silently sighed. "What did she look like?"

"She was nice," Mackenzie said. "And pretty."

"Yeah, her friend thought so, too," Zoe added.

Mackenzie giggled. "He likes her, I could tell."

"I know," Zoe chuckled like a schoolgirl that had a secret. "I think she likes him, too. They're both too scared to tell each other."

Mary held Zoe's hand. "Was this friend of hers nice to you?"

Mackenzie nodded enthusiastically. "Very. He helped when she tried to bring us to the hospital."

Zoe yawned. "It was so early; the sun wasn't even up yet."

"I don't like getting up that early," Mackenzie said.

"They tried bringing you to the hospital?" Mary shifted uneasily. "Did they hurt you or something?"

"No Mommy, we weren't hurt," Mackenzie answered. "They were trying to get us to you."

"That's when those men in the car came up and...and..." Zoe's voice trailed off.

"And what?" Mary encouraged.

Zoe sniffled. Wiped her eye. "They grabbed me and Mackenzie. And...and...it's all kind of fuzzy after that."

"Is that when you got hurt?" Mary's body stiffened with maternal protectiveness. "Did those men hurt you?"

"I don't know," Zoe said.

"They hurt the tooth fairy," Mackenzie chimed in. She rubbed her forehead as if trying to loosen a piece of her memory. "I think...I think...they punched her and then took us."

Mary did her best to calm the distress that infiltrated her tone. "What did those men look like?"

Zoe squinted. "I don't remember."

"Me neither," Mackenzie said.

"Where was that friend of hers?" Mary asked more pointedly than she'd intended. "You said he was with you."

Mackenzie thumbed over her shoulder. "He was waiting in the car."

Mary exhaled sharply as she looked up at the ceiling in frustration. "I don't understand," she mumbled. What had happened to her daughters? Who was this woman who claimed to be the tooth fairy? Why were they kidnapped? "What did they want?"

"They wanted this, Mommy." Zoe reached into her pocket and pulled out a coin.

"We each got one," Mackenzie pulled out hers.

Someone gasped. The detective stepped forward to get a better look.

Mary gingerly pinched Zoe's coin between her fingers. "Where did this come from?"

"My animal bank," Zoe answered.

"Mine didn't have any," Mackenzie said. "Only Zoe's had them."

"Animal bank?" Mary asked curiously.

"Yeah, Mommy," Mackenzie confirmed. "The ones we bought with our own money, remember?"

The trauma from being hurled through the window had thrown Mary's memory into disarray. "I think so," she answered doubtfully. She paused to collect her thoughts. "Whose coins are these?

"He gave them to us," Mackenzie said. "He needed to keep the rest."

"You mean these belong to the tooth fairy's friend?"

"Yeah." Zoe nodded.

"Why did he need to keep them?" Mary asked bluntly.

"That's how he gets paid," Mackenzie said.

"Paid for what?"

"To take people on his boat," Zoe commented.

Mary flipped the coin over. "You mean people give him this coin to go on a boat ride?"

"Something like that, I guess," Zoe said.

Mary stared at the coin. "That's an awfully expensive-looking token for a simple boat ride."

One of the police officers cleared his throat as he stepped to the side of the bed. "May I see it?"

"Sure." Mary held out her hand.

The officer studied the coin. Wonder deepened the wrinkles on his forehead. Apprehension paled his skin ever so slightly. "Charon," he muttered.

"What did you say?" the detective asked.

"Charon," the officer said again. "The mythical Greek figure who ferried souls across the river Styx. The dead would pay him a coin for passage." He paused. "That's why, long ago, people would place a coin on a dead person's eyes or mouth before they buried them."

The detective clucked his tongue with doubt. "I don't think some ancient man is actually operating a boat to take the dead across the river."

The officer shook his head apprehensively. "It would be hard to believe. But these coins are old and when she said boat," he handed the coin back to Mary, "it was the first thing…."

"Well, let's throw that theory out of the discussion," the detective said. "I don't need another whacko asserting to be something they're not. I've got enough mythical figures on my hands, especially the one claiming she's the tooth fairy."

"I'm just saying that it could be something worth looking into," the officer said.

The detective brushed away the officer's suggestion. "We'll discuss it later." He looked at Mackenzie and Zoe. "What else can you tell me about this man?"

"I'm hungry," Zoe said without acknowledging the detective.

"Me too," Mackenzie agreed. "I don't want to talk about this anymore."

"Can we watch television with you, Mommy?" Zoe snuggled into Mary.

"Of course," Mary said fondly. A gesture at the detective to end the discussion. "There's nothing I'd rather do more than to be with the two of you."

Mackenzie smiled. "What should we watch?"

"Where's the remote?" Zoe lifted her head off Mary's shoulder.

A nearby nurse handed Zoe the small, black device.

"Thank you," Zoe said.

"It's not your turn," Mackenzie stated.

"Yeah, it is." Zoe aimed the remote at the television and with the press of a button brought it to life.

"No, it's not." Mackenzie's brows crinkled. "Mommy, tell her it's my turn."

"It's not your turn," Zoe said. "You picked that movie with the dog the last time."

"No," Mackenzie shot back. "You got to watch that pirate movie."

"We never finished it."

"That doesn't mean…"

Mary half-smiled as she glanced over at the detective. He shrugged his shoulders with hopelessness. They may never get to the bottom of this. Maybe Mackenzie's and Zoe's memory was already disintegrating.

At the moment, Mary didn't care. Happiness strolled though her heart and spread to every corner of her being. She was safe with her daughters and that's all that mattered.

26

THE SUN HAD quietly worked its way below the horizon. Its invisible hand brushed the sky in a palette of pinks and reds. Varying hues of orange rubbed the clouds' soft bellies. Ahead of Charlie, the colors varnished the river in a glossy sheen.

He looked at it. Tried to take it all in. Tried to let it flatten his emotional rollercoaster. Somehow slice away the peaks of anger. Lift up the valleys of bleakness. A grunt. His thoughts were elsewhere.

Charlie repeatedly punched the boat's steering wheel with frustration. How had he let it happen, not once, but twice? Let Aryssa fall victim to that jackass, Sammy, and his henchmen. He thought back to the moment when he had been staring down the barrel of that gun. Should he have taken the bullet? Shook his head. Never would have made it without getting killed.

He thought about the seconds that had ticked by as Aryssa stopped fighting and went limp. Could she be alive? Or was she dead? If she wasn't dead, would she be soon? Maybe she was being held captive, but for what purpose?

Charlie let the wind slap his face as a way of punishing himself for his failures. Maybe the repeated blows would knock the fog of doubt out of his mind. Somehow force him to just pick a spot and start the search. But how? He had no idea where she was being kept. No idea where to look. No idea if she was even alive. Charlie had hoped that the drive down the river would somehow clear his mind. It had helped in the past; so far it wasn't helping at all tonight.

The sun had strolled even farther down the nocturnal steps when his hands began to suddenly tingle. He opened and closed his fists several times, but the sensation wasn't going away. In fact, it began to trickle up his arms. What was happening?

Along either side of the river the numerous apartment buildings, warehouses, shipping yards, bars and restaurants fought back the evening's advances. Lights flicked on and shimmered off the water. Yet, in the midst of it all stood a dark spot. A black hole in the city's starlit presence. Charlie drew closer to the void and recognized it for what it was. The abandoned factory.

The tingling grew stronger. He had felt this before. It had been happening over the last several months, each and every time he'd passed the factory. Tonight was no different. Then again, something *was* different. An image flashed across the television screen of his memory. That moment in Aryssa's apartment when he'd dumped the coins out onto her table. Was the sensation one and the same? How was it possible?

The closer he got to the factory, the more the feeling brushed against his curiosity. Should he pull over and investigate? Snoop around the gargantuan building? Forget every rumor and story he had ever heard and simply step inside? What was he expecting to find?

Charlie glanced up the river. At the twinkling lights. The darkening sky. Maybe he should just go back to the marina and wait for a client? Or go back home and then what—watch the tube? Remain alone with his thoughts while they slowly squeezed the last spoonfuls of optimism from his decaying hope?

A discontented sigh. He turned his attention to the factory, only to realize that the distance was closing fast. Back to the river and the way home. What to do?

The tingling in his hands and arms was even stronger. Almost unbearable. Curiosity lifted itself out of its burrow and nudged the wheel. Charlie couldn't hold back. Before he realized what he was doing, he had swung the boat's bow toward the factory.

Charlie spotted a metal ladder fastened to the sea wall. He maneuvered the boat to the bottom of the ladder, shut off the motor and let the fiberglass hull gently bounce against the rotting tires that were anchored into the metal. He quickly tied down the boat using the dock cleats embedded in the wall.

He grabbed the ladder and then froze. A head appeared over the top of the wall and just as quickly disappeared. "Is that you, boatman?" called the male voice.

"Who's asking?" Charlie questioned cautiously.

"Me."

"Who's me?"

"The one who's asking."

Charlie drummed his fingers along the metal rung. Swallowed the annoyance coating his tongue. That voice sounded familiar. "Johnny, is that you?"

Silence.

Charlie smiled. It had to be him. He slowly ascended the ladder. "I know it's you, Johnny."

"No you don't," the voice responded.

"Umm, yes I do."

"How do you know?"

"Your voice," Charlie replied. "I know it when I hear it."

The voice deepened. Cadence slowed. "I was faking it. This is my real voice. See…you've no idea who this is."

Charlie clicked his tongue and kept climbing. "Johnny?"

"Yes."

"See, it's you, isn't it."

"Aww, damn." Johnny snapped his fingers. "You got me."

Charlie reached the top and stepped over the wall. "What are you doing here?"

Johnny nervously paced back and forth. "What am I doing here?" Squeezed the glass bottle in his hand. "What are *you* doing here?"

"I don't know." Charlie looked at the factory and then turned his attention back to Johnny. "I was kind of pulled here."

"Me too."

Charlie watched Johnny walk a few steps, turn and walk the same distance in the other direction, only to spin around and do it all over again. He motioned to the liquor bottle in Johnny's grasp. "Have you been drinking tonight?"

"No."

"What's that, then?"

"Bottle with water," Johnny answered.

"Looks like a vodka bottle to me."

Johnny held it up before his squinting eyes. "So it does." A pause. "I filled it with water."

"Water?"

"Yes, water." Johnny thrust it toward Charlie. "Wanna taste it? I'll let you, if you don't believe me."

Charlie bit his lip with disgust. No way was he going to put his lips to that thing. "I believe you. Why water?"

Johnny kept pacing. "To prevent them from finding me."

Charlie scratched his scalp. "Water does that?"

"I know it does," Johnny answered. "The more I drink it, the more it dilutes me. The more dilution, the less chance they have of finding me. If I can't be found, then they can't make me do what they want me to do." He paused the length of a heartbeat. "Don't you get it?"

"I think so." Charlie quietly nodded. "What do they want?"

Johnny slugged some water from his bottle. Wiped his mouth with the back of his forearm. "What do they want, you say?" He pointed. "For me to go in there."

"The factory?"

Johnny paced. "Yeah, into that forsaken place." Waved his arm wildly. "There's something in there they want me to get. But I don't want to go in there. No sir, I don't." he shook his head. "But they're trying to make me. Made me come this far." Looked at Charlie with feral eyes. "I'm making my final stand here." Another swig from the bottle. "I'm not going to let them get the best of me. Not tonight, no sir."

"I get it," Charlie responded. The factory loomed before him. His boat gently rocked below. It would be so much easier to climb down and drive away. Yet there was something preventing him from doing it. Something pulling him into that damn building. Was it the same thing that Johnny was experiencing? Did those mysterious people Johnny always talked about have some influence over Charlie, too? He shook the thought away. If not that, then what was it?

Johnny looked up toward the night sky. "I'm not going in there." He bent forward to stretch his back. Then just as quickly looked up again. "You hear me? Not going to do it."

"Think they heard you?" Charlie tried to sound as understanding as possible.

Johnny shrugged. "Don't know and I don't care."

Charlie once again looked at the factory and let its foreboding presence engulf him. "I know you've been in there." He paused to see if Johnny would resist. He kept on pacing. "Is there anything that I should know about?"

"Don't want to talk about it." Johnny shook his head. Tapped his chest. "You know that he'd be fine with it." Gestured toward Charlie. "Maybe you too—then again, maybe not." He looked down at his shoes. "Don't do it. Don't go in. I'm not, but maybe he will because they go through me to get him." Johnny grabbed the sides of his head. "I need to walk. Walk away. Just walk away." Johnny turned and scrambled along the sidewalk that wound its way along the river.

Charlie silently watched as Johnny disappeared down the throat of the night. That tingling sensation, that overbearing pull, hadn't disappeared with Johnny's presence. Or when Johnny walked away. His warnings didn't have any effect on it, either. Charlie couldn't resist. He'd hate himself if he didn't at the very least take a peek inside. He exhaled any remaining pieces of doubt and began to follow the sidewalk that led to a set of double doors.

Would they be locked? If so, would that stifle his curiosity? Or would he find the courage to search for another way into the place? He was less than fifty yards away when one of the doors slowly opened.

Charlie's heart skipped a beat. Alarm shot liked a lightning bolt across his network of nerves. He leapt behind a nearby bench, took cover and froze.

A lone figure warily slid outside the door and kept close to the wall. It looked left, then right. Scanned the grounds. Turned its attention along the top of the building. Who in the hell was this?

The figure began to run down the walkway leading right to Charlie. It drew closer. And closer. Why was this person outside the abandoned factory at this time of night? What should Charlie do now?

27

SAMMY RACED DOWN the steps, his thoughts running faster than his feet. He burst through a metal door and scampered along the dimly lit hallway. Fiddled with the ring of keys with annoyance until he found the right one, then jammed it into the door's lock at the end of the corridor and threw it open. It slammed shut behind him when he entered.

Apprehension gelled the air in the room. The three bouncers were huddled near the makeup counter. The women were standing in a loosely knit group. Even though they were decked out in trendy clubwear, any suggestion of sensuality had been sucked out of them. Some fiddled with their fingers. Others had their arms pressed against their chest and uneasily rocked back and forth on the balls of their feet. Uncertainty stooped their shoulders while anxiety was etched into the lines on their faces.

Sammy grunted and stormed up to the bouncer from the club. "What do you mean, 'she's gone'?"

The other two men took a half step backward, seemingly trying to distance themselves from the fray. Sammy shook his finger. "Oh no, you don't." Glared at all three of them. "You're all a part of the problem." A tense pause. "So where is she?"

"I don't know," the bouncer said.

"What do you mean, you don't know?" Sammy questioned even more harshly.

The bouncer's tone was pressured. "I said, I don't know." He pointed at the counter. "One minute she's doing her makeup and the next she's gone."

Sammy snapped his fingers. "Just like that? Poof! Disappears, right into thin air."

"Yeah, something like that," the bouncer replied.

"Do you realize how stupid that sounds?" Sammy huffed. "No one just disappears."

"She did." The bouncer folded his arms across his chest. "We've torn this pace apart and she's not here."

"Then she must've gotten out." Sammy squeezed his gut to keep it from blowing apart with rage. "Did you look?"

The bouncer pointed at the door Sammy had just stormed through. "You mean out there?"

Sammy thrust his hands on his hips. "Where else would I be telling you to look?"

"It was locked and someone was watching it," the bouncer stated. "There's no way she could've made it past without us knowing."

"She must've if she's not here!" Sammy fired back. "Did you check the security cams?"

The bouncer nodded. "Yeah, we did."

"Well?" Sammy questioned impatiently.

"Nothing. They showed nothing."

Sammy looked over the women. "Did she talk to any of them?"

The bouncer shrugged. "Not really." He made a half-hearted gesture toward one of the blondes. "Maybe her."

Sammy stepped in front of the woman. "I know all about you and where you're from, Kamelia." He straightened his shoulders. Glared coldly to convey his frustration. "Did you talk with her?"

"With who?" Kami answered.

"Aryssa." Sammy grumbled. "The one who's missing."

Kami shook her head while she stared at the floor. "I know of no girl," she answered in her thick accent.

"He said that you talked with her." Sammy pointed at the bouncer. "Did she tell you anything?"

"I know nothing."

Sammy repeatedly smacked the back of his hand into the palm of the other. "I think you're lying to me." He paused. "Where'd she go?"

Kami kept shaking her head. "Know nothing. Only do what I'm told."

"Someone in this damn room had to have seen something." Sammy stood over Kamelia and raised his arm. "Last time! Where did she go?"

Kami coward. "I know nothing. Honest. Nothing."

The steam of Sammy's aggravation felt as if it were ready to blow through the top of his head. He needed answers and he needed them now. Several cries burst from the other women. A muffled scream from another. He was about to slam his fist into Kamelia's face, but a movement out of the corner of his eye forced him to pause. "What's wrong with her?"

"Who?" The bouncer's gaze homed in on the woman chained to the mattress.

"Yes, her," Sammy said with fire scorching the edges of his voice.

The bouncer scoffed. "She didn't want to do it." He paused. "Demanded more money. So I had to take matters in my own hands after she slapped me."

"She slapped you?" Sammy questioned tersely. "What the hell happened?"

"I told you, she was being a little bitch. Started insisting on more money. When I told her no, she thought she could be disrespectful." The bouncer brows crinkled. "Had to teach her a lesson."

"Son of a…" Sammy bent down for a closer look. "You've got to be kidding me. She can't go out looking like that."

The bouncer's complexion turned red with anger. "If she would've just listened, then…"

Sammy ran his hand over his head. "Did I not tell you how important tonight is?" He paused as if to wait for an answer, but instead continued. "Didn't I? Let me reiterate once again the large sum of money that they paid for us to be there." A huff. "Now I'm down two women. Any idea how I'm going to fix this?"

The large man in the black shirt cleared his throat and said nothing. The bouncer was quiet, too. The third kept his head down.

Sammy glanced at his watch. "We leave in less than an hour. Do you understand that?"

"Yeah, I get it," the bouncer responded. "Just like we're supposed to."

"That gives you plenty of time to go out there and look for her."

The bouncer pointed toward the door. "You mean out there?"

"I mean exactly that," Sammy answered matter-of-factly. "You screwed this up, now go and fix it."

"Out there?" the bouncer questioned with a tinge of fear. "You want me to go out there?"

"I want all three of you to go," Sammy commanded. "Do

you have any idea what could happen if she manages to get away?" He let the question hang in the air. "Any idea what the Network will do to us if we get busted?"

"But, out there?" The bouncer tipped his chin toward the door. "That place gives me the creeps."

"You've got flashlights, phones and your guns," Sammy said. "What would you rather be, a little scared or a little dead?" Looked at his watch again. "Time's ticking." A huff of displeasure. "This needs to happen now!"

The bouncer sighed. The other two dawdled. Any sense of urgency seemed to have passed over the men.

Sammy pulled out his cell and found the contact he wanted. Tapped the *call* icon. "What the hell is wrong with you?" His voice exploded with rage. "Now! Do it now! We leave in about fifty minutes and she's got a head start."

The men finally sensed Sammy's resolve. They gathered their things and rushed out the door.

Ariek's voice was on the other end of the line. "Did you get it straightened out?"

"We've got a bigger problem than I thought," Sammy said. "A much bigger problem."

28

THE MYSTERIOUS FIGURE was getting closer. Bare feet slapped against concrete. A feminine grunt rose above her chugging breath. Who was this person? Were those shoes dangling from her hand? The movement, the breathing, the thin silhouette—didn't look like someone Charlie should fear. Still, this wasn't the time to take any chances.

Charlie scrunched tighter against the bench just off the sidewalk, hoping his bulky frame would manage to blend with its shape. He watched as the figure drew closer. And closer. Something was off. Was that a dress she was wearing? Hair flowed behind her as she ran. Was it—could it be? He stood up. "Aryssa?"

The woman screamed. Jumped sideways and chucked her shoes at Charlie. They skidded across the ground a few feet to his left. "Aryssa, it's me, Charlie."

The woman's posture stiffened. Her chest heaved as she tried to catch her breath. "Charlie?" Leaned forward in the dark. "Is that really you?"

Charlie took a couple of cautious steps. "Yes," he said reassuringly.

Disbelief stuttered off Aryssa's tongue. "What…what are you doing here?"

"I was about to ask you the same thing."

"Thank…" Aryssa leapt into Charlie and wrapped her arms around him tightly.

Charlie hugged her back. He relished the way Aryssa clung to him. Savored the warmth of her body and the smell of her hair. For a brief moment the world seemed to stand still. She was alive. He quietly exhaled with gratitude and lowered her to the ground.

Aryssa brushed her hair off to the side. "I'm…I'm so glad to see you." She glanced back at the factory. "But, of all places."

Charlie's body tingled with sudden yearning. He couldn't take his eyes off the way her mini-skirt hugged her curves. Exposed her toned legs. The way her makeup highlighted her eyes. The way her dark lipstick defined her lips. He opened his mouth to say something, but quickly discovered that his tongue flopped like a fish out of water.

Aryssa must've noticed the look on his face. She giggled. "You've never seen me like this, have you?"

"No, I guess not."

"That's a good thing," Aryssa said. "It makes you all— well, you know—all the more likeable."

Heat rose from under Charlie's collar. He slowly exhaled to try to blow it from the furnace of his lungs. "Umm…"

Aryssa grabbed Charlie's hand. Her demeanor morphed into something more frantic. "I didn't choose to wear this without a reason. I was forced into it."

"Forced?" Charlie questioned uncertainly.

Aryssa nodded. "They wanted me to be a part of…" She lowered her head. Sniffled.

"Part of what?" Charlie rubbed Aryssa's arm.

"A sex ring." Aryssa looked up at Charlie. Fear poured from her eyes. "That's why Sammy wanted those coins so badly. To pay for his latest shipment of women."

"You mean like prostitutes?"

"More like slaves." Aryssa paused. "They buy and sell these women as if they're a commodity." She swiped a finger below her eyelid. "They get them from all over the world and treat them like..." The rest if her words became lost in the night air. "They're forced to put out every day."

"As in sex?"

Aryssa nodded silently.

Charlie tapped his chin. "They were going to make you do it, too?"

Aryssa shivered. "Or else." She swiped at her lid again. "Don't even want to think about it."

"But, you got away." Charlie instinctively pulled her close to protect her. "How did you manage it?"

"You know, it's a little complicated." Aryssa leaned her head against Charlie's chest. "I'm glad to be out of there." Sniffed. "I just...I worry about the others."

The sensation that had brought him here in the first place still vibrated through his extremities. He opened and closed his hands several times. What was causing it? Was it Aryssa? It didn't go away in her presence. In fact, it had grown stronger the closer he got to the factory. Was it something in there? "Should we go back for them?"

"No," Aryssa said. "I don't want to go back in there." Sliced her hand through the air. "No way." A sharp exhale. "But the others...I...I don't know what to do."

Charlie was being pulled toward the building as if he were a fish on a hook. "I think..." he hesitated. "I don't know what it is, but I need to go in there. There's something..."

"No, please, Charlie," Aryssa pleaded. "We've got to get out of here. Let's regroup and figure out a better way."

There was something tugging at his very soul. Charlie stepped toward the factory, but forced himself to hold back. "I don't know what it is, I need to…"

Aryssa yanked on Charlie's hand. "Come on, we can't. There's got to be a better way."

"But…" Charlie froze. The factory door swung open. The beam from a flashlight swept the area. Then another shined out from inside the building.

Aryssa gasped.

"Shhh," Charlie hissed with his finger crossing his lips. He pulled Aryssa toward the bench.

"It's them."

A large man stepped outside. The other swept a beam along the side of the factory.

"Who?"

"The ones who were watching over us," Aryssa whispered. "That's…that's…" her voice faltered. "The one who punched one of the girls." Her hand covered her mouth. "We've got to get out of here."

"Hold on," Charlie commanded. "Maybe they'll go back inside."

"I'm not going back," Aryssa said. "You don't understand; they'll kill me, then you, if they find us." She propped herself onto her haunches as if ready to spring across the ground like a scared rabbit.

"My boat," Charlie stated. "I've got my boat."

"You do?" Aryssa sank back down. "Let's get the hell out of here."

Charlie kept a tight grip on Aryssa's hand. He hesitated to make a move. The men didn't. Their flashlights swept over the ground and inched closer to Charlie. A third man stepped out of the factory.

"There's another one," Aryssa whispered.

The beams were only a few yards away. Charlie couldn't hold off any longer. It was now or never. He pulled Aryssa's hand and started running.

"Hey!" one of the men shouted.

"It's her!"

Aryssa gasped with fright, but she kept up with Charlie. Charlie led her to the wall and forced her down the ladder.

Bang! A gun went off. The bullet struck the wall near Charlie, sending shards of concrete bursting through the air.

"Shit!" Charlie bellowed. He threw himself over the wall just as another shot rang out.

He slid down the ladder and dropped into the boat. Pulled a knife from his pocket and slit one of the ropes. "Undo that one!" he yelled.

Charlie started the motor. The engines roared to life and he immediately slammed the throttle. The boat's bow rose and lurched forward like a frightened gazelle. "Get down!"

They were nearly a hundred yards from the wall when several more gunshots blasted behind Charlie. A bullet whistled through the air somewhere over his head. Several pierced the water around him. He kept the engines screaming and angled the boat toward the far side of the river.

More gunfire, but it was becoming more and more distant. No signs of a bullet striking his boat, the water, or for that matter, him. Charlie glanced over his shoulder to find Aryssa lying facedown on the deck.

"Are you okay?"

Aryssa didn't move. Was something wrong? Had she been hit?

"Aryssa!" Charlie screamed over the whine of the motor and the rush of air. "Aryssa!"

She didn't move. Charlie's heart freefell into the pit of despair. He couldn't let go of the steering wheel. Couldn't stop until they were farther away. "Aryssa!"

29

THE SCREAM OF fear bellowed from deep in the valley of Aryssa's mind and churned like a violent storm across the landscape leading to her ears. The roar of the motor and the wind of a tornado rushed over her. A bullet had ripped through the side of the boat, leaving a gaping hole in the seat cushion. Bits of fiberglass, stuffing and vinyl had viciously tumbled in front of her as she fell to the floor. Her panic-stricken heart hadn't stopped pounding against her ribs. Guns, bullets, money, kids, prostitution…how in the hell had she gotten into this mess?

Aryssa kept herself glued to the boat's deck.

"Aryssa!" Was someone yelling for her? There was no way she was leaving the safety of the floor. No way she was getting up and risk being pierced by a bullet.

"Aryssa!" Was that Charlie's terrified voice echoing from behind all that noise? "Are you okay?"

She took a moment to try to calm her mind. Run a full body-check. She was on Charlie's boat. Away from those men. Felt no pain, so she hadn't been shot. Were they finally safe?

"Aryssa!" Charlie's scream came more into focus. "Tell me you're okay!"

"I'm fine," she answered. "Are we away from them?"

"Yes," Charlie said. "You're not hurt, are you?"

Aryssa slowly rose to her knees. Looked out to the darkened patch of shoreline. The space between it and the boat was rapidly growing. Couldn't see anyone standing on the wall. A sigh filled with relief as she slid onto the bench seat. "I'm fine."

"Damn it!" Charlie shrieked. "You scared...I thought you were dead."

Aryssa gestured with her hand. "All this noise and my mind racing like...like it..." She paused. In no mood to try to explain it. Slid closer to Charlie. "What about you? Are you okay?"

"I'm good," Charlie answered. A sharp exhale. "That was damn close."

"Too close," Aryssa agreed.

Charlie tipped his chin and turned his focus onto the river. He didn't say anything more. It looked as if he was trying to let the tense moment drain out of him.

The space that fright had occupied in Aryssa began to disintegrate. Anger filled the vacancy it had left behind. Bits and pieces of the last couple of days filtered out of her memory. Mackenzie and Zoe getting kidnapped. The botched exchange. Nearly being sold into prostitution. She thought of the other women. Of Kami. The way that bouncer had punched the young woman. Aryssa was weary. Tired of being pushed around. Tired of the threats. Tired of all that Sammy had been trying to do to her.

The furnace of rage kicked on. The memories of all that had happened became the fuel that stoked the flames. "Where are we going?" Aryssa asked with scalpel-like sharpness.

"To the marina to dock this thing," Charlie answered. "After that, we're going to the cops."

"And tell them what?"

Charlie rolled his hand. "All of this. Everything we, and especially you, have been through."

"Do you think they'll believe us?"

"Why wouldn't they?"

Aryssa rubbed her temples. "We've got nothing to show them. No evidence, no pictures. Nothing, except for my word."

"That's something," Charlie commented with a heaping spoon of optimism.

"It's not enough." Aryssa steadied herself as the boat jumped a few waves. "By the time they start an investigation, Sammy and whoever else he's working with will be long gone."

Charlie kept his focus on the river. "What about the factory?"

"What about it?"

"You were in there. In some kind of room."

Aryssa bowed her head. "By now they all know that I escaped."

Charlie slowly nodded. "No use in getting the cops to go there." A sharp exhale. "If they're smart, they'll have it cleaned up in no time at all."

"Besides, that place is huge," Aryssa said. "I have no idea where I was or how I managed to find my way out."

Charlie clicked his tongue. Said nothing for several long seconds. "What do we do now?" A pause. "I can't let this go."

"Neither can I," Aryssa said, bitterness stinging her lips. "We need to find them. You know, catch them in the act."

The boat struck a couple more waves. "How are we going to do that?"

"The Cad," Aryssa answered. "They're taking the girls to the Cadillac Hotel."

"How do you know?"

"The bouncer," Aryssa said. "He was one of those men chasing us. I don't think he meant to say it, but he did."

Charlie eased back on the throttle, allowing the boat to slow down. "What makes you think that they're not going to abandon that, too?"

"Money," Aryssa said confidently. "It's a gathering of important people. High rollers. They said it themselves when they told us to get ready." She pointed toward the city skyline and the direction of the hotel. "There's no way that Sammy will put a stop to it. His ego won't let him. Besides, he probably overextended himself to get those girls and he's going to squeeze them for every last drop so he can get all the money he can."

Charlie silently nodded as he seemingly let Aryssa's comments sink in. "What are you suggesting?"

"That we go to that party."

Charlie's brows arched with surprise. "And what, rescue them?"

Aryssa gripped the seat cushions to calm her frustration. "Kind of." She paused to swallow her doubt. "It'll be too hard to get them all out of there. But if we make sure they are there, then we can get the cops involved."

"And if they're not, then what?"

Aryssa shrugged. "We're dead in the water and they get away."

Charlie seemed lost in thought. "Risky exposing ourselves like that."

"It is, but we've got to do something," Aryssa said. There was no way she was letting this go. "I can't think of any other way."

"Neither can I." Charlie slowed the boat even more as the

lights around the marina and those that lit up the several docked boats grew into focus.

Aryssa sighed quietly. The lights that twinkled off the water lifted some of the doubt that clung to her. But underneath the facade, her anger continued to simmer. Was the fury influencing her judgment? Was it leading them both into something they wouldn't return from? She looked past the shimmering surface and deeper into the dark water. A place where uncertainty lurked. What were they going to find at the hotel? What would they do if they found everything they were looking for?

30

POP! POP! POP!

Somewhere far behind Johnny, gunshots cracked the stillness of the night. He turned to look into the black veil that covered the factory, but was too far away to make out any movement. Couldn't spot any commotion. A few more pops sounded off and then everything went silent. It didn't take long before the screaming of an engine splashed into Johnny's ears. Way out toward the middle of the river a boat-shaped shadow sliced across the glass-like surface.

Johnny slugged some water from the liquor bottle, wiped his lips with the back of his hand then sighed. Should he have stayed back there with the boatman?

He shook his head to the negative. It was better here, away from…from that place. That factory. A shiver rippled through his body. He was better off; still, he couldn't stop himself from rubbing his chin with uncertainty. How much better off was he?

Something kept pulling him toward it. Nudging him. Even at this distance it wasn't letting up. Another gulp of water to try to drown the sensation. He took a desperate step backward, but before his foot could touch the ground, he pulled it back. "Damn," he muttered.

That sound of gunshots had been reverberating deep in his

mind. It released some kind of infection that slowly began to spread. That tiny organism fed off the sound and doubled in size, then soon doubled again. It began to multiply more rapidly, spilling out of his subconscious and swirling down his throat and into his lungs. The very act of breathing allowed it to cross into his bloodstream and swarm into his gut.

Johnny tried to turn away from the factory. Tried to forget he had heard those guns. Tried to deny the illness that was swiftly overtaking him. He lifted the bottle toward his quivering lips, but the bottle slipped from his grip and hit the ground with a solid thud.

The infection was robbing him of his strength. The world around him began to sway. The river lost its shimmer and the city's lights flickered. His legs felt like they were the consistency of melting rubber. Before he could tighten his thighs, he lost all control and dropped to his knees. The jarring pain ratcheted up his torso and through his ribs. Like a falling tree, he fell forward and smashed his face against the sidewalk. Stinging pain skewered his lip while the metallic taste of blood seeped over his tongue.

Johnny smacked his lips, then licked them with animalistic fervor. A low growl rumbled from deep inside his throat. The liquor bottle was out of his reach. He tried to fight what was happening, but it was too late. There was no stopping it. The predator had been awakened.

He rolled onto his back and clenched his teeth. "No...I can't...can't do..."

A dagger of pain impaled Johnny's spine, causing him to violently arch his back. He writhed. Moaned in agony. Nothing was giving him relief.

He opened his mouth to scream, but an invisible pair of hands seemed to wrap around his throat and choke the air out of him. An ink as dark as the hidden caves of night filled his eyes. Pinpricks of pain slid from beneath his cuticles. A muffled sound like the crackling of cellophane bubbled from under the layers of his skin.

Johnny's entire body contracted and gripped him in the throes of anguish before releasing him. He gasped and went limp. Time passed—how much, he didn't know. He never knew. Johnny lay on the sidewalk until his strength outmuscled the pain. Until he could freely move his arms and legs.

He exhaled sharply, rolled over and rose to his feet. Gazed at the reptilian scales that covered his hands and arms. At the pointed nails protruding from his fingertips. Chuckled with delight. He was back.

Johnny looked down at the tattered clothes clinging to his body. Grunted with disgust. He blew into his cupped hands, then brushed them over the frayed fabric. Within a few heartbeats the shredded garments morphed into a finely tailored black suit. He dabbed his finger in the blood clinging to the corner of his mouth and touched his tie. The bright red color of the blood crept across the silk fabric until it soaked every last fiber.

He lifted his nose, sniffed, then smiled. Opportunity weaved itself into the nearly imperceptible current wafting though the air. It was going to be a busy night. He could feel it trickling through the marrow of his bones. Another sniff. Death was dancing somewhere on there, too. His salivary glands frothed with animalistic lust, causing him to chuckle with delight. It was time to find where it was all going down.

31

SAMMY TIPPED HIS glass toward Ariek. "You look like you could use one of these." He took a sip of his scotch. "It helps."

"I've tried," Ariek said flatly. "Not feeling it."

"Of all nights," Sammy said somewhat sarcastically.

Ariek's brows furrowed. "There's too much at stake. It's better I keep my head clear."

"All the more reason." Sammy swirled the drink and reveled in the way the ice cubes chattered against the glass.

"How many have you had?"

Sammy chuckled. "Does it matter?"

"Yeah, it does."

"Since when have you become more uptight than me?" Sammy sipped his drink. "You're supposed to be the calm one."

Ariek slid his hands into his pockets. "Since she managed to escape. You do realize the problems she could bring us?"

"The key word here is *could*." Sammy leaned against the balcony's railing and gazed down at the crowd in the Cadillac's lobby. "But she won't. Not tonight."

"What makes you so sure?"

"For starters, she doesn't know we're here." Sammy pointed at the bouncer from the club who was sitting in a chair near the hotel entrance. "He assured me that the girls had no idea where they were going."

"It's a loose end." Ariek tapped the railing with his palm. "I hate loose ends."

Sammy tented his fingers over his chest. "So do I, but we can't let it stop us. Not tonight."

Ariek scoffed. "The sooner we get this over with, the better."

"We're going to get through this." The scotch had effectively numbed Sammy's stress and allowed his confidence to take root. "I can feel it. Just think of the money." A pause. "Keep your eye on the prize."

Ariek gripped the rail. "There will be no prize if we get busted."

"We've been through too much crap to come this far and have it fall apart," Sammy said. "It's our time." He exhaled a breath of annoyance. "Think about it, Ariek, just think. We're on the verge of some serious money and some serious recognition from the Network." Triumphantly extended his arm over the crowd. "A few more of these and we're more than just sitting pretty. I'll be damned if I allow some stripper to ruin it for us."

"She could." Ariek audibly sighed. "She knows too much."

Ariek's negativity bore into the container housing Sammy's frustration. "There's nothing I can do about it right now!" He looked down at all the activity swirling in and out of the bar, hoping he hadn't spoken too loudly. A couple sitting on a couch in the lounge looked up, but quickly reengaged in their conversation.

Sammy slowly lifted his glass to his mouth. Let the liquor coat his tongue before swallowing it. "I agree that these are some tense moments. But we can't let it go to our head, or we'll lose all we've worked for."

"I agree," Ariek said.

"We couldn't have stopped tonight if we wanted to," Sammy said. "And, quite frankly, I don't want to."

"All I'm saying is that this could explode in our faces at any moment," Ariek explained. "We've got to be ready for the worst."

"And we are," Sammy said. "No one is going to find that room in the factory."

"Maybe. Maybe not." Ariek braced his elbows on the railing. "Aryssa could lead the cops to it."

"She could be dead for all we know." Sammy swirled his drink. "They didn't see any movement after they shot at that boat."

"That's beside the point," Ariek stated. "We can't take the girls back there."

"Where do we take them, then? It's not like we have a lot of options."

"Harmony House," Ariek answered.

"You mean that dump on Michigan Avenue?"

"I know the owner." Ariek fiddled with his fingers. "He has a few rooms tucked in back in case…well, you know. We can lay low for a few days until we figure our next move."

"I still say our place is best," Sammy said confidently. "I guarantee you that Aryssa doesn't' know how she got there. And even though she managed to find a way out, I'm certain she doesn't remember how she did it."

"What about that boat?"

Sammy scrunched his face. "Pure luck. She probably flashed some guy for a ride." He chuckled. "He probably got more than he bargained for with all those guns going off."

"What if it was more than a coincidence?" Ariek's question dripped with concern.

Sammy sighed. Ariek was quickly killing his buzz. "Fine. Call your friend and we'll take the girls there, if that'll ease your mind."

Ariek grumbled through pursed lips. "It will." A pause. "We've got to strip that place clean, in case it's discovered."

Sammy clenched his jaw to contain his frustration. "How about you take care of that and I'll take care of things here." He took a sip of his drink and listened to the laughter that drifted up from the crowd. To the chatter of endless conversations and the upbeat music that seemed to bolster everyone's elation. The infectious rhythm spread throughout the space, making even Sammy bounce off his feet. "Can't you see that the girls are finally doing what they're supposed to be doing?"

"I see it," Ariek replied. He was busy scrolling through his phone. "I'm just trying to keep our investment secure."

"And I'll make sure it functions the way it's supposed to."

"Speaking of which, is that woman still chained to the wall?"

Sammy nodded silently. "What else was I going to do with her? She's no good for tonight."

Ariek grumbled again. "I'm not going to be the one taking her to the emergency room if she's seriously jacked up."

"She'll be fine," Sammy said confidently. "Regardless, I'm not taking her, even if she needs it." He took a long sip from his drink. "I've had a very serious conversation with the men. I thoroughly explained that workers who don't work don't bring us money." A pause "If they want to get paid then they'll have to think twice before smacking around the merchandise like that again."

"Let's hope so," Ariek replied. "We can't afford any more screw-ups."

"She did have to be put in her place, though," Sammy

said. "I could tell she was going to be a feisty one when we first got her."

Ariek held his phone to his ear and looked directly at Sammy. "It's my friend who owns Harmony House."

Sammy tipped his chin in acknowledgement. "We're not totally abandoning the factory."

"I know," Ariek confirmed. "This is temporary."

Sammy drained his drink with a tip of his head. Pointed to the bar as he looked at Ariek. "I'm going down to check on everyone."

Ariek nodded his understanding. "Hello? Hey, it's me…"

Sammy rattled the cubes in his empty glass; the alarm telling him that it was time for another. He exhaled slowly and realized that his stress was practically gone. All that crap from earlier was behind him and now he needed to keep his focus on the future. So what if Aryssa escaped. Did she know where to find him and the girls? Sammy shook his head. He made his way along the balcony and descended the elaborate staircase that lead into the lobby and toward the bar. Could she find that room inside the factory? Another shake of his head.

Even if Aryssa accused him and Ariek, it's not like she had any evidence. It was her word against his. Who would any reasonable person believe—a stripper and a possible junkie, or a respected businessman? Besides, she keeps to herself. There's no way she would pursue any of this.

Sammy made it a point to stop by the bouncer sitting near the entrance. "Hey," he said. "Make sure you look over every person who walks through those doors. We don't need Aryssa or the cops barging in here."

"What do I do if I see her?" the bouncer asked.

"Any sign of her or the cops, you call me." Sammy held up his cell. "Delay them as best you can, but more importantly, don't draw any unnecessary attention by doing something brash."

"Will do," the bouncer replied.

Sammy sighed. His earlier reluctance gave way to a small sense of security. "Better to be safe," he whispered to himself. On the balcony above him Ariek nonchalantly gave a thumbs-up.

Sammy waved his reply. Now to get the girls to the places they needed to be.

32

ARYSSA'S HEART THUMPED wildly. Dread trickled across the network of nerves that ran underneath her skin. She did her best to hide all the internal chaos that fought to break through her calm façade. Maybe she should've just thrown on some sweats, stayed home and persuaded Charlie to do the same. A sigh. Too late now.

She slid onto the stool at the end of the bar and let Charlie scoot her forward so she could be closer to the bar's edge. Readjusted her leather jacket and then nonchalantly picked a piece of lint off Charlie's suit jacket as he sat next to her. She tried to keep her interest on Charlie in hopes of simply blending in. Then again she couldn't help herself. It didn't take long before her attention wandered amongst the faces of the crowd. Her gaze eventually drifted beyond those that blocked her view of the Cadillac's lobby. Past the ceiling that covered most of the bar. Across all those seated in the lounge. It took several minutes, but someone did manage to catch her eye.

Aryssa nervously whispered into Charlie's ear. "That guy over there."

"What guy?"

"In the lobby; it's hard to see him from here." Aryssa steadied her voice. "The one sitting in the brown leather chair near the entrance."

Charlie slowly tilted his head. "I think that..." He leaned sideways. "I really can't..." Took a little longer to try to figure out who she was talking about. "That gargantuan one?"

"Yeah."

"What about him?"

Aryssa silently clucked her tongue. "He's a bouncer at the club. One of the ones that held me in that room."

Charlie's body stiffened. The muscles around his jaw tightened. "Are you sure that it's..."

"It's okay." Aryssa rubbed the back of Charlie's arm to calm him. His protectiveness eased some of her anxiety. "It tells me that we've come to the right place."

Charlie's eyes darted around the room. "Anyone else we should be worried about?"

Aryssa peeked over Charlie's shoulder. "Nothing I can see." She didn't recognize anyone sitting at the bar. "I'm glad I listened to you."

The way she had been stroking Charlie's arm seemed to ease his tension. "You mean coming through the back?"

"How'd you know about it?"

Charlie shrugged. "I just did. Figured that if this was the place, then there'd be someone watching the front."

Aryssa sighed. "That means there are more of them around here somewhere."

"I don't know what I'm looking for," Charlie said. "This place is packed."

It was true, there were people everywhere. Sitting and standing. Talking. The music weaved through the voices and drifted above the crowd. It was hard to pick out a single person from the forest of the many. "I'm still not..."

"Hey folks." The female bartender, wearing a black-and-red vest, smiled and laid a black coaster in front of Aryssa, then Charlie. "What are you drinking this evening?"

Aryssa gently bit her lower lip. She definitely could use a drink after everything she had been through. "Bourbon old fashioned on the rocks."

"What kind of bourbon?"

"Dealer's choice," Aryssa answered. "As long as it's top-shelf."

Charlie looked at her from the corner of his eye with an arched brow. "I was feeling a beer, but now I'm not so sure."

"Why not?" Aryssa questioned.

"You're making me feel so unmanly."

"Trust me, you don't look it." Aryssa gripped his arm. "Besides, after everything that's happened today," she leaned close to Charlie, "I needed something a little more—you know, hard-hitting. Time to throw prim-and-proper out the window."

Charlie was quiet for the length of a heartbeat. "Better make that two."

"Coming right up," the bartender said.

Aryssa watched the bartender walk to the illuminated liquor shelf and select a bottle of bourbon. She wondered what brand the bartender had chosen, but the thought quickly disintegrated when Charlie spoke.

"What's next?" Charlie spun to face her. "Sit here for a bit?"

Aryssa nodded. "I guess. Maybe I'll recognize someone besides that bouncer."

"Seeing how this is the place, I'm surprised you haven't spotted any of the women."

"I wasn't with them for very long." Aryssa brushed a strand of hair behind her ear. "I sure hope I can recognize them now that they're all decked out."

Charlie shifted in his seat. "It's a big hotel; they could be anywhere."

"It's possible." Aryssa casually ran her finger around the edge of the coaster. "Is there another bar?"

"There's a restaurant on the top floor."

"A restaurant?" Aryssa paused. "How did I not know about that?"

Charlie shrugged. "I don't know."

"I guess that's a place they could be." Aryssa took a moment to consider the possibility. "I don't know why, but it just doesn't seem like the right fit."

"It's not as casual as this place and I bet not as crowded," Charlie said. "I think we should sit here and see how things unfold."

Aryssa nodded her agreement. "We give it an hour or…"

The bartender stepped up to Aryssa and set her drink on the coaster. She then did the same for Charlie.

"Thank you," Aryssa said. She gazed at the eye insignia molded into the large ice cube and the way it seemed to float in the amber liquid. "This looks incredible."

The bartender smiled her appreciation. "Would you like to start a tab?"

"No, I'll pay for it now." Charlie pulled fifty-dollar bill from his wallet and slid it across the bar.

"Be right back with your change."

Charlie lifted his drink. "Cheers."

Aryssa tapped her glass against his. Took a sip and let the sweetened liquor dance across her tongue. "Maybe a suite."

"A suite?" Charlie questioned. "Like one of those honeymoon things?"

"Kind of, but not as tacky," Aryssa answered. "Don't some

hotels have those fancy rooms with a hot tub, a great view and a decked out bathroom? You see them in movies."

"We're not in a movie."

"I know, but this is a high-end hotel," Aryssa reasoned. "I bet it has one of those rooms for people who need to entertain. You know, people with money and a need to do so."

Charlie sipped his drink, letting his nose scrunch ever so slightly. "Let's say this place has one and that's where everything is taking place. How are we going to find it?"

"Good question." Aryssa sighed. Had she hit a dead end? The air began to leak out of her balloon of enthusiasm. Now what? "Maybe if we sit here long enough we'll see someone heading to the elevators."

"And then what?" Charlie sat his drink on the bar. "Follow them?"

"We'd have to," Aryssa answered in a tone dripping with doubt.

"A little risky, don't you think?" Charlie wrapped his thumb and forefinger around his glass. "They know who you are."

"The girls will keep quiet," Aryssa said.

"That's not who I'm worried about," Charlie interjected. "You and I both know that there's more of Sammy's crew somewhere out there."

Aryssa solemnly gazed at her glass. Things were looking bleak. They had managed to find seats at the back of the bar. Had avoided the bouncer in the lobby. How long could they sit and wait before someone would recognize her?

Charlie noticed Aryssa's defeated expression. "Let's give it some time. You never know what might pop up."

Aryssa took a consolatory swig of her old fashioned. Nodded her agreement, but suddenly stopped. A voice managed to punch through the noise of the crowd, hook her attention and urge her to spin around.

Was it her imagination, or had she actually heard a thick Eastern European accent?

Aryssa focused on the direction of the voice, hoping she could confirm what she had heard. Two well-dressed couples were gathered around the high-top table directly behind her. A waitress slid by with a tray of drinks. Two men were laughing over something one of them had said. Another man, wearing a gray suit, approached two women who were standing near the bar. A couple hugged and…

Aryssa froze. Could it be? There in a booth along the wall. She tapped Charlie's leg. "It's her."

Charlie spun slowly. "You see someone?"

Aryssa nodded. "The blond in the booth. Black dress with the busting cleavage. Sitting with the balding guy in the white dress shirt."

Charlie casually glanced in the direction Aryssa was describing. "How do you know her?"

"It's Kami. The only woman I talked to in that room."

"Are you sure?"

"Very," Aryssa answered with certainty. "We've got to get her out of here. She's the proof we need."

"Hold on," Charlie cautioned. He held Aryssa's hand to stop her from leaping off her seat. "You can't just run up there."

"What am I supposed to do, then?"

"You don't know who could be watching," Charlie said. His eyes ran over those standing near the booth. "We need to be careful." A pause. "I've got an idea."

33

CHARLIE NEEDED TO be absolutely sure. He—no, they—couldn't risk discovering the woman wasn't who Aryssa thought she was. Worse yet, what if there was a guard nearby? He cautiously followed Aryssa and diligently watched for any sudden movements. Any last bits of doubt disintegrated when Aryssa stepped up to the table without so much as a hint of trouble.

The blonde's eyes widened. Surprise arched her brows. Jaw slackened. She quickly regained her composure, glanced at the man on the other side of the table, then back to Aryssa.

"How are you, Kami?" Aryssa infused her voice with astonishment. "It's been such a long time."

"It has," Kami said in her thick accent. "Of all the places."

"What's it been? Something like three, maybe four..." Aryssa let the unfinished sentence hang in the air.

"At least," Kami answered. "Why you come here when you have the night off?"

Aryssa sat her drink on the table. "Oh you know, just wanted to check this place out." She gestured over her shoulder. "Have you met Charlie?"

Kami shot a nervous glance past Charlie into the crowd. "I'm Kami." She extended her hand. "Pleasure to meet you."

"Likewise." Charlie gently shook Kami's hand.

Kami turned to the man across from her. "And this is…"

The balding man cut her off before she could say his name by quickly extending his arm. "Nice to meet you both."

Charlie shook the man's hand first, then Aryssa followed. The balding man casually looked at his watch. "I hate to be rude," he gestured toward Kami, "but we really should be going."

Kami seemed to reel backward at his sudden insistence, but quickly regained her composure. "Yes, I think so," she responded politely. "Maybe we go now."

Aryssa leaned forward. "So soon?" Charlie nudged the small of her back. She took his cue and slid into the booth next to Kami. "I was really hoping we could catch up."

"Maybe another time; unfortunately we're running late," the man said more firmly.

"Late," Charlie said. "I hate being late. Never like it when other people are late, either." He purposefully paused. "A sign of disrespect, don't you think?"

"I agree." The man started to scoot his way out of the booth. "Then you'll understand why we need to be on our way."

Charlie stepped to the edge of the seat and effectively blocked the man from getting out. His irritation welled up in his throat. "Looks like you're going to be extremely late to wherever you were planning on taking her."

The man's brows furrowed. "Who are you to tell me what's…"

"A bit of advice," Charlie intruded. "In a matter of minutes this place will be crawling with cops." He held up three fingers. "You can stay and try to explain yourself." Curled one of the fingers into his fist. "Leave through the back and simply go straight home." Closed the second finger. "And if you try to warn Sammy, well, I'm sure you can guess what will happen."

"I paid good money for tonight," the man said defensively. "I deserve to…"

"Really? You want to argue about this right now?" Charlie tapped his wrist. "Time's ticking."

"I think you're bluffing," The man stated spitefully. "For all I know you could be trying to take away what's mine."

"What's yours?" Charlie's voice grew hot with anger. "She's a human being, not a possession." Balled his hands into fists. "I'm about to add a fourth option. Me taking you out back and pounding some sense into you."

The man's shoulders curled with defeat. He looked over at Kami, then toward Charlie. "Fine. I don't need any of this." He tried to squirm through the tiny space Charlie had left between him and the edge of the seat. "I expect my damn money back."

After a few seconds of letting him struggle, Charlie stepped back. The man stood up, his face as red as a cayenne pepper. He straightened his white dress shirt and scurried away toward the back exit.

Kami gulped her wine. "You shouldn't have done that. What happens if he tells?"

"He won't," Charlie said reassuringly.

"How do you know?" Kami asked.

"His doubt." Charlie answered simply. "He can't say for certain that I was lying. I'm betting he's more worried about explaining himself to the police." A pause. "Call it self-preservation."

Kami sighed. "Are the police really coming?"

"Not yet," Aryssa said. "But they will be."

Kami swiped her finger under her eye. "This is too much.

What if the police work for them?"

Aryssa laid her hand on Kami's shoulder. "No way. Not here."

"It happens," Kami said. "Where I come from, it happens."

Aryssa opened her mouth, but nothing came out. She glanced at Charlie as if pleading for his help.

A sudden pressure crawled onto Charlie's shoulders. He needed to get Aryssa and Kami out of here before someone noticed. "Look, we came for you. We want to get you back home."

Kami shook her head. "My sister. What about her?" She sniffled. "If they find out, they'll kill her."

"She's going to be safe," Charlie said.

"You don't know that."

Charlie sighed. "You're right, I don't." He paused. "But they say that to scare you." Tapped his temple. "It's a mind game to make you stay and do what they tell you."

"He's right," Aryssa said. "The man that brought you here—I know him. He doesn't have that kind of connection to get your sister." She caressed Kami's arm. "I'll bet he doesn't even know that she exists."

Kami sipped her wine. "I don't know. Maybe I go back to room and wait for the next one."

"I told you there's a room," Aryssa said to Charlie. She held Kami's hand. "Where is this room?"

Kami gestured toward the ceiling. "Twentieth floor. It's very big." She tapped her glass. "They have two of them for tonight."

"Two of them?" Aryssa said with a hint of surprise.

"Yes, two," Kami confirmed. "I should go now."

"No. No you shouldn't," Aryssa said determinedly. "No

woman should be forced to do what they're making you do. Charlie and I came here to expose all of this."

Charlie held up a phone. "We're making the call once we get you out."

Kami sniffled. "Where will you take me?"

"Somewhere safe," Aryssa answered. "Someplace they don't know about." She brushed a strand of Kami's hair off her face. "I got out and then risked coming back here to help. If I can do it, then…"

The strain to get things moving weighed heavily on Charlie. "I hate to sound pushy, but we should…" He thumbed over his shoulder. "We've got to go before someone notices."

Aryssa held out her hand. "Please, you've got to trust me."

Kami set her wine glass on the table. Bowed her head. Her chest fully inflated then slowly collapsed. She finally lifted her gaze to Aryssa and smiled ever so slightly. "We go," she whispered. "Thank you."

"You're doing the right thing." Aryssa's voice was filled with relief. "It'll work out for the best, you'll see." She grasped Kami's hand and helped her out of the booth.

Charlie grabbed Aryssa's free hand and began to snake his way through the crowd. Could he get the two women out of the hotel without drawing attention? With the way things were going, it sure seemed like he could.

34

SAMMY CASUALLY SET his drink on the high-top table that stood just inside the bar. He slowly scanned the room and within a minute or so spotted three of his women. Each one of them was sitting close to her client. Each woman thinned her lips into a smile, as if she truly meant it. Focused her attention. Winked. Stroked an arm and most likely an ego. Effectively primed their men for what lay ahead. In essence, doing everything that was expected of them.

Two of them had already escorted their client upstairs to one of the suites. Sammy checked his watch. Right about now they were indulging the men in their deepest fantasies. Doing things their wives were either too scared to do or were flat-out incapable of doing. By the look of these men, maybe it was more like too prudish to even consider. Sammy chuckled. Despite everything that had happened earlier, tonight was going off without a hitch.

He looked over his shoulder at the bouncer sitting near the entrance, then up to Ariek, who slowly paced along the balcony with his phone pressed to his ear and finally to one of his other men sitting at the end of the bar with his back pressed against the wall. His attention was glued to the nearest television. Sammy quietly huffed his displeasure and made a mental note to tell him to keep his focus on the task at hand.

Some of his men were out of his sight, like the two brothers who were upstairs watching over the rooms. The bouncer out back, near the alley. Not the brightest of the bunch and damn if he didn't smoke like a chimney. Hopefully he was doing what he was supposed to be doing and not taking one of his frequent naps in his car.

The chatter of the crowd, the driving music, the flowing drinks and the sexual tension that saturated the atmosphere— all of it uplifted Sammy's mood. Still, he yawned and tried to rub the fatigue from his eyes. It had been a long and stressful day, and it wasn't over yet. There were still a few women unaccounted for. He would have to wander through the bar and find them. But first things first.

Sammy pulled out his phone and logged into the account. As if he hadn't checked it already, but he felt the need to make sure that there were no sudden discrepancies. Everything looked on the up and up, except—what was this? Why was the final tally lower from when he had last looked? He anxiously scrolled through the accounts. Who had suspended their payment? Why had they taken their money back?

It took several minutes to find the amended account. Of all the people, why him? This was his third, maybe fourth, time using Sammy's services. Always had paid. Kept quiet. Seemed satisfied. What woman had he chosen to be with?

Sammy balled his hands into fists and squeezed his frustration. That damn blonde from Bulgaria. The one who had been talking to Aryssa. Should've known there'd be a connection. He immediately scanned the crowd. Where in the hell was Kami?

Several people milled around the hotel entrance. It was too crowded to clearly see all the way to the back of the bar. He needed to find her and it needed to be done now. Sammy started to make his way through the throngs when something snagged his attention.

Three people were weaving through the couches and chairs in the lounge toward an exit at the far end of the lobby. They moved with too much purpose—more like a little too frantically. A man with long dark hair, dressed in a suit. A blonde in a sexy dress and…was that…that…Aryssa?

Sammy motioned to the bouncer sitting at the bar, but his concentration was focused on the television. "Damn it."

He scampered to the boundary that divided the bar from the lobby just as the long-haired man swung open a door. "Hey!" Sammy yelled.

The man turned his head just enough for Sammy to know that it was Aryssa's friend from the alley. And there was that blonde Bulgarian, Kami. The third had to be her. "Aryssa!"

"ARYSSA!"

It was purely instinctual. Aryssa swung around to look behind her. Her vision fell on the man who had screamed her name. Sammy.

Aryssa gasped. "It's him."

"Inside," Charlie demanded. He yanked Aryssa across the threshold and into the stairwell. Motioned at her purse. "You've got to call now."

Aryssa didn't hesitate. She pulled out the phone and with the press of a button the screen lit up.

Charlie glanced out the tiny window in the door. Shook his head. "This way," he whispered with urgency.

"What is it?"

"He's coming."

A jolt of fright singed Aryssa's nerves. Her legs went numb, causing her to stumble. Kami's breath anxiously chugged behind her.

"Make the call," Charlie said.

Aryssa struggled to keep her attention on the phone and her feet moving forward. Her thumb trembled. She somehow managed to press the three numbers.

"Hello, this is nine-one-one. What's your emergency?"

Charlie bound up the flight of concrete steps at the end of the corridor.

Aryssa purposefully stomped up them in order to keep her balance. "Um…hello. I have an emergency."

"How can I help you?" the dispatcher asked.

"I'm at the Cad," Aryssa answered. "I mean the Cadillac." Took a quick breath to steady her voice. "There's a man with a gun."

"Has someone been shot?"

"Not yet." Aryssa swung to the left, ran across the landing and jumped onto the next flight of steps. "He's running a prostitution ring and threatening to…"

The phone slipped from Aryssa's grasp, bounced off the metal railing and fell end-over-end down the shaft between the steps. It struck the bottom and burst apart.

Disbelief froze Aryssa. She leaned over the railing and stared at the broken phone scattered across the floor as if it were the victim of a horrific car crash.

"Come on," Charlie stated. "We've got to keep moving."

Aryssa sucked in a breath and followed Charlie upward. Had she given enough information? Had she convinced the dispatcher to send the police?

CHARLIE WAS READY to lead Aryssa and Kami up the next

flight, but instead stopped. The heavy thundering of feet fell like torrential rain from somewhere above. "We're almost there," a male voice spoke.

Was it security? More of Sammy's men? Someone unrelated to everything that was taking place? Charlie couldn't take the chance. Somewhere below he thought he could hear another set of footsteps stomping upward. Was it Sammy? He had no choice.

"Follow close and move fast," Charlie whispered urgently. Without waiting for a response he swung open the wood door and sprang out onto the balcony that overlooked the hotel lobby.

Some thirty feet away a man spun around to look upon the trio. His hand holding his cell phone dropped to his side. Jaw slackened, but then quickly tightened. He scowled as he thrust his arm forward and pointed. "Stop right there."

"Ariek!" Aryssa screamed.

Kami tried to hold back. Charlie pulled on Aryssa's hand, dragging both Aryssa and Kami forward. There was only one way off this balcony and that was through the man with the phone. Charlie leapt and balled his hand onto a fist.

Ariek's menacing glare morphed into shock. Brows arched. Mouth dropped open. Before he could react, Charlie's fist connected with the bridge of his nose.

Ariek's head snapped. Blood splattered. He flew backward into the wall and crumpled onto the carpet.

Charlie's heart pumped confidence into his veins and it readily mixed with the irritation already swimming in his blood. He wasn't going to let anything stand in his way. Even that large man in a black shirt that crested the elaborate staircase at the end of the balcony and ran straight for him.

The bouncer in the black shirt swung. Charlie easily side-stepped the punch, allowing the man's momentum to carry him forward right into Charlie's driving knee.

Agony exploded from the bouncer's mouth. He managed to quickly recover, wrap his tree-trunk-sized arm around Charlie's leg, plant his own foot and drive Charlie backward.

Charlie threw an uppercut into the bouncer's face. Than another. And another. It wasn't slowing his momentum. In a matter of seconds Charlie's lower back careened into the railing. Pain rifled up his spine and into his shoulder blades. A punch to the bouncer's ear did nothing to slow him.

The man in the black shirt kept driving Charlie backward as if he were a lineman on a football team. The railing buckled. Shifted. Charlie wrapped his arm around the bouncer's neck just as the railing broke.

Aryssa's scream filled Charlie's ears. He was suddenly weightless. Air rushed by his head. The world flipped and twirled like an uncontrollable gyroscope. He managed to spin the bouncer underneath him just as they both came to a crashing halt.

Bones snapped. A bolt of pain ripped though Charlie's pinned arm. The bouncer blew out a breath followed by a barely audible moan then fell silent. Even though Charlie had landed on top, the jolt of striking the floor ripped into his core. The shock wave roared into his head and jumbled his circuitry. Static filled his eyes. Disconnected his consciousness. Then everything went black.

35

SAMMY WAS STOMPING up the flight of concrete steps when the two brothers descended onto the landing above him. Their breaths chugged like an old Buick.

"What's going on?" the taller brother asked.

"She's here," Sammy responded bitterly.

"You kept saying that over the phone. Who's here?" the portly one said.

"Aryssa and that guy of hers." Anger curled the edges of Sammy's voice.

"You mean that dancer?"

"Yes, that one." Sammy bound up the last couple of steps and yanked the wood door open.

Ahead, near the far end of the balcony, two men were tangled in a fight. The railing suddenly gave way, sending them both tumbling to the floor below. A collective cry went up from the crowd in the bar. Aryssa screamed, "Charlie!"

Kami, that blonde from Bulgaria, was standing near the railing. Her eyes were wide with shock and her hand covered her gaping mouth.

"I want them both." Sammy javelined his arm forward. "Then we get the hell out of here."

Sammy bound toward Kami. He couldn't allow her to get away and expose everything he had spent so long putting together. She was cautiously creeping toward the edge of the balcony in order to get a glimpse of the damage below, seemingly unaware that he was closing fast.

Ariek was heaped on the floor. He slowly tried to prop himself against the wall. Sammy grunted. There was no time to stop and help. Sammy needed a smooth exit and it needed to happen fast.

Sammy snagged Kami by the arm and yanked her across the balcony.

Kami screamed and tried to jerk free of his grasp. Sammy squeezed even tighter and threw her against the wall. "How dare you!"

"I no run," Kami said in her thick accent.

"Yes, you did," Sammy responded with a hiss. "And your sister will pay dearly."

Shock crinkled Kami's expression. "You no touch my sister!" She squirmed. Tried to kick Sammy. The taller brother latched onto her.

"Take her to the van," Sammy demanded. "We're going back to…"

The taller brother didn't let Sammy finish. Instead his rage bolted across his face as he grabbed Kami by the scruff of her neck.

Sammy held out his hand. "Don't damage the…"

"Does it matter right now?" the taller brother questioned tensely.

"I guess not."

"I thought so." The taller brother let his fury rifle through his arm and out into his hand as let go of Kami's neck and immediately slapped her across the cheek. Her head snapped, eyes glazed with confusion. The opposition that had tensed her body softened to conformity. The taller brother forcefully led her toward the elaborate staircase that descended into the lobby.

Sammy pointed at Aryssa. "You tried to screw me over." Gestured at the portly brother. "I don't care what happens to her." He took off down the balcony toward the staircase.

"Neither do I," the portly brother mocked.

CHARLIE WAS UNCONSCIOUS, maybe even dead, on the lobby's floor. Kami was being dragged away. One of Sammy's men was in front of Aryssa, essentially boxing her in like a cornered animal. The cold fingers of dread curled around her heart and made it thump with desperation. The venom of numbness leaked into her veins and fanned out through her limbs.

"Remember me?" the portly brother taunted. His sinister smile scrunched his burnt cheek. "Got lucky once. Not going to happen a second time."

Aryssa tried to swallow her fright. "Wasn't luck." She tried to leap sideways, but the portly man was too quick and matched her movement. Her path to freedom was choked off.

"Not as quick as you think." The portly brother stepped toward Aryssa. Pushed her closer to the edge of the balcony. A balcony with a broken and missing railing. "You weren't when you were tackled in the alley, neither."

His mocking tone ignited a flame of anger deep inside Aryssa. The will to fight spread. "You needed a gun, a bag over my head and the element of surprise." She baited him with a nonchalant flick of her hand. "Too short and too soft to do it like a real man. Must be too scared to take on a woman."

The portly brother grunted his displeasure. "You little bitch." He sprang toward Aryssa with wrath bursting from his eyes.

Aryssa shifted her weight to the right but quickly stepped left. The portly brother bought the fake only to realize Aryssa wasn't moving in that direction. She planted her left foot and drove her right knee into his gut with everything she had.

A gust of pain exploded out of the portly man's mouth. His eyes widened. Face reddened. He managed to stop himself from tumbling over the balcony's edge and spun.

Aryssa anticipated the spin. She regained her balance, side-shuffled toward him, cocked her leg and rifled her foot into his chest.

The man's brows molded into an arch of bewilderment. He stumbled backward and lost his balance. Before he could register anything else he toppled over the balcony's edge and plummeted to the floor. *Splat!*

The crowd gasped. A few people screamed. Aryssa looked over the edge and down the thirty or so feet to where the shorter man was lying face down with his limbs sprawled across the floor. He desperately tried to dig his fingers into the stone tile, as if he were trying to claw his way toward the exit.

One of the bouncers ran out from the bar. He angrily glanced up at Aryssa, then turned his attention to the portly brother and finally at the one under Charlie who wasn't moving at all.

Aryssa sucked in a deep breath and stood tall. She pointed at the bouncer and yelled. "He's one of them!"

The music kept playing. Some of the bar crowd was rushing toward the exit. Others gazed in horror. Still there were some inside the bar who had no idea what was happening. "He's one of them!" Aryssa shouted again.

Irritation slid off the bouncer's face. Uncertainty made him cock his head.

"He's a part of the sex ring!" Aryssa screamed. "He's responsible for enslaving women and beating them! There are other women in this hotel being forced to have sex, as I speak."

Aryssa's words were a spear that pierced the bouncer's chest. He stepped away from the portly man who was trying to slither across the floor. Spun to look at the crowd who, he quickly realized, were staring at him. Some appeared to have already made up their minds about what was happening.

The bouncer opened his mouth to speak, but his jaw froze in place, allowing nothing but silence to pass over his tongue.

"Is it true?" A voice piped up from the crowd.

"A sex ring? In our city?" questioned another.

"How many have you forced...?"

The bouncer took three or four steps backward. Kept his hands out in front of him. "I...I don't know anything about..."

"It's true!" Aryssa yelled. "I watched him beat a woman senseless!" She gestured at the men spread across the floor. "Two of those men are part of it, too."

Several in the crowd fidgeted while others whispered to those standing next to them. Murmurs overflowed with irritation. The tension that bound the group became even tighter.

The bouncer must've sensed it. He sprinted through the lounge and toward the rear of the lobby.

"Get him!" someone shouted.

Five or six men took off after him. Aryssa watched the men chase the bouncer toward the exit. The very exit that she, Charlie and Kami had ran into only minutes earlier. The matter quickly fell from her concern, because there was something far more important to attend to.

Aryssa looked down on Charlie. He still wasn't moving. She couldn't tell if he was even breathing. Was he dead? Angst nearly tore her heart in two. "Charlie!" She bolted toward the staircase leading into the lobby and ran right to him.

THE ABSOLUTE DARKNESS that surrounded Charlie was so thick that it engulfed the horizon of his consciousness. It squeezed him on all sides, found a way beneath his skin and before long it weighed heavily in his limbs. The faint chatter of voices floated from somewhere in the distance. It grew a little louder. A little closer. There were a lot of voices. Maybe hundreds. Was it coming from inside his head? Nothing about it was relaxing; in fact it was rather harsh. Uninviting. He tried to cover his ears, but his arms wouldn't respond to the command.

"Charlie!" The voice rose above the chatter.

Who was calling his name? Charlie tried to open his mouth. Tried frantically to thrust the air from his lungs. Not even a whimper managed to pass across his vocal cords.

"Charlie! Please wake up." The voice sounded more desperate.

Electric pain skewered his wrist and shot up into his shoulder. At the same time something soft brushed across his cheek.

"Charlie…"

The darkness, the chatter, the heaviness seeping into his skin, all of it was sucked into a vacuum. For a microsecond nothing existed. Then he opened his eyes to a bright light that flooded his awareness.

Aryssa was kneeling over him and gasped in relief. "Charlie…are you okay?"

He was on his back, staring at the ornate ceiling way above

Aryssa's head. The ceiling of a hotel. The...the Cad. Charlie exhaled. Several other people were standing over him. To his right someone was struggling to crawl away. To his left a large man wasn't moving at all. The dam holding back the events from up there, up on that balcony, burst open and it all came rushing into him.

"Say something, please," Aryssa pleaded as tears pooled in the corners of her eyes.

Charlie gasped and sat upright. "What the hell just...?"

"Oh, my god." Aryssa threw her arms around him and squeezed tight. "You're alive."

"I am," Charlie affirmed. He wrapped his good arm around Aryssa and reveled in her embrace. "At least I think I am." He paused. "How did I end up down here?"

"Take it easy," a man in a blue blazer said. "The ambulance will be here soon."

"Ambulance?" Charlie tucked the bad arm into his side to protect it. "I don't think I need..."

"You definitely need one, especially after a fall like that." The man in the blue blazer knelt by Charlie's side. "And the cops too."

Aryssa pulled back and nodded. "He's right. You're hurt and there's so much to sort through." She softly stroked his hair. "We've managed to rescue some of the girls."

"Some?" Charlie couldn't stop the disappointment from infiltrating his tone. "What about the others?"

"There were two in the bar." Aryssa gestured through the crowd. "Security is upstairs looking for some of the others."

Charlie rubbed his temple. "Can you trust them? They could've been bought off."

"Possible, but I doubt it." A tear trickled down Aryssa's cheek. "The cops will be here soon. Let them deal with it."

She tipped her chin toward the burly man lying on his back. "You've taken care of one." The portly man trying to crawl away grunted in pain. "That one is not going anywhere."

"We'll make sure of it," said a dark-haired man wearing a white dress shirt. Two other men looked down on the man trying to crawl away like hawks eyeing their prey.

Aryssa motioned up toward the balcony. "And Ariek isn't going anywhere either." A smile creased her lips. "You got him good."

A memory behind a dissipating cloud. Someone trying to stop him up on the balcony. Charlie's punch that crumpled him to the floor. He sighed. There was something missing. More like someone. "Where's Sammy?"

Aryssa's head bowed momentarily. "He got away."

"He got...?" Tension held Charlie's tongue. His blood thickened with anger. "Where's...?" he couldn't remember her name. "You know, your blonde friend from..."

"You mean Kami?" Aryssa sniffled. "They snagged her and took her with them."

"Where?"

Aryssa shrugged. "Maybe to the factory. Somewhere else? I'm not sure." She readjusted her knees. "I think he may have said something about going back to that room."

Charlie glanced at his deformed wrist, sucked in a breath to try to relieve the pain and then braced it against his gut. "Maybe we should..."

Aryssa shook her head. "You're hurt. We're not going anywhere until the medics get here."

"It could be too late by then," Charlie reasoned. "We need to get there now."

"You mean leave?" the man in the blue blazer questioned. "Don't think that's a good idea. There could be so much more wrong with you."

"I agree," Aryssa said. "Let the cops handle it from here."

Frustration boiled up in Charlie. He couldn't sit here and do nothing. Couldn't just let it be handled by someone else. Couldn't let it remain unfinished. He used his good hand to clutch his temples with his middle finger and thumb. It was kind of like repairing his boat. Never leave things unfinished and expect someone else to do it for you.

The pain from the fall was already waning. His memory of the events was sharpening. The steam of determination rose from his smoldering frustration. It swirled into his limbs and then up into his head. Charlie grunted and rose to his feet.

"What are you doing?" Aryssa questioned.

"Hey man, you should sit back down," the man in the blue blazer said.

Charlie took a deep breath, then exhaled sharply so he could steady the teetering. He braced Aryssa's shoulder. "I'm going after Sammy, to finish this once and for all."

"But..." Aryssa stammered.

"Send the cops to the factory," Charlie interrupted. "They'll eventually find that place where they held you captive. I need to get there before they manage to slip away for good."

"But you're hurt!" Aryssa gingerly held his injured arm. "There could be something more..."

Charlie held up his once-injured wrist. He wiggled his fingers. "I'll be fine."

Aryssa's mouth fell open in shock. "How's that possible?" She pointed. "It's not... it's...it's straight. How'd you...?"

The man in the blue blazer stepped backward. "No way. I swear it was..."

"You coming or not?" Charlie said to Aryssa.

Aryssa wavered. "Are you sure that it's a good idea?"

"Now or never," Charlie said firmly.

Aryssa looked at Charlie, the crowd and then at the man who was lying on his back. Something grabbed her attention. She knelt, lifted his shirt and pointed at a metal object tucked into his waistband. "What about this?"

Charlie didn't flinch. There was too much happening and his mind was still a touch foggy. "Grab it and let's go." He stepped backward toward the door.

"Are you sure you should be doing that?" the man in the blue blazer asked hesitantly.

Aryssa ran after Charlie, cupping the gun in her hands. "I guess it's now or never."

Charlie scampered to the exit with Aryssa in tow. Sirens blared from somewhere down the street. It echoed through the surrounding buildings joining the chorus of flashing blue and red lights that bounced off the windows.

"This way," Charlie said. He clutched Aryssa's elbow. "We've got to get there before he leaves."

"What do we do if he's not there?" Aryssa asked tentatively.

Charlie shrugged. "Then I guess he's gone for good."

36

A CLOAK OF silence hung heavily in the taxi. Even though it was invisible, Aryssa could almost feel its starched, sound-dampening texture. Smell the acrid odor of its fibers woven with the threads of exhaustion, pain, death and everything else that had taken place in the hotel lobby. She shifted in her seat, hoping to find a position that made her feel a little lighter. Maybe a little more energized. She shivered. Then again, maybe it had something to do with where they were going and the gun she was holding. These were things she didn't want anything to do with, but destiny had bound them to her anyway.

Aryssa looked over at Charlie. Whatever spell that had roped his thoughts was suddenly broken. He turned his attention on her and smiled ever so slightly. "Something on your mind?"

"Yeah, a lot," Aryssa answered.

"Like what?"

Aryssa hesitated, then gestured toward Charlie's wrist. "Like that. No one can mend a broken bone that fast." An uneasy pause. "I'm questioning myself if it was even broken?"

Charlie opened and closed his fist. Laid his hand in his lap. "Maybe you saw it from a wrong angle."

"That's bullshit and you know it," Aryssa stated decisively.

"It was definitely messed up. I know it, you know it and everyone in that room who saw it knows it."

"It's fine now."

"It wasn't back there," Aryssa thumbed over her shoulder. "What gives?"

Charlie was silent for several seconds, then he shrugged. "I really don't know."

"What do you mean by that?" Aryssa uneasily ran her hand over her thigh. "How can you not know? It's your body and what happened wasn't anything close to being normal."

"I get that," Charlie responded. "I don't know why or how it happens."

"So it's happened before?"

Charlie slowly nodded. His features lost vibrancy and simply became blank. A distant stare that could be measured in years. "Twice," he eventually said.

"So this is the third?"

"Yeah," Charlie answered. "Both times they somehow fixed themselves within a matter of minutes." He wiggled his fingers. "If I cut myself, it heals quicker than I can snap my fingers. It happens all the time when I'm wrenching on the boat."

"But, why?" Curiosity clung to Aryssa's voice. "I mean, how is it possible? No one I know can do that."

"I've never met anyone either," Charlie said. "I just don't know what would happen if I was shot or seriously burned."

"What about your parents? Maybe a relative had the ability."

Charlie rested his head against the seat. "I've never had..."

"Alright," the cab driver said. "We're here." He scrunched down into his seat as he peered out the window. "Are you sure this is where you want to go?"

"This is the place." Charlie took some money out of his wallet and passed it up to the driver. "Keep it."

"Much appreciated." The cab driver's smile stretched his Fu Manchu. The wrinkles atop his balding head deepened. "Don't get anyone who wants to come here this time of night."

Aryssa swallowed her uneasiness. Maybe this wasn't such a good idea. She leaned toward Charlie. "Don't you think we should let the cops handle this?" Tried to disguise the worry in her tone. "We don't even know where we're going."

Charlie gazed out the cab's window. "He's here. I know it." He slowly rubbed his hands together. "There's something else in there. Something that I…" his voice faded into silence.

"Something else?" Aryssa asked in a tone that hinted at not wanting to know what it could be.

The cab driver turned in his seat to look at Aryssa. "This was the place to work back in the day. Employed a whole lot of people." Clicked his tongue. "Even my dad."

"Your dad worked here?" Aryssa nestled into her seat.

"Not in the factory itself, but in the offices," the driver said in his raspy voice. "He helped manage the books."

"Like an accountant?"

The cab driver tapped his temple. "He never went to college to make it official, but was smart enough for sure. Ran that department for years."

Something clicked inside Aryssa. Could the cab driver be familiar with the room where she'd been held captive in the factory? "Were there offices in the basement?"

The driver squinted as if he were trying to cleave a piece of his memory. "I'm pretty certain there was a basement. It's been a long time, but my dad took me there when I was young." He paused. "If my memory serves me, there must be two if not three floors that were once used for offices."

Aryssa looked out into the darkness at the same time Charlie did. "Are you sure?" Charlie asked. "All I've ever seen is that factory. Nothing out there looks like any kind of office building to me."

"That's because it was built to be hidden." The driver flicked his wrist. "They wanted to keep those white and blue shirts separated, so they made a whole different group of buildings." His head bobbed with certainty. "They're connected, you know. There's a tunnel in the basement that runs underneath the lot."

Charlie looked over at Aryssa with his chin jutting forward. He slowly nodded. She could almost hear the gears turning in his head. "Think it's still there?"

The cab driver shrugged. "Parts of it, I guess."

"Maybe that's where I was taken?" Aryssa questioned.

"If it's going to be anywhere, that's got to be it," Charlie said confidently.

"You two really thinking of going in there?" The driver chomped on his gum. "Ain't the thing I'd be doing this time of night."

"I've heard the rumors," Charlie said.

"Those ain't no rumors. What you heard is true," the cab driver said.

Aryssa fidgeted. "What's true?"

The driver huffed. "Place is haunted. Plain and simple. Not even the bums go in there." He paused as if trying to remember what he had heard. "There's something deep inside that place. Something that ain't right."

"Like what?" Aryssa asked.

"I just know folks talk of some strange shit. Weird kind of things. Things that shouldn't be in existence." The cab driver paused. "They know not to get close to that place."

"Close?" Aryssa rubbed her sweat-drenched palms over her thighs. "Like that office building?"

The driver shook his head vigorously. "Somewhere inside that factory. Down below the main floor." A tense pause. "That's all I know."

"Aryssa laid her hand on Charlie's shoulder. "Do you really think this is a good idea?"

Charlie stared out the window for several silent seconds. "Where are those offices buildings you mentioned?"

The driver pointed. "Back in there." Motioned to the far right of the factory. "You see that break before you reach the end?"

"Kind of." Charlie opened his door and stepped out onto the darkness. "Through there?"

"Yeah," the driver responded. "Stick to your right and you'll come upon a section of the building that doesn't seem like it quite fits with the others. That'd be the place." He rested his hand on the window frame. "Don't really know what you're expecting to discover."

Charlie braced his arm atop the door. "Neither do I," he mumbled. "But there's something in there that I need to find."

Aryssa slowly climbed out of the cab and kept the gun hidden underneath her leather jacket. The factory was a silent and gigantic menace. She swallowed hard. Should she back out? Was Charlie really going to go in there?

"If you ask me, I'd at least wait the couple of hours till daylight. Maybe even bring a few more people." The cab driver shifted the lever forcing the transmission to clunk through several gears. "You know, strength in numbers." The engine revved and the cab lurched forward. "Good luck."

Aryssa watched the red taillights disappear down the

street. She walked over to Charlie and stood by his side.

"Maybe it's best if you go home," Charlie calmly advised. "I can't risk you getting hurt over this."

Could Aryssa simply walk away and leave Charlie? Would she regret not going in and possibly finishing this once and for all? Despite her fear, that flame of determination started to burn brighter. She sighed. "I'm not going home."

"I think you should," Charlie insisted. "It's not safe."

"Everything that's happened over the last several days hasn't been safe." Aryssa defiantly folded her arms over her chest. "I'm not running away from it now."

"But..."

"But nothing," Aryssa purposefully cut Charlie off. She sliced the fear from the edges of her voice. "If Sammy's in there, then we finish this together."

Charlie glanced toward the factory, then back at Aryssa. He sighed and seemingly expelled any last fragment of doubt with a harsh huff. "I'm not going to win this argument, am I?"

Aryssa stood her ground. "You're not."

"Damn you," Charlie whispered. "Alright," he held out his hand, "let's do this."

37

CLICK.

Sammy snapped the cuff around Kami's wrist. He fought to catch his breath as he stepped back from the bed. The blonde Bulgarian kicked. Writhed. Screamed. She had put up a fight, but succumbed to the inevitable. Should've known that she was no match against two men.

"Now what?" the taller brother questioned. His chest heaved like an accordion. He kicked the mattress, jolting Kami from her contorted position. "Shut up already."

Sammy cocked his leg, ready to do the same, but let his foot drop back to the floor instead. All the other things that were occupying his mind smothered his frustration over Kami. Everything around him was disintegrating. All his work turning to dust.

"Any word from your brother?"

The taller one pulled his phone from his pocket. "Nothing."

Sammy tapped his cell and was greeted by his screen saver. No calls. No texts. Where in the hell was Ariek? Those two should be here by now. He ran his fingers over his head. Grabbed a wad of hair. Was this really happening?

"What do you want to do?" the brother anxiously rocked back and forth on the balls of his feet. "The sooner we get out of here, the better."

The pressure to leave was squeezing Sammy from all sides. His thoughts were in disarray, buried under what felt like a pile of scrap iron. He glanced around the room. At the makeup counters, the closet full of clothes, the showers and finally the mattresses scattered across the floor. He gestured toward the door leading to the hallway. "We've still got that room."

The taller brother cleared his throat apprehensively. "That one in the factory you've talked about?"

"Yeah, that one."

"That's your business, not mine." The taller brother shook his head. "You can't pay me enough to go there."

Sammy sighed. He'd thought about this very scenario before. Tried to come up with a plan if things went south. Maybe blow up the place, except that finding bomb material was out of the question. Or trash it to make it look like the homeless camped here. But he was faced with a bigger problem. The two shackled women. What to do with them?

The taller brother must've known what he was thinking, He swiped his finger across his throat. "It's the only way."

Sammy bit his lip. Had it really come down to this? Was it in him to off these two women? Sammy used his finger and thumb to mimic a gun. "What about?"

The taller brother nodded. "That'd work too."

The gun in Sammy's pocket had been digging into his hip. Dread coated the cold steel and frosted his skin in a patch of inevitability. "What do we do with the bodies?"

"Just leave them," the brother responded. "It'll be a long time before someone finds them."

"Don't know if..." Sammy hesitated. "Don't want to chance anything connecting us to this place."

"Then we pack it all up and take it with us."

"That'll take too long," Sammy reasoned. The gangrenous tips of sinister's fingers dug into his rationality. There had to be a way to kill the women without any direct contact. "I say we burn it."

"Burn it?" The brother folded his arms over his chest. "You mean all of it?"

"Yes, all of it."

"But you've put so much into this place."

"Doesn't matter." Sammy slashed his hand through the air. "We need to abandon everything."

"You sure about that?"

"Very." Sammy nodded. "Go and get those gas cans from the generator. We're lighting this place up." He tipped his chin toward the women. "By the time we're through, no one will know who they really are."

The brother's eyes lit up. "Be right back."

CHARLIE CUPPED HIS hands over a window and peered through the pane of glass. A sigh. It was just as dark, if not darker, inside as it was outside. A grunt of disappointment. They were no closer to finding that room than they were ten minutes ago. And the fifteen or so before that.

The sharp hiss of frustration sliced through Aryssa's lips. "It's like looking for a needle in a haystack."

Charlie tried to shrug off the heaviness of defeat that had been piling on his shoulders. "This place is bigger than I thought."

"They could be anywhere," Aryssa said. "That's even if they're here."

That pins-and-needles sensation was bristling through

Charlie's hands and arms. It was stronger than what he had felt on the boat. Why was it happening? Could it have something to do with Sammy? Or was it something else?

Charlie looked over his shoulder. Back at the broken windows and locked doors they had already passed. In front of him there was more of the same. He leaned against a windowsill. Was it hopeless? "I know he's here," he said in a tone filled with conviction. "I just don't know if we can find him."

Aryssa stood close. "We've tried." Her head slumped forward. "I don't think we will."

Charlie silently nodded. Was it time to give up? Inevitability was seeping beneath his skin and knocking on the gates of understanding. "I guess we should…"

Wham!

A door flung open no more than fifty feet away.

Charlie's entire body tensed. Aryssa gasped and flattened herself against the building.

A figure emerged from the door and darted away from them.

"Who's that?" Aryssa whispered.

"I don't know." Charlie grabbed Aryssa's hand and crouched. "We're going to find out."

The shadowy figure kept tight to the wall, scurried across a section of the lot and disappeared behind the door in a nearby building.

Charlie cautiously led Aryssa to the partially opened rusted door. Pale light seeped through the tiny crack. Everything was silent save for the distant hum of a motor.

"What's going on?" Aryssa whispered behind him.

Charlie slowly pushed it open. "It's a stairwell." He quietly stepped across the threshold. "Must've gone down."

"You sure?"

"Yeah." Charlie squeezed Aryssa's hand and then slowly descended. He kept close to the cinder-block wall. The air became cooler and the tension thickened. The dread solidifying his legs made them heavier with each step he took.

At the bottom was a long hallway. A lone bulb, surrounded by a barely visible haze of dust, dangled from a wire every twenty feet or so. The drone from that motor was a little louder. It all pointed toward the room at the end of the corridor.

Charlie warily stepped past broken doors and shattered glass. Did his best to avoid the random shards that would crunch under the weight of his shoes. A tattered chair lay on the floor like a skeletal corpse of a long-lost adventurer.

They passed a small conference room. The faint light from the bulbs revealed its decaying walls and barely legible graffiti. Charlie reached the end of the hall and put his ear close to the opened door. The motor chugged, its pistons snapping from the explosion of gas, like a dragon flicking its claw.

Aryssa squeezed his hand. The sheen of nervousness glazing her palm oozed onto his. Charlie slowly inhaled and peered around the threshold.

The noise from the large generator made the walls tremble. A few bulbs hung precariously from the ceiling and struggled to spread their light to the four corners. From the far end of the room Charlie heard someone's feet shuffle. Within a few seconds a plastic gas can slid across the dirt-encrusted floor. Then another.

Who was in there? More importantly, why was anyone in there? Charlie leaned even farther across the entry. A man moved a box off to his side. He grabbed what looked like another gas can, shook it and then flung it against the wall.

There was something familiar about that man. Charlie

pulled back behind the safety of the doorframe and thought for a moment.

"What's wrong?" Aryssa asked in a barely audible whisper.

"I think I recognize him."

"You do?"

Charlie tipped his chin. "I'm pretty certain it's that person who tackled you in the alley."

Aryssa's hand squeezed a little harder. Anger seemed to smolder from her fingertips. "You mean that tall…?"

"Yes." Charlie nodded his affirmation. "The very one."

"What's he doing?"

"Digging through some boxes." Charlie paused. "Whatever it is, I'm sure it's nothing good."

"Is Kami in there?" Aryssa asked with concern sliding from her voice.

"I didn't see anyone else." Charlie gestured toward the inside of the room. "I have a feeling she's back wherever he came from."

"What's he doing here, then?"

"As best as I can tell, he's looking for something. Maybe gathering supplies?" Charlie slowly exhaled. "I have a feeling he won't be staying much longer."

"Let's hold back and follow him."

Would it be best to wait and then follow? Charlie thought for a moment, but anger was urging him forward. This man had to have come from somewhere and that somewhere had to be the place where Kami, and maybe even Sammy, were hiding out. Had to be somewhere behind that door they had first seen him run out of. Would it be better if he took this person out and made it one less to tangle with? Or was it better to follow him and find out exactly where everything was located? Charlie balled his hand into a fist. If this was actually the person who had kidnapped Aryssa and those two kids, then he had to pay. Pay dearly for what he had done. An animalistic rumble slipped into Charlie's tone. "Wait here."

"What are you going to…?"

Charlie didn't answer. He slipped across the entrance and quietly crept across the floor toward the figure.

The man pulled another plastic gas can off the shelf. He strained to lift and place it behind him. Perhaps it was a sixth sense, or maybe it was the nearly imperceptible sound of Charlie's feet that tipped him off, but he lifted his gaze and looked right at Charlie.

The surprise that arched the man's brows was the only response he could muster. Before he could react, Charlie leapt forward and swung the battering ram of his fist into the man's gaping mouth.

Air burst from the man's lungs. Blood splattered. Eyes rolled backward. Charlie sprang to land a second punch, but the man collapsed inward, buckled like a deck of falling cards and crumpled to the floor.

38

SAMMY SWUNG THE bottom-heavy garbage bag full of toiletries as if it were a bowling ball. It slid across the floor and slammed into the wall near the exit. He then started pulling dresses from the closet and stuffing them into another bag. Removing them one by one from the hangers quickly stoked his aggravation. How could such a simple task be so tedious?

He managed to pull off a few more, but his anger got the best of him. Letting go of the bag, Sammy wrapped his arms around a bunch of clothes and tore them from the metal rod. He stomped over to the shackled women, dropped the clothing in a pile and went back for more.

Before long he had several haphazard piles around the women. Sammy grabbed several bottles of nail polish remover and dumped the liquid atop the clothes and a few of the empty mattresses. He stopped to catch his breath. The gears of determination were spinning faster and that forced the engine of his resolve to push harder. The decision had been made and the wheels were in motion. Now more than ever he wanted this done and over with.

Sammy pulled out his cell and sharply exhaled. Still no word from Ariek. And still no gas cans. What was wrong with everyone? Was Sammy the only one managing to keep it together?

He noticed the doors leading to the backrooms. The rooms where the bouncers hung out. Could they be trusted to have cleaned up after themselves? He shook his head. Even if they did, they were bound to have left something any half-decent detective could use. He squeezed his fists and stormed off to make sure it was taken care of.

ARYSSA'S HEART THUMPED wildly. She could feel it pounding against her bones as if it were trying to escape her chest. She followed Charlie down several steps, through a few doors and along a dimly lit hallway. They stopped at another metal door that seemed to be shut tight.

"This has got to be it," Aryssa said with spoonful of nervousness.

"Look familiar?" Charlie whispered.

"Kind of." Aryssa rubbed her temple, trying to break free a piece of her memory. It might have happened only a few hours ago, but she felt as if she'd escaped several days ago. Then again, the crush from that tooth had clouded her recollection. "I'll know for sure when we get inside."

Charlie put his hand on the knob and hesitated. He slowly twisted it, causing his head to cock with surprise. "Thought it would be locked."

"Me too."

Charlie slowly pushed the door open and peeked through the small crack.

A sharp but pungent odor spilled from the room. Aryssa sniffed.

"What's that smell?" Charlie leaned back from the opening.

"I'm not..." Aryssa sniffed again. There was something

familiar about the odor. Reminded her of the dressing room at the club. "Nail polish?"

Charlie scrunched his nose. "It's strong."

"It is," Aryssa confirmed. "But is anybody in there?"

Charlie put his ear close to the door and remained perfectly still. Once again he looked through the crack. He placed his palm flat against the metal and slowly pushed it open.

Aryssa held her breath as the space between the edge of the door and the doorframe grew larger. That sharp odor poured out even stronger.

Charlie cautiously stepped into the room. Gazed to his right, then his left. Silently jabbed his finger toward something inside.

Aryssa crept through the entrance and turned to where Charlie had been pointing. She gasped with shock. Was it really...? Kami was shackled to one of the mattresses. So too was the young woman who had stood up to the bouncer.

As quietly as she could, Aryssa scampered around the piles of clothes and knelt next to Kami. "Are you okay?" she whispered.

Kami halfheartedly nodded. A tear tried to crawl over her lid. "He's here."

"Who's here?" Aryssa responded. "Sammy?"

"Yes."

"Where is he?"

Kami tipped her chin toward the backrooms. "Somewhere in there."

Aryssa motioned toward the rooms with a glare. "Charlie." She put her finger over her closed lips.

Charlie tipped his head with acknowledgement.

"He's in there." Aryssa waved him closer. "What do we do?"

"Please, no leave me," Kami begged. "He's going to kill us." She sniffled. "I know it."

"We're not leaving you," Aryssa said reassuringly. She looked up at Charlie as he squatted by the mattress. "How do we get her out of these?"

"Need a key." Charlie scanned the room. "We could use a small piece of metal, or maybe," snapped his fingers, "a pin of some sort."

"How about a bobby pin?" Aryssa suggested.

"You got one?"

Aryssa pointed toward the makeup counter. "Maybe in one of those drawers."

Charlie quietly picked up the metal chain. Walked his fingers toward the cuff and studied the lock. "It might work."

Aryssa swallowed the dread that had dried her throat, stood and scurried over to the counter. Quietly pulled open a drawer, only to find it empty.

So was the next one. Aryssa opened another drawer and exhaled her relief. There were three—no, make it four—of them scattered across the bottom. "Found some." She pinched them between her thumb and forefinger and held them up for Charlie to see.

Creak!

A nearby door slowly opened and a figure stepped through. Sammy's brows arched with surprise, then quickly furrowed with anger.

Before Aryssa could fully process what was happening, Sammy dropped whatever he was carrying and lunged at her.

Charlie yelled, "Aryssa!"

Sammy grabbed Aryssa and flung her to the ground.

Aryssa landed on one of the piles of clothes. Dresses scattered. The gun fell out of her jacket and slid across the floor.

The solid thud of hitting the ground sent reverberating pain echoing through her body.

Before she could fully process what had just happened, something clicked. There was the momentary scraping of metal on metal and then a sudden…

Poof!

A ball of fire erupted from one of the piles of clothes. The flame serpentined across the floor to ignite another heap of clothes.

Bam! Bam!

The thundering hammer of gunfire exploded in the room.

Aryssa screamed and covered her head. Kami shrieked. Charlie dove.

Bam!

Aryssa's ears rang. Unfiltered panic shredded her nerves. Would she be shot and killed? She curled into a ball and leaned against the wall. Her body tensed tighter than a watch spring. Nothing happened. Were those footsteps? Did a door just slam shut? After a few seconds she dared to lift her head out from under her arms. No sign of Sammy. Where'd he go? Did he leave?

Kami's screams snagged Aryssa's attention. She was frantically kicking her shackled legs, trying to beat back the fire that was eating away the end of her mattress.

Charlie leapt to his feet, peeled off his jacket and started pounding the flames. "Anyone hit?"

"No!" Aryssa yelled.

"Me neither," Kami gasped.

Aryssa still had the bobby pins between her fingers. She jumped to Kami's side and buried one of them into the lock. She desperately picked at the mechanism, but the pin suddenly snapped. "Damn it!"

Charlie continued to beat at the flames. They weren't gaining strength, but they weren't showing any signs of weakening. A cloud of smoke was already creeping across the ceiling.

Aryssa grabbed another bobby pin and inserted it into the lock. She eased back on her aggressiveness and tried a little more finesse. Without realizing how she had done, there was a sudden click. The cuff popped open and Kami's arm was free.

"Help me…please help…" Kami squirmed and pulled on the other locks. "Get them off me!"

Aryssa's confidence blossomed. She realized someone had to go after Sammy. He couldn't be allowed to get away once again. She yelled at Charlie, "Go get him!"

"These flames," Charlie said. "I can't leave…"

"I've got this."

"What about her?" Charlie pointed at the chained woman who was barely moving.

Aryssa motioned toward the exit. "Go! Go! Go!"

Charlie hesitated. He slapped the flames a few more times then tossed his suit coat at Aryssa's feet. "You better be right about this."

"I'll be fine." Aryssa stuck the pin into the second of the four locks and got it to click open. "Just go and get him."

Charlie took a deep breath then sprang toward the door. He jerked it open and disappeared.

The smoke in the room became thicker, its dark hands effectively dimming the overhead lights. Aryssa tried her best to remain calm as she picked at the lock binding Kami's ankle. She looked at the young woman lying on the next mattress who had managed to wake up. Her eyes were wide with fright. The pressure to rescue both women suddenly coiled around Aryssa. Would she have enough time to do it?

39

SAMMY SLAMMED THE door, sprinted to the end of the hallway and paused. Did he lock it? His heart and lungs battered against his ribs. He glanced over his shoulder. Too late to go back and check. Besides, he had a more important decision to make. Which way to go?

Up the steps and out to the car or into the factory? Sammy uneasily swiped his hand over his head. Where was Ariek? Why hadn't that brother returned? Had he taken off and left Sammy to fend for himself? Maybe they both had abandoned him. "Son of a…" he muttered.

Sammy leapt up a step, then another. Before he lifted his leg onto the next step he stopped. If Aryssa had found this place, then the police wouldn't be far behind. What if the taller brother had been caught? Were the cops up there waiting for him?

He listened for any kind of noise. Footsteps. Talking. The squawk of a radio. Silence swallowed everything around him, even the thump of his heartbeat. Sammy glanced up into the stairwell. Should he risk it? A huff of frustration blew past his lips. As soon as it reached the air in front of him it disintegrated into a cloud of doubt.

Sammy quietly retraced his steps and peered down the darkened hallway that led into the factory. More importantly to that one place in particular.

The hair on the back of his neck wavered with dread. A chill coiled around his spine. It didn't matter that he was responsible for putting it all together and that he had helped detain the first captive. It still wasn't his first choice as a place to hunker down. Then again, it would do for a day or two. Desperate times called for desperate measures.

He tapped the flashlight icon on his phone and lifted the beam into the darkness. The light traveled only a few feet before it was devoured by the blackened abyss. He knew the way, but still wanted the light to help guide him. If only he had grabbed a flashlight before darting out of the room. It would've made things so much easier.

Sammy gripped his gun tightly and took off at a steady pace. He didn't make it very far when...*Boom!* The sound of metal slamming against brick rolled down the hallway and drifted over him.

CHARLIE THREW OPEN the metal door, allowing it to slam into the wall and ducked off to the side just in case Sammy was there with his gun. After a few seconds he exhaled with relief. The hallway was empty.

He sprinted to the end of the corridor and stood before the split. Up the steps or keep moving forward? Which way would Sammy have gone?

A dim light bounced off the walls deep in the throat of the hallway. The faint echo of footsteps rolled across the floor. It had to be Sammy.

Charlie took a second or two to allow his eyes to adjust to the darkness, then sprang forward after the light. He couldn't let Sammy get away. Not this time. Not ever.

FLAMES LICKED THE sides of the mattress. Patches of burning embers grew outward across the tattered fabric. The smoky cloud rolled into every corner of the room. It became denser. Darker. Aryssa coughed as she crouched low next to the young woman's shackled wrist. Kami was on the other side of the woman, grunting in desperation.

Aryssa's bobby pin snapped. "Shit!"

"Hurry…please," The young woman pleaded.

"Almost got it," Kami said.

The sting from the smoke spread across the dried surface of Aryssa's eyes. She desperately swiped her wrist across her eye sockets, hoping to find a little relief.

Kami coughed and rubbed her face with her shoulder. "Come on, already."

Aryssa snagged the last pin and hunkered closer to the floor. Brought her face nearer to the lock. Did her best to slow her thinking in order to corral the unyielding screaming that roared inside her head. She softly pushed the pin downward and gave it a little twist.

Click. The lock sprang open. The young woman pulled her arm free and snagged a water bottle off the floor. She uncapped it with her teeth, then tossed the water across the burning mattress. "The flames!"

The writhing yellow and orange flames slithered along the edge of the mattress. The free-flowing specter grew larger. Brighter. Its new found strength allowed it to reach onto the top of the mattress in order to feed its relentless need for more fuel. "Oh god! I'm going to…"

Aryssa ripped off her leather jacket and beat the flames. They hissed and dodged her blows. In the end they were no match against Aryssa's determination. Another swing and the flame sputtered, then morphed into ash. She swung again, forcing the last remnants of its life to go up in smoke.

Aryssa's focus immediately fell to the lock that gripped the young woman's ankle. She held her breath and delicately inserted the pin into the hole; it took only ten or so seconds before it sprang open. She glanced over at Kami who raised her arms in triumph.

"Got you, you bastard."

The girl sat up and rubbed her eyes, then her wrists before aggressively coughing.

Aryssa stood and kicked at the pile of burning clothes, scattering them across the floor. She knelt before the last locked limb. Kami took a knee by her side.

"Do it," Kami encouraged. "You're faster."

Again Aryssa held her breath. Coughed against her tightened lips. Carefully inserted the pin into the lock. The mechanism was firmer than the others and it forced her to squeeze the pin a little harder. She applied a little more pressure. Then a bit more. The pin started to bow.

"It's not turning," Aryssa said.

Kami slid even closer, as if to shield Aryssa from the smoke. Anticipation oozed from her cheeks. "You can do this."

Aryssa eased the pressure, then slowly reapplied it. A little more. Then even more. "Come on, already," she commanded.

The lock refused to give up its prisoner. Fire crackled. Smoke pressed tighter into the room. Aryssa backed off the tension and slid her finger down the pin to curb the chance of it snapping.

Aryssa once again pushed against the locking mechanism.

Then pushed even more. The pin dug into her flesh. She fought back the pain and gave even more. Nothing happened. The stubborn lock refused to budge.

Kami stroked her shoulder. "You got this."

Aryssa huffed her frustration and gave it a final push. *Snap. Click.*

The pin broke. The lock opened. Kami immediately pulled back the clasp from around the woman's ankle.

"Thank you," the young woman said. She rolled off the mattress, grabbed the edge and hoisted it upright.

Aryssa slid backward. Kami leapt up to help. Together they flipped the mattress onto a burning pile of clothes. The last remnants of the pile's smoke bellowed out from around the mattress's singed edges.

The woman sprang over to a metal object that was partially tucked under a smoldering pile of clothes. She pointed it at Aryssa and Kami.

Aryssa's heart tore from its moorings and fell into a pool of shock. What was she doing with the gun?

Kami's eyes went wide. Alarm froze the expression on her face. "What are you...?"

The young woman's brows curled with disbelief. "Oh...I didn't mean to..." She looked down at the gun, then back to Aryssa and Kami. "Umm, sorry about that." She lowered the gun to her side. "It was kind of a knee-jerk reaction to..." She sighed. Shoulders drooped as if a burden had suddenly been lifted. "I guess I should explain." A pause. "I'm a cop."

"A cop?" Aryssa asked.

"Yes," the woman answered. "I've spent almost an entire year trying to..." She rubbed her eye. Coughed. "I'll explain later." Quickly motioned toward the remaining burning piles. "We should take care of that before it's..."

Aryssa grabbed a nearby mattress and tossed it onto one of the piles. Kami did the same with another smoldering heap. All three worked together and within minutes the last of the flames fell victim to their efforts.

The young woman dragged a chair to the far wall, stood on it and smashed the windows near the ceiling with the butt of her gun. Kami ran into the bathroom and happened to find a few tattered wash clothes. She soaked them with water from the showers and passed them out.

The once-thick smoke began to dissipate. The young woman coughed. "I can't thank you enough for what you did." She stepped off the chair. "I owe you a lot."

Kami smiled, wrapped her arm around the woman's back and gestured toward Aryssa. "I think we both owe her."

Aryssa wiped her face with the wet cloth to hide her embarrassment. She stepped close to the two women and embraced them. Silence wrapped them in a blanket of gratitude. Aryssa eventually stepped back and looked at the young woman. "Are the cops coming?"

"Not until I can make a phone call," the woman responded. "I need to find a phone."

"I don't have one," Aryssa advised.

Kami shrugged. "Nothing."

They all glanced around the room. "We're not going to find one in here," Aryssa said firmly. "But there's something else we need to worry about."

"What's that?" the young woman asked.

"Charlie. He went after Sammy. We need to find him."

Kami leaned into Aryssa. "He's a good man." Glanced at the young woman. "She's right. We need to find him."

The young woman sighed and bowed her head as if she were lost in thought. "I still need to contact my handlers. It's been too long since I checked in."

Aryssa walked to the exit and gazed down the hallway. Sammy was long gone. So was Charlie. Where were they? Was Charlie alright?

40

METAL GROUND AGAINST metal. The harsh noise of wheels groaning under the weight of whatever they were carrying. *Boom.* Did something close? The rigid metallic sound clawed its way up the steps and slammed against Charlie as he peered down into the cave-like stairwell.

Charlie had relentlessly pursued Sammy. Did his best to move as stealthily as he could as he drew closer and closer. He had followed that dim light through twisting hallways, across vast spaces and around all kinds of giant machinery. Now here he stood. A drop of sweat trickled down his back. Many more clung to his forehead. Sammy was somewhere down there—where exactly, he didn't know.

A faint, early morning light lay siege against the shadows that reigned over the factory's interior. The few remaining pinpoints of starlight poked through the fading night sky and were framed within the ceiling's gaping holes.

Those giant machines were beginning to show their individuality as the darkness slowly receded. So too was the immense area filled with inanimate objects of a bygone era. Only a few feet away from Charlie, a bent stool lay on its side like a fallen soldier. There was the three-legged, rusted desk that seemed to fight against gravity in order to remain upright. He could smell the acrid odor of decaying metal and the pungent smell of aged grease mixed with the long-forgotten clamor of men and machines, clinging to the specks of dust that lazily drifted through the air.

Charlie slowly rubbed his palms together. An electric jolt zipped along his nerves sending a shiver across his sweat-soaked flesh. He wiped the sudden chill from his shoulders, then crossed his arms over his chest so he could hold in his body heat, even though a dank humidity was completely surrounding him.

That tingling sensation in his hands was stronger than ever. It had infiltrated his arms, swirled into his chest and pooled in his lower back. Somehow it pushed him forward. Persistently shoved him toward the steps.

Charlie resisted. What exactly was urging him to move down the stairs? He needed to know before going any farther. He looked to the walls, the ceiling, the machines and even across the battered floor. Waited for the smallest of hints, but they all remained mute, as if the slightest sound would shake the factory's foundation and send everything crashing into a heap of useless metal and concrete. The quiet was its way of refusing to reveal the things that were hidden in its darkest recesses—its way of choosing to protect the secrets that resided beneath the floor.

Minutes ticked by before Charlie's curiosity got the better of him. He needed to know what was down there, where Sammy had gone and why he had chosen to come here. He grabbed the solid metal railing and hesitated. There was something else that didn't seem right. Something that existed underneath that tingling sensation. Whatever it was, it cooled his spine and allowed tiny flecks of dread to cling to his frosted bones.

Charlie couldn't wait any longer. He shook caution away

and began his descent into the pit of darkness, which washed over him like a pool of ink. He made it to the bottom and cautiously walked the short distance to a large metal wall that blocked his path. Except this wall had wheels on its bottom and a handle near its edge.

He carefully placed his palms against the wrinkled and dented surface. The metal was unusually warm. A warmth that wasn't overly inviting. It seeped beneath his skin and morphed into hundreds of tiny pricks of needle-like pain.

Charlie yanked his hand away and shook it. What to do now? He slowly exhaled. He had come this far; there was no turning back.

He wedged his fingers into the space between the metal's edge and the wall and pulled. Wanting to keep things as quiet as possible, Charlie increased the tension until it gave way. It groaned deeply as the space slowly opened. He stopped when there was just enough room to squeeze through. A rush of warm air spilled through the opening. A warm and pleasant yellow light illuminated the gigantic room on the other side of the door. He took a deep breath and stepped across the threshold.

ARYSSA LED THE two women to the end of the hallway. The smoke's sinewy arms crept along the ceiling, clouding the already dim bulbs.

Kylee, the young-looking cop, coughed. "Which way?"

Kami pointed up the flight of steps. "That goes to the outside."

"Are you sure?" Kylee asked.

"She's right," Aryssa interjected. "I just don't know if it's the right way to go."

"If it takes us out of here." Kylee brushed her free hand through her hair as uncertainty stiffened her fingers.

Aryssa sighed. Indecision was eating away her ability to think rationally. She glanced down the pitch-black hallway leading into the factory. "So does that."

Kyle coughed again. "It looks like it leads to some kind of building."

"The factory," Aryssa confirmed.

"That made them scared," Kami said.

"Scared?" Kylee questioned. "Who was scared?"

"Those men that watched us," Kami answered. She shuddered. "I think they were afraid to go there. Eyes...I saw it in their eyes."

Kylee placed her foot on a step. "I don't think that's the way we should go." She paused. "It makes sense that Sammy would want to get out of here as quickly as possible. And the fastest way is up."

Aryssa gestured into the darkened corridor. "I went that way when I escaped."

"You did?" Kylee leaned against the wall with her foot still on the step. "You went all the way in there?"

"Yeah," Aryssa answered. "It took awhile, but I found my way out."

Kylee looked up the flight of steps. "And this leads outside too, doesn't it?"

"To parking lot," Kami said.

"The path of least resistance," Kylee stated. "It's got to be the way he would go."

It seemed too easy. Too convenient. "Maybe," Aryssa said simply. "The guards may have been scared to go that way, but it doesn't mean that Sammy wouldn't do it." She coughed. Gestured back down the hall toward the room that had been their prison. "Sammy and the others had managed to refurbish this place to fit their needs. They could've built something similar to that room, or maybe a place to hide, somewhere in there."

Kylee nodded. "This place is huge. Trying to find another room like that one would be damn near impossible, especially with just the three of us searching for it."

"I don't want to go in there," Kami said with dread layering her voice.

There was some truth to what Kylee had said. How impossible would it be to find this other hideout? That's if it even existed. Still, there was something else that bothered Aryssa. "What about Charlie?"

Silence pinched the women's lips shut. It was as if they had been suddenly rendered mute. Aryssa fidgeted. The others didn't move. Time was quickly becoming of the essence. A decision needed to be made and it needed to be done sooner rather than later.

Kylee broke the stillness. "We've got to get help. We can't do this alone."

"We can't leave Charlie behind, either," Aryssa said with desperation clinging to her tone. "He might need our help."

Kami stroked Aryssa's arm. "We don't know where he is." Her eyes filled with concern. "It's best to look outside."

"She's right," Kylee agreed. "I say we go up and out." She hoisted herself onto another step. "It's what I'd do."

Aryssa hesitated. Something kept poking her thoughts. Kept pulling her away from the easier solution. She rubbed her temple. Still, she couldn't let her doubt stand in the way of a majority decision. She tipped her chin. "Let's go."

Kylee immediately spun and bound up the steps. Kami followed close behind. Aryssa grabbed the railing and stopped to peer into the shadow-filled corridor one last time. Had Charlie followed Sammy in there? If he did, then why would Sammy go there in the first place? She shook the questions away and leapt up the steps.

41

THE HONEY-COLORED BULBS hanging from the girders coated Charlie in a layer of sweetened warmth. It seeped through his skin and numbed that tingling sensation he had been feeling in his hands and arms. It swam into his head, making him yawn. How many hours had he been up? How long had he been strapped into that adrenaline-fueled rollercoaster?

He thought about that moment he had lost Aryssa in the back alley. How he had to make that split-second decision to abandon those kids. How he had aimlessly driven his boat along the river. That off-chance of docking outside the factory, then stumbling upon Aryssa. That relief that morphed into terror when bullets had zipped over his head as they sped away. The confrontation in the hotel, falling off the balcony, the gun going off in that room, the flames and now this. He looked to either side and then up across the ceiling. What was this place, anyway?

Charlie yawned again. Fatigue weighed on his lids and nestled into his limbs like a dog napping by a fireplace. He started to walk along the extra-wide corridor that shot straight as an arrow under the factory floor. Was this a basement that had been used for some kind of storage? Maybe it had been a dedicated area that serviced those machines above.

Whatever this place used to be, those warm lights nudged

the questions from his mind. He tried to rub the sleepiness from his eyes. If only he could find someplace to sit. Some sort of soft chair would do, but there wasn't anything like it along the walls. Not even a broken stool like the one he had seen upstairs. A soured sigh escaped his throat. Maybe he could just lay right on the floor, close his eyes for a few minutes and rest.

Except that wasn't what he had come here to do. What was happening to him? Why was he feeling so tired? He exhaled sharply to expel that exhaustion, took a couple of steps only to feel it come back.

A thick paste of slumber oozed into his head. His limbs became heavy. Charlie couldn't resist. He knelt and reached out toward the floor, started to close his eyes, but something made him hesitate. A distant noise, maybe voices, echoed from down the hall. He slowly stood and listened.

Faint at first, it became louder the more he focused his attention. It wasn't one voice, but several. It sounded like an entire crowd. Feet shuffled. Furniture squeaked. Odd as it was, there was no laughter, but rather the conversations seemed strained. Heavy. Nothing lighthearted about any of it. What was going on?

A jolt of realization zipped through Charlie. Sammy. Was he somewhere down there, simply waiting, maybe even hiding? Charlie rubbed his temple with doubt. Didn't he follow Sammy down here in the first place? So he had to be here. But where?

Charlie tried to refocus his energy despite the clinging fatigue. He couldn't risk being surprised, or worse yet, shot. He tightened his quads for fear that his legs would buckle under the strain of weariness.

The concrete floor, the white plaster walls—all of it mo-notonously stretched forward, only to disappear into the distance. Charlie forced himself to press forward. He stumbled, leaned against the wall to keep his balance, yet the more he moved, the more his surroundings stayed the same. However there was one thing that kept changing. Those voices. The chatter from that hidden crowd was becoming louder. He was getting closer to someone, but whom? How was it possible that he could hear so many people, but not see a single person?

Charlie cautiously crept forward. Should he turn back? He had made it this far; what use was there in stopping now? He glanced over his shoulder to find that the metal door he'd used to enter this place was almost the length of a football field behind him. How had he covered so much ground so quickly? Or had he lost track of time and had been down here longer than he realized?

After a few more minutes the plaster wall gave way to what appeared to be a thick sheet of plexiglass embedded with a single column of evenly spaced holes that ran from the floor to the ceiling. Behind the transparent wall was a small room that looked like a prison cell. A bed with a torn mattress and a lone metal chair were its only inhabitants.

Charlie walked several feet to the end of the small room, only to come upon another identical plexiglass wall enclosing another cell decorated with the same austere accommodations. On the other side of the hallway he saw a similar row of prison-like cells. What were these things used for?

He passed another cell, then another and another after that. Each housed a bed and chair. That chatter was still coming from somewhere in the corridor. He was getting closer to it, but who exactly was he getting closer to?

That all-too familiar tingling sensation managed to bully its way upward from the deepest depths of Charlie's extremities. He shook out his hands and crept forward. Passed another cell. Then another. On and on it went, until he was about to totter past another when a movement made him freeze. He was about to spring backward, but it was too late. A middle-aged woman sitting in the lone chair lifted her head out of her hands. Her cheeks were sunken. Lips blue. Mouth fell open as her eyes widened with hope.

"It's you!" The woman lifted herself out of the chair and limped to the plexiglass wall. "You're the one."

Confusion folded Charlie's tongue. "I'm the...?"

"Yes," the woman answered with an assured tone. "I was told that I'd know when I saw you. And...and...it's true. I just know."

Charlie stepped back from the glass. "I don't know what you're talking about."

"It's him." An elderly man, with a stooped back, was standing behind the plexiglass wall on the other side of the hall. He pointed at Charlie with an arthritic finger. "You're the one."

A younger man wearing a backward-facing baseball cap was standing with his skeletal-like face pressed against the glass in the cell next to the old man. "Yo, man. You here to take us?"

"Oh my god!" A woman wearing a blue denim skirt, in the next cell over, bounced on the balls of her feet. "I can't believe it."

"You can't believe what?" someone curiously asked from a cell near where Charlie stood.

The lady wearing the denim skirt tapped the glass in front of her. "He's here."

"Who's here?"

"The one we're supposed to find," the blue-jean woman

said.

"Are you sure?" a male voice asked.

"Yes," the man wearing the baseball cap shouted. "It's like she said," he pointed at the middle-aged woman standing in the cell behind Charlie. "You just know."

"I'm Marjorie," the middle-aged woman said. "You've got to have me on your list."

Charlie scratched his temple. "List? I don't have any list."

"How do you not have a list?" Marjorie thrust her closed hand forward. "How do you know who's supposed to give you this?" She uncurled her fingers to reveal an object in the palm of her hand. It wasn't just any object. It was the coin.

Charlie silently gasped. The old man held a coin between his warped fingers. The guy in the baseball cap held up his, as did the woman in the denim.

That tingling he'd been feeling in his hands finally made sense. But how…how did these people end up here?

"I've got one too," someone said.

"So do I," said another.

More voices called out, confirming they had a coin.

"You've got to get us out of here," the man wearing the cap said. He pounded his fist against the glass. "Can't you bust this thing?"

Marjorie followed Charlie as he walked to the other end of her cell. "Please. I can't handle this place any longer." She wearily looked out into the hallway. "They keep trying different things to take these coins from us."

Charlie studied the coin in the woman's hand. "What kind of…?"

An obese man was crammed into the corner of his cell on the other side of the wall that separated Marjorie's room from his. "You're the boatman."

"Hey, it's the boatman!" someone yelled.

"The boatman? For real?"

More and more people called out. Still others screamed for Charlie's help. There was pounding on plexiglass. Kicking of chairs. The noise grew steadily louder as the news of Charlie's presence spread.

A tall man, wearing a gray suit, leapt out from what must've been a nearby cell. Anger scrunched his face. Nostrils flared as if fire was ready to bellow from them. "You all need to shut up!" he screamed.

No one heeded his demand. Instead, more and more people began to yell. Pounded the glass. Pleaded for their release.

The man in the gray suit stopped in the middle of the wide corridor. Slowly turned to face Charlie. Daggers of rage shot out his pupils. Brows furrowed. Shoulders tensed. "You're not wanted here." Without giving it a second thought, he ran straight for Charlie.

Charlie stood his ground. Tightened his body. Primed his arms and fists with fury.

The gray-suited man moved like lightning and struck with the speed of a snake.

Charlie quickly ducked to the side, but he wasn't fast enough. The blow caught the edge of his jaw, causing him to stumble backward. Before he could counter, a second blow was rocketing toward his face.

ARYSSA STEPPED OUT into the vanishing night, where a sliver of orange sliced the edge of the Eastern horizon. Kami and Kylee were standing near the middle of what had once been a parking lot.

Kami threw up her arms and let them smack against her

sides. "I don't know."

"They could be anywhere," Kylee said to no one in particular.

"We should go," Kami pleaded. "Just get out of here."

Aryssa gazed around the lot. Nothing stirred from inside the other buildings. She stepped up to the group. "You see anything?"

"Nope," Kylee responded. She gestured toward the large wall of the factory. "If they're in there, we will never find them." Pointed toward the city. "Don't even want to try and guess."

Kami tipped her chin at the factory. "Too big."

Aryssa grunted with frustration. "Damn it! Now what are we supposed to do?"

Kylee swiped a strand of hair from her face. "The sooner we get help, the better." She paused. "We're simply wasting time standing here."

"She's right," Kami agreed. "We must go."

Aryssa pinched the bridge of her nose. It made sense. The longer they waited, the better chance that Sammy would get away. "I guess you're right."

Kami's smile cracked the mask of worry that had clung to her face.

"Which way do we go?" Kylee asked.

Aryssa pointed at the decayed road that separated the factory from the office buildings. The very road she and Charlie had followed into this place. "That way will take us out."

Kylee nodded. "Let's do it."

Kami immediately took the lead with Kylee following. Aryssa was about to step forward to join them, but stopped. She couldn't do it. Just couldn't. Charlie was somewhere inside that factory. She was almost sure of it. Even though she harbored a small cloud of doubt, it wasn't enough to keep her going with Kami and Kylee. "You guys go on."

Kylee spun around "What did you say?"

Aryssa licked the moisture of certainty onto her lips. "I'm staying."

Relief drained from Kami's face and was replaced with lines of anxiety.

"I don't think that's a good idea," Kylee said. "There's no telling when we'll be back."

"I'll take that chance," Aryssa said. "Charlie's in there. I know it. I don't know how or why I know, but I do, and I'm not leaving him to fend for himself."

"What if he's not?" Kami said. "You would waste time staying here."

Aryssa tapped her stomach. "My gut. I…I don't know how else to explain it."

Kylee sighed and her shoulders stooped. She glanced at the factory, then to Kami before lowering her head just enough to appear she was struggling with some kind of decision. "Are you sure it's telling you that?"

Aryssa nodded. "Feels way more right than it does wrong."

Kylee exhaled sharply. Had she reached some kind of verdict? She placed her hand on Kami's shoulder. "Do you think you can find your way to the police?"

Kami's eyes widened. "Alone? You want me go alone?"

Kylee hesitated before answering. "Yes. The day is breaking. You'll be much safer."

Kami's head bent forward. "But…but I…"

"Don't doubt yourself," Kylee said. "I need you to tell them everything that's happened. I'm…" she glanced at Aryssa, "…we're counting on you."

Kami took a deep breath that expanded her chest and after a few seconds she let it deflate like an accordion. "What happens if they no believe me?"

"They have no reason not to," Aryssa chimed in. "You saw what happened at the hotel. The police are there sorting through all of it as we speak and that means all the cops in this entire city are waking up to the news at this very moment."

"She's right," Kylee said. "There's no way that they won't believe you." A pause. "You've got to do this."

Kami expelled a long sigh. She eventually lifted her head and slowly nodded. "I will. I'll get them here."

"That's my girl." Kylee wrapped her arms around Kami.

Aryssa walked over and did the same. "You got this."

Kami hesitated for the length of a heartbeat before turning and trotting down the road. Once she disappeared around the corner, Kylee turned to Aryssa. "I hope your gut is right about this."

"I know it is," Aryssa said confidently. "Follow me."

"Where to?"

"Around the back by the river," Aryssa answered. "There's a way into this place that I think will help us."

42

SAMMY SAT IN an office he had purposefully built between two of the prison cells in the factory's basement, his head buried in his hands. He thought about what to do next. Cut his losses and run? Get out of the city? Remain tucked away down here for a few more days? He lifted his head and realized his cohort in the gray suit wasn't sitting at his desk. In fact he wasn't in the room at all.

The distant echoes of commotion spilled into the office. Even though Ariek had been better at it, he could clearly hear the rapidly expanding chorus of voices bursting from the prison cells. The yelling and screaming. The demands and pleading. Something was happening outside the office. What in the hell was going on?

Sammy grabbed his gun and stepped out into the commotion. The shock of seeing him, Aryssa's friend, quickly turned into burning rage. How had he found this place? How had he...?

CHARLIE PLANTED HIS foot to stop from stumbling. He leaned back just enough to cause the gray-suited man's punch to fall short.

The man struck with his other hand, but Charlie managed to block it before it found its mark. He jammed the next one and stopped the one after that. The back-and-forth rhythm was suddenly disrupted when the man's leg caught Charlie off guard.

Charlie was thrust sideways and slammed into the hardened glass wall, causing it to reverberate from the impact. The obese man on the other side leapt backward. Charlie lifted his arms, but it wasn't quick enough to stop the punch to his head.

Charlie's brain rattled. Stars flashed across his vision. Scalp stung with burning pain. Instead of standing, Charlie dropped low as the next punch rocketed over him and smashed into the glass. The gray-suited man grunted. He stepped backward, recoiling from the pain that had to be shooting through his hand.

It was the waver Charlie needed. He mustered his strength, shot upward and with a roaring uppercut caught the gray-suited man on the underside of his chin.

Teeth gnashed. Head snapped. A gush of pain burst out of his throat as he flew through the air and landed hard on his back. His head smacked the concrete floor with a solid thud. A disorientated groan oozed over his lips.

The man reached for the back of his head. He tried desperately to brace his feet on the floor so he could stand, but the soles of his shoes slid haphazardly under the unsteady movement.

Charlie took a quick breath. Then another. And another. It was his chance to finish the fight, yet he couldn't get his lungs to fill with enough air. Couldn't get the life-sustaining energy to his limbs. The strength inside him was faltering. He couldn't find the means to recover from the fight. He looked up at those honey-colored lights. The very ones that seemed to be slowly devouring his vitality. How was that possible?

Charlie heard the screams. The chorus of yells. The despondent pleas from all those prisoners. Those souls who had tried to move on, but were instead being held captive against their will. And for what purpose? The answer immediately revealed itself on the illuminated pedestal in his mind. The coins—they were being held captive for those coins.

Darkness spiraled on the outer edges of his periphery. Was this it? Was this the way things were destined to end for him? Images floated across his vision. The boat. The sound of its well-tuned motors. The way the wind whipped against him while he zipped along the river. And of Aryssa. He sighed happily over her affectionate voice. Her deep beauty. The way she smiled when he was with her. How his tongue had tied itself into knots when he first tried to talk to her. All the things they had been through.

The images spurred a reptilian anger that burned deep inside Charlie. An inextinguishable pilot light to the furnace of his existence burned brighter. Hotter. An animalistic rage crept upward from the depths of Charlie's being and swirled into his limbs.

Charlie shook away the circling darkness and pounced on the gray-suited man. He raised his arm and buried his fist into the man's face. Raised it again and struck. And again. And again.

Blood splattered. The man moaned in agony, tried to lift his teetering extremities only to pass out altogether. Charlie labored to raise his own arm, but exhaustion pulled his fist to the floor. His chest heaved. Head stooped. Charlie struggled to roll himself off the man. He plopped on the ground and gulped for air.

The prisoners roared with delight.

"He got what was coming to him!"

"Way to go!"

"Get me out of here!"

"Hurry up, before someone else comes!"

Charlie needed a minute. Maybe more. He was too weak to stand. Simply too exhausted to move. He fought against gravity just to stop himself from falling over.

"Look out!" Someone yelled.

There was a movement in his periphery. Someone was briskly walking toward him. Charlie strained to turn his head. Was it really him? Was it…yes, it was. It was Sammy.

Sammy moved with purpose. Anger pounded off his soles with each step. He was gripping a metal object and with a swift movement of Sammy's hand, came that undistinguishable clack of a loaded gun. He pointed it directly at Charlie. "I've had enough of you and Aryssa!"

ARYSSA MOTIONED WITH her arm for Kylee to hurry. She pointed down the darkened steps and whispered. "You see that?"

Kylee slowly nodded in agreement. "Is it really…?"

Yellow light weakly spilled across a small section of the wall and floor at the bottom of the stairwell.

"Yeah, it is," Aryssa answered.

"What do you think it's to?"

"We'll never know unless we check it out," Aryssa said.

"We've come this far."

Aryssa kept her hand cupped on the railing and hugged the wall with her shoulder as she descended the steps. Kylee was close, so close that she could feel her breath stroking her neck.

She reached the bottom and cautiously covered the distance that led to a metal door. A warm light drifted through the partial opening.

Aryssa's heart thumped wildly. What was on the other side? Was Charlie somewhere behind it? She leaned close to the opening and listened.

Seconds morphed into minutes. "Did you hear that?" Aryssa whispered.

Kylee moved closer. Eventually shook her head. "I don't hear anything."

Aryssa rubbed her ears. Listened again, but was greeted only by silence. She sighed. "Maybe it was my imagination."

Kylee gestured toward the opening. "Take a peek."

Aryssa maneuvered to look around the edge of the door. That warm light filled a barren hallway that stretched deep into the distance. Except that it wasn't totally empty. There was someone sitting on the ground hundreds of feet away. Could it be?

She gasped. "I think it's Charlie."

"You see him?"

Why was he on the floor? Panic swept through Aryssa. She instantly slipped into the large corridor. "He needs help."

Kylee grabbed Aryssa's arm. "Hold on," She whispered urgently. "It might not be safe."

Aryssa stopped when she heard Kylee's warning. She looked again at Charlie, but this time she saw someone approaching him. Was that Sammy? What was he pointing at Charlie? "I think he's got a gun."

Kylee stepped to Aryssa's side. "Who's got a...?"

"Sammy." Aryssa pointed at the men. "He's going to kill Charlie. We've got to..."

Kylee must've heard the desperation in Aryssa's voice. Must've seen what was about to go down. "Move." She pulled Aryssa's shoulder and jumped in front of her. "Stay close and be as quiet as you can."

43

SAMMY TIGHTENED HIS grip on the pistol and started off with a determined stride. His gait morphed into a scamper, then a run. His focus narrowed along the barrel, through the site and right onto the very person who ignited his anger. He still had several yards to go before he could get an accurate shot.

He needed all of this to be over. Needed a break from everything that had gone down. Needed to regain some semblance of control. And it all came crashing on that one man. The person who had been consistently bringing him so much grief. The one person along with Aryssa, he needed dead.

"I've had enough of you and Aryssa!" Sammy screamed as he squeezed the trigger.

Bang!

CHARLIE'S RESERVE OF adrenaline was bone dry. His limbs felt as if they were filled with concrete. He tried to get his legs underneath him so he could stand and defend himself, but they struggled to move. All his strength had been devoured by his fight with the man in the gray suit. And more particularly, those damn lights. What felt like the weight of an automobile was somehow parked on his chest, making him struggle to keep himself upright.

He was defenseless. Stuck out in the open with nowhere to hide. Summoning any last bits of might left in him, Charlie desperately jerked his shoulders to his right, then threw himself to his left. Everything seemed to move in slow motion.

Bang!

A bullet struck the concrete floor only a few feet from him. Bits of concrete splattered through the air. The sharp blast bounced off the walls and drilled into Charlie's ears.

Charlie landed on his left shoulder, tucked his arms into his chest and rolled onto his back. The momentum jolted him upright. All he had to do was leap onto his feet in order to have a fighting chance. His sudden burst of movement was deceiving. Charlie barely made it onto his knees when he noticed the gun was aimed right...

Bang!

Searing pain burrowed through the muscle and bone in Charlie's chest. The force of the bullet thrust him backward and knocked the air out of his lungs.

"Charlie!" a woman yelled.

Sammy lifted his gaze toward the screaming voice, his face scrunched with rage. He turned his attention back to Charlie.

Bang!

The burn tunneled into Charlie's shoulder while blood splattered out the hole.

Bang!

A gun went off somewhere behind Charlie. Sammy's face suddenly elongated with shock. An explosion of blood leapt out from the middle of his chest. His arms flailed outward as he stumbled to regain his balance.

Bang!

Sammy's body recoiled from the piercing intrusion. His feet lost contact with the ground. He flew through the air and landed on his back. Legs and arms trailed in front of him, and he fell in a lifeless heap across the concrete.

"Charlie!" the woman screamed again.

Who was calling him? It sounded like Aryssa, but how was that possible? Charlie tried to turn around to look upon her face, but his body buckled, causing him to collapse to the floor. He attempted to suck in a breath, desperately tried to look behind him, except his strength had disintegrated. Tried again. Nothing happened.

The glass-walled cells, the screaming prisoners, those overly warm lights had somehow tunneled from his sight. It wasn't long before he was surrounded in the shroud of darkness and soon the black cloak of death completely covered him.

"ARYSSA...WAIT...!" KYLEE YELLED.

Aryssa heard the warning but kept running, even as the sound of Kylee's gun went off and the bullets whizzed by her head. She kept running as Sammy flailed and fell to the floor. She ran by small empty rooms enclosed in what appeared to be glass. Briefly noticed the chairs. The beds. The emptiness. Her screaming thoughts over Charlie's well-being ricocheted off the bones of her skull and despite all the noise inside her head, everything around her—her footsteps, Kylee's voice, the echo of gunshots—was muffled into silence. And even though there wasn't another soul around except for Charlie, Sammy, Kylee and herself, that very silence only became magnified the closer she got to him.

Aryssa ran up to Charlie, flung herself onto her knees and pulled his head into her lap. Tears streamed down her face.

She sniffled. Her body convulsed with shock and trembled in horror.

"Charlie!" Aryssa yelled. "Please open your eyes."

Kylee kicked Sammy's gun toward the wall and placed her fingers on the side of his neck.

Aryssa focused her attention, her grief, her very soul on Charlie. "You can't be dead." She cradled his head even more closely. "Please, don't be…"

44

SOMETHING WAS OFF. A strange awareness drifted through Sammy. It gently trickled into his core. That burning anger he'd had toward Aryssa had dissipated and was replaced with something else—maybe it was more like nothing at all.

Neither happiness nor sadness took precedence. Neither rage nor love could dominate. There was no pain, but at the same time he felt something. It was there, somewhere—he just couldn't describe exactly where, or what type of feeling, for that matter. At best it was an undeniable sensation of neutrality. An odd kind of balance that simply defined existence. Sammy looked up at the honey-colored lights. Why was he lying on his back?

He took a deep breath letting the warm air caress his lungs and spread through his body. Oddly, it was a warmth he had never noticed before. Sitting up, he rolled onto his feet and brushed the bits of dirt and dust off his pants. There was an almost weightless sensation in his arms. For some strange reason his movements felt almost effortless.

He noticed the woman standing at the glass wall in her cell. And the obese man in the one next to her. Sammy had gotten better at hearing the distant murmur of voices, but had never been able to differentiate between them. Now he could hear the individual people yelling. Pleading. Demanding. And he could actually see them too. What had he finally done to make this happen?

Sammy glanced over his shoulder toward the sniffles and tears. His focus narrowed onto her—onto Aryssa. She was cradling her friend's head as his lifeless torso was splayed across the floor. Sammy forced a scoff from his throat, then compelled his cheeks to scrunch into a smile. Her friend had what was coming to him.

Another person was nearby. It was that...that young woman who had been shackled to the mattress. How did she manage to escape? How did she find her way here? She was kneeling next to Aryssa. The wick on the candle of Sammy's anger cindered, then snuffed out, leaving a thin trail of smoke filling his room of composure.

Someone else was lying on his back a few feet from Sammy. Whoever it was, wasn't moving. Not even a flicker of life pulsated though his pale skin. Sammy allowed his vision to skip over the man's torso, across the two bullet holes in his chest and then up to his face.

Sammy gasped. Jumped backward away from that...that person on the floor. His jaw slackened with shock. "It can't be," he muttered.

"Believe it," the woman standing in the nearby cell said. "You're one of us, now."

Sammy shook his head in disbelief. "I can't be...no way!"

"Yes, you are," Someone else stated.

Several prisoners laughed. Others jeered.

Sammy desperately patted his chest. Didn't feel any bullet holes. Didn't feel any pain. He was alive and safe. Wasn't he? Panic trembled across his nerves. "Just...just wait a minute..."

He remembered firing his gun, not once, but twice. Then another gun had gone off, too. Burrowing pain had suddenly skewered his chest. Had he been shot, or was he imagining it all?

He looked down upon the man, a man who looked like him, lying on the floor. At the woman with her fingers pressed against his neck. She shook her head.

Sammy covered his mouth with his hand. "No…no way. No it can't be…I can't be…"

"Oh, it can," spoke a voice that crackled like a burning log from behind Sammy.

The hair on the back of Sammy's neck stood erect with dread. He spun toward the voice. Gasped with fright. "Who in the hell are you?"

The gargantuan bald-headed man stepped forward on legs the size of tree trunks. Scales were embedded in his skin. Eyes as dark as the deepest depths of space and void of any emotion. Black suit. Blood-red tie. He pointed at Sammy with a sharp fingernail. "I'd like to think your worst nightmare."

Sammy warily stepped backward, trying to keep some separation between him and this…this reptilian-looking thing. His heart hammered against his ribs, but he confidently straightened his shoulders. "Maybe you are or maybe you're not." He feebly flicked his hand. "I've no need for you."

"No need for me?" the reptilian man chuckled with delight. "I don't care about what you think you need. I'm here for one thing." His eyes narrowed. "And that's you."

"Me?" Sammy tented his fingers over his chest. Did his best to prevent fear from wrinkling his voice. "What have I done to you to make you want me?"

The reptilian man gestured with his thick hands to the prison cells on either side of him. "Do I need to spell it out for you?" He licked his lips. "They aren't yours to keep."

Sammy swallowed hard. He tried to stand his ground with

a firm tone. "They're not yours, either."

The reptile's hands curled into fists that resembled wrecking balls. His entire body became taut with anger. "Your insatiable greed has created an imbalance." He took a heavy step forward. "Those coins weren't meant for you; they were meant to be possessed by those to whom they were given. Their very destiny is wrapped in those coins."

"Well…well…" Sammy stepped backward on trembling legs. "If you ask me, someone's been taking them and selling them for large sums of money." He bit his lips. "And it wasn't me. So I don't know why you're accusing me of doing…"

"They belong to one man," the reptilian man huffed. The heat of annoyance in his furnace-like breath rippled the air. He pointed toward Aryssa's friend. "They belong to him."

ARYSSA WAS SITTING on the floor hunched over a body. She embraced the man's head and caressed his face. The tears trickling down her cheeks pinged Charlie's heart with the ache of longing.

Sammy had stopped halfway between Aryssa and the reptilian man. Even though Sammy fought against it, the unmistakable weight of uncertainty burdened his posture. Buckled his legs. The ambiguity glazing Sammy's face made it appear that he was trying to decide which way to run. Then again, was there anywhere he could run that would allow him to get away?

Charlie looked at the reptilian man. "It's been a long time."

"That it has," the reptile responded.

Charlie glanced at the prisoners in their cells, their faces pressed against the glass. Coins clutched in hands. The yelling and jeering had stopped and was replaced with a solitude of silence. The iron claws of tension gripped the air. The hostages seemed to be waiting for what was to come next. Charlie sighed. Realization knocked on the door of his reason. It was all beginning to make sense.

The steady decline in business over the last several months. These imprisoned souls and their coins—coins that were to be used as payment to travel across the river. Charlie knew that he could walk up and take any, if not all, of those coins. But, he reasoned, Sammy could not.

Sammy was holding these people captive and torturing them in order to steal those coins. Once he successfully had them in his possession he would sell them on the open market. Use the money to further expand his business. Would it be for drugs? More prostitution? Power? Charlie waved the notion aside. It didn't matter because Sammy hadn't found the way to convert them from the realm of the dead into the domain of the living.

The reptilian man looked up at the warm lights, then settled his dark eyes on Charlie. "I knew something was wrong, but I couldn't figure out what it was."

"I guess now we know," Charlie confirmed.

The man in the gray suit moaned. His hand brushed over his cheek. Head shifted to the side ever so slightly. Was he waking up? Sammy took a small step backward. The rigidity that had bound his muscles looked as if it had eased. Or had it?

Charlie ran his hand through his long black hair and looked over at Aryssa as she gently cradled a man's head. A head and a body that looked very familiar. He bent down for a closer look. Slowly exhaled. It…it was his head.

The instantaneous shock flashed as if it were a blown circuit. Charlie rubbed his cheek with doubt. He had never drifted out of his body before, but had always figured it was possible.

"You exist in two realms," the reptilian man stated. "It's why you see things the way you do. It's why you can take those coins and bring them into this world." A pause. "But I'm only telling you something that you already know."

Charlie nodded. "I think I somehow knew that." He cleared his throat, "I guess I never fully thought about it."

"This duality is what defines you," the reptile said. "It's given you choices."

"Kind of figured that it did."

What was it about Charlie's past that made him who he was? As far back as he could remember he had taken souls across the river. He always had bridged that gap between the living and the dead without thinking about it. It was simply like breathing, it just happens. At the moment though, he was completely on the side of an existence he wasn't overly familiar with. He gestured at the prisoners. "I think it's high time that I get them out of here."

The reptilian man nodded. He pointed his thick, steel cable-like finger at Sammy. "And I need him."

"Me?" Sammy shook his head. "We've been over this. You don't..." Held his arms in front of him as if to push the reptile away. "Where can you possibly take..."

"You'll find out soon enough," the reptilian man said sharply.

Sammy's brows arched. "I don't think so." Stepped backward. "I go where I want to go."

"Not for you to decide." The reptilian puffed his chest. "You've created your karma. Now it's time to pay your debt."

"I owe nothing."

"You owe more than you think."

"Says who?" the words had barely left Sammy's mouth when in one fluid motion, he spun and sprang toward that metal door and the end of the hallway.

The reptilian man coiled and leapt. Within the blink of an eye he snatched Sammy's arm and flung him to the floor.

Sammy hit the ground hard, forcing the air to burst from his chest. He writhed in pain. Tried to jerk his arm free, but the reptile's grasp was too strong.

Charlie tipped his chin toward the man in the gray suit, who was clutching the back of his head. "What about him?"

"He'll be going to someplace special." The reptilian man effortlessly dragged Sammy across the floor before clutching the nape of the gray-suited man's neck.

"Let go!" Sammy yelled. He dug his heels into the concrete. Tried desperately to pull his arm fee. He writhed. Jerked. Grunted.

The reptile's brows furrowed with rage. He yanked Sammy upward, twisted his arm and pulled him close. Sammy yelped in pain. "You're mine now," the reptilian man hissed. "Do that again and I'll rip your arm out of its socket and make you feel a pain the likes of which you've never felt before."

Worry thickly coated Sammy's face. His body softened into pacification. He allowed himself to be led down the hall while the reptile dragged the man in the gray suit.

After several steps, when Sammy thought the reptile had dropped his guard, he tried to jerk free of the reptilian's grasp.

The reptilian man responded by effortlessly pulling him close. "What do you think you're doing?"

"You can't do this!"

"I can and I will."

"No!" Sammy stopped and pulled backward. "You've got

no authority to…"

In one lightning-quick movement, the reptilian man released Sammy's arm and punched him in the face.

Sammy's head snapped sideways. A grunt of pain before his body went limp.

The reptilian man caught Sammy by the shoulder as he sank to the floor. He readjusted his grip before looking over his shoulder at Charlie. "Don't take too long."

"Too long?"

The reptilian tipped his chin in acknowledgement. He turned away from Charlie and started to drag his prey down the corridor. "Before you're stuck here and can't get back."

Charlie quickly nodded, then ran to the first cell he saw. He fiddled with the handle that was notched in the glass.

"I think you need to pinch those two levers together," Marjorie said.

Charlie squeezed. "Are you sure that…" the lock popped.

Marjorie exhaled a sigh of relief as she pushed the door open. "I can't thank you enough." Under the warm lights she labored to lift her arm and hold out the coin. "You want this now?"

"Later," Charlie answered. He gestured at the prisoners on the other side of the hall. "Help me set the others free and get them out of here."

Marjorie nodded. "Where are we supposed to go?"

Charlie pointed down the corridor leading to the metal door. "That way." He paused to recharge his voice. "It'll take you into the factory and then out to the river where you can wait."

Marjorie slowly pivoted her head to look at the seemingly endless rows of prison cells. "There's so many. I…I don't think I have the strength to do it all."

"You don't have to," Charlie said. "Get a few open and let them take care of the next ones."

Marjorie nodded her understanding. Took a heavy step forward but her shoulders sagged under the oppressive weight of her surroundings. Gait staggered. "This is harder than…"

Charlie braced Marjorie by her arm. "We've got to get everyone out from under these lights. Away from this place before it's too late."

Again Marjorie nodded. Took a deep breath which seemed to fill her with determination. She patted Charlie's hand with reassurance and then trudged across the corridor toward the cells.

Charlie's window was shrinking. He jumped to the next cell and popped the lock allowing the rotund man to exit. He then looked back on Aryssa. To the young woman who had been shackled. To Sammy's contorted body with its red-stained shirt. Then finally at himself lying lifeless on the floor. An invisible hook pierced Charlie's gut and pulled him toward his body, the very one that was slowly starting to disintegrate.

How much time did Charlie have before he became totally separated from his body and never be able to return? Would he be able to free these prisoners if he did reconnect? Would he have enough time to lead these souls out of this oppressive prison? Guide them to where they needed to go? The pull grew stronger, causing him to stumble sideways. Could he resist it? Did he really want to?

Aryssa sniffled and held Charlie's lifeless head closer to her chest. The young-looking woman with the gun put her hand on Aryssa's shoulder. Charlie saw the hive of activity grow as more prisoners were released from their cells and in turn helped free the others. A steady line of people were already slowly making their way down the corridor toward the metal door.

Charlie could feel the intense pain from the gunshots. Feel the burning hole in his chest. His shoulder. Even if he did go back, would he survive? Would he ever be with Aryssa? The uncertainty multiplied. He looked at the crowd then to his body on the floor. Did he even have a choice? After all, he did exist in two worlds.

45

THE MOON CHOSE to keep itself hidden below the horizon. Maybe she felt the need to take a break from her motherly duties. Or maybe she was just too tired to climb upward into the clear night sky. Whatever the reason, she wasn't stepping out onto the world's shadowy stage.

In the distance a dog barked. Crickets chirped. Somewhere nearby a car rolled over a bump in the road. A cool breeze ruffled the leaves of a large tree. Aryssa inhaled deeply, reveled in the quietness and savored the slight chill of fall's awakening breath. Even though it was several weeks away, she was already opening her eyes from her nearly year-long slumber.

Aryssa ran her fingers across the pocket of her jeans. Made sure the vial was still there. In her other pocket was the night's bounty. There were still several more houses to visit. More teeth to pull out from under pillows. But before tackling the next home, she needed to make a stop.

"Come on," Aryssa whispered. She darted off the sidewalk and across the lawn to the side of the house with a ladder leaning against it. One of its windows was covered with a sheet of plywood.

She crept to a partially opened window and looked over her shoulder at Charlie. "I'll be right back."

Charlie nodded. "I still don't know why I can't go with you."

Aryssa quietly scoffed. "You know why."

"I can be quiet."

Aryssa brushed his cheek with her fingers. "Oh honey, you and I both know what would happen if…"

The window suddenly slid upward, sending a wave of surprise smashing into Aryssa. Charlie jumped backward and was about to run.

"It's about time you showed up," Zoe said with a smile.

Confusion coated Aryssa's tongue. "About time? How'd you know that…?"

Zoe shrugged? "I could smell it."

"Smell it?"

"Yeah." Zoe pointed at Aryssa's pocket. "You've got three new ones in there. And the crushed ones in there."

Aryssa's jaw dropped with shock. "How'd you know that?"

Zoe scratched her head. "I just do."

"But, that would mean…"

"Hi Aryssa!" Mackenzie said enthusiastically. She appeared next to Zoe and slid her head out the window. "Where's Charlie? I know he's here."

"You do?" Charlie stepped up behind Aryssa.

Mackenzie lifted her hands and wiggled her fingers. "They tingle when you're close by."

"They do?" Charlie's tone was tinged with doubt.

"Yeah," Mackenzie answered. "Happened the last time. Felt it even more this time."

"Are you sure?"

Mackenzie nodded. "Very."

"Is it the coins?" Aryssa asked curiously.

"I think so."

Charlie massaged his cheek. "Have you ever driven a…"

"Mom says thank you," Zoe said. "She still doesn't believe that you guys exist."

"Hey, I was supposed to tell them," Mackenzie stated.

"No you weren't," Zoe fired back. "It was my turn."

"No, it wasn't."

"Yes, it was."

"That's what you said last…"

"Girls," Charlie said in a stern voice, "you're going to wake the neighborhood."

"She always does this," Mackenzie muttered, as if trying to get in the last word.

"No I don't," Zoe countered.

Aryssa sternly held up a finger. "Hey, you two." She tried to bury her smile. "Not the time for arguing."

"We're not arguing," Zoe said.

"Yeah, it's disagreeing," Mackenzie stated.

"Whatever you want to call it, let's save it for after Charlie and I leave."

"Okay." Mackenzie sank back into the window. Within a few seconds she giggled. "Mom tripped on the stairs today."

Zoe chuckled. "She was carrying this box and it went flying."

Aryssa leaned forward with worry. "Is she alright?"

"Yeah. It was only a box of papers," Zoe confirmed.

"They went everywhere," Mackenzie added. "As high as the ceiling."

"Mom wasn't happy, though."

"Yeah, she said a bad word."

"A lot of them."

Charlie was smiling. He tapped the windowsill and looked up at the nearly finished siding. "Are they close to being done?"

Mackenzie nodded. "I think so. Mom says that they're doing a good job." Her eyes slightly narrowed. "She also says they sit around too much and watch the paint dry."

"Why would they want to watch paint dry?" Zoe questioned. "That seems boring."

"Yeah," Mackenzie agreed. "Why watch it when you could just touch it."

"It's a figure of…" Aryssa dropped the explanation. Best to leave it alone before she was forced to give a lengthier description. "It looks like it's all coming along nicely."

"I like my room," Zoe said.

"Me too," Mackenzie added.

Charlie reached through the window with a coin pinched between his fingers. "Give this to your mom."

Mackenzie took it. "I will."

Charlie gave another coin to Mackenzie and then one to Zoe. "One for each of you."

"Thank you," Mackenzie said gratefully. "Mom says so too, even though she won't believe us."

"That's okay," Aryssa said. "Adults are like that sometimes."

"I'm not going to be like that," Mackenzie added.

"Me neither," Zoe said.

"Is your mom using them like I told you?"

Mackenzie nodded. "I don't get it. She doesn't believe, but she goes to that place and gets money for them."

"As long as she is doing that, that's all that matters," Charlie said.

"Money for the house and our…our…" Zoe yawned.

"Our college," Mackenzie interjected. "Mom says it'll be for our college."

Zoe rubbed her eyes. "I'm tired."

"Me too," Mackenzie said.

"It's late," Aryssa chimed. "You two need to get to bed."

Mackenzie yawned. "That means you're leaving."

"We'll be back," Aryssa said.

"When?" Zoe asked.

"Sooner than you think." Aryssa grabbed Charlie's hand. "We've got a long night ahead of us."

Visiting Mackenzie and Zoe had brightened the candle of Aryssa's affection. They were two kids who made her feel happy. Reaffirmed the joy in the work she had been doing all along. But now there was someone who stoked the fires of her passion. Made her feel incredibly alive. She kissed Charlie on the cheek.

Zoe gagged playfully.

"Ewww," Mackenzie spewed.

Aryssa whispered into Charlie's ear. "I have a little surprise for you when we get back. A little something before the sun rises."

Charlie smiled. Tightly embraced Aryssa with his muscular arms. "Nothing would please me more than to be with you."

THE END

Thank you for reading *Enamel*. Please consider leaving a quick review to let me know what you thought. If you enjoy gripping, psychological thrillers keep reading for a special preview of *Chain of Salt and Water*, Book 1 in my A Cure to Kill for series.

www.timsabados.com/books

The Chain of Salt and Water

1

ANTHONY FORCED HIS mouth open to scream, but the sound struggled to make its way from an area deep between his shoulder blades. Like a weighted bubble, it travelled the curve of his back and wedged itself in his throat. He gagged on the fear that clogged the passage leading to his lungs. He coughed. Retched. Sucked for air. Any air. His throat spasmed. The electric shiver of panic rode the nerves from his neck out into his arms. His fingertips went numb. If only he could get his ribs to expand. His lungs to inflate. Even a tiny bit.

He thought of a balloon inflating. Imagined it as if his life depended on it. The rubber growing thin and taught. A small intake of air. He managed another. The next was a little deeper. He exhaled. The whimper of air that escaped his lips fell listlessly into the darkness.

From deep inside his head the ringing started. It was faint, distant. It grew louder. And louder. Pushed outward on his ears. Sharp as a steel razor. A harsh-pitched vibration like the tips of a cold tuning fork. His eardrums quivered with pinpoint precision. And louder. Sharper. The pain was unbearable. Anthony tried to grab his ears. To shut it off. Block it. It only got louder. If only his ears would explode and make the torture end.

Again he tried to lift his arms. They wouldn't move. His

legs were stuck, too. Not even a twitch. Something pinned them with the force of a two-ton robot. Shackled like a prisoner to his own bed. A giant specter had climbed on top of him and held him down. It tightened its frigid grasp on his arms. Sank its weight onto his chest. Brushed its arctic-frost breath across his cheek. Was this the end? Was death claiming dominance over him?

If only he could open his eyes, then maybe—just maybe— it would all go away. They were glued shut. Sutured closed. He forced his right eye partially open. His left eye wouldn't budge. The tension in his chest, his throat, his head, was excruciating. The ringing in his ears was unforgiving. It was all ready to burst like a valve pushed beyond its limit.

Pop! The sound was abrupt. Brief. It was as if his soul had ripped itself from his body. The blockage in his throat was gone. So was the pressure on his chest. And the ringing in his ears. His head was clear. He could open his eyes. He could breathe. His arms and legs moved freely. Nothing weighed them down. Is this what death feels like?

A vast expanse of pitch-black nothingness greeted him. The world was plugged to a deadened silence. There was no sound except for the static vibration of his consciousness grazing the tips of the hairs inside his ears. He reached out in the murky soup, not sure which way was up or down. Forward or back. The blackness was absolute. His eyes were open but registered nothing. He couldn't see his hands in front of him.

An invisible web of loneliness hung in the air. It clung to his body. Draped itself over his head. It wrapped him tighter and tighter. Pressed him on all sides like a vice. The vampire sadness burrowed through his skin and fed on the life force within his being.

Anthony shook his arms. Ran his hands across his neck.

Twisted his torso side to side—all to rid himself of the draining sensation. He took a deep breath and stepped forward. His legs were as heavy as anvils. *Thump. Thump.* His feet fell roughly on the ground. Lumbered. It was like he was wearing flat-soled boots filled with lead. He extended his hands out in front of him and blindly felt his way through the velveteen darkness. Time passed, or so it seemed. There was no way of telling how long.

A concrete step materialized before his feet. His toes grazed its edge. Another step appeared, then another, and another after that, until a complete spiraling staircase descended into the dimly lit depths. The musty smell of decaying grime oozed from the damp, haunting gray walls. It all looked familiar. Had he been here before? A stagnant breath of air rose from the unseen depths and stroked the back of his neck, making his hairs cower in fright.

Someone spoke. Then someone else. A deep male voice in a tone so thick that his throat must be coated in years of layered soot. The garbled speech of the two men rode the moribund currents from somewhere deep below. Anthony stood frozen in place. His arms hung like icicles. The voices were too far away to make any clear sense. He needed to get closer. Who were they? Was it safe to go down there? Before he realized it, he had already taken his first step into the unknown depths.

Anthony carefully placed his foot on the next step and slowly crept down into the abyss with leopard-like stealth. The conversation grew louder, but it was still a jumbled mess. Another step. He tried to make out their words. Step. His ankle buckled. He yelped. A burning pain shot along the outside of his shin. The conversation stopped. Anthony flattened himself against the wall, trying to shield his vulnerability. He covered his mouth, attempting to mute the panic that filled his rapid breaths.

Thump...thump, thump. The clatter of footsteps echoed off the concrete walls. It fell like rain from somewhere above him. *Thump.* They grew closer. Louder.

He hobbled down a few more steps and stopped. There were two or three people waiting somewhere at the bottom. Behind him several more were coming. A nervous perspiration beaded on his forehead. A trickle of sweat scurried down his cheek. He was stuck. Exposed and out of place. He ran his hand over the top of his head and looked down into the pit. Then up toward the approaching footsteps. Trapped. Nowhere to hide.

Anthony threw himself against the gray wall and wrapped his arms across his chest. He cowered in the faint shadows that lay between the aura cast by the pale lights. Sliding his back down the wall, he came to rest with his knees crammed into his chest.

"Come, come...we're getting closer," the voice hissed. Chugging like a diesel engine, the approaching stranger inhaled and exhaled several times before he spoke again. "No need to worry; this is where you want to be. You've made the right decision...I can see it on your faces."

From around the bend three silhouettes emerged in the grainy light. A man of hulking proportions led the group. He was larger than an offensive lineman. No neck. Arms that couldn't rest at his sides. His black suit fit snugly against his body. The blood-red tie followed the curve of his barrel chest. Anthony squeezed his knees tighter.

The leader's words crackled in the air like a dry log on a fire. "You'll be more than glad you chose this path. More than glad...you'll see." The man smiled, exposing his bone-white teeth. Valley-deep furrows crinkled across his bald forehead and around the sides of his mouth. They were getting closer. Anthony was trapped. He pushed harder against the wall. Squeezed his legs tighter into his chest, hoping he could just disappear. The dampening chill of fright seeped into his skin and sent shards of icicles piercing the matrix of his bones.

Anthony wanted to bury his head in his arms. If he didn't look up, maybe the man wouldn't look down. But he couldn't stop himself. Some unseen force yanked his gaze toward the approaching trio.

The leader's body practically filled the corridor. His reptilian eyes were devoid of any twinkle. Empty of emotion. Solid and black. Lifeless. If he had a soul, it was lost behind those inert visual organs. Two people blindly followed him. One male and one female.

The college-age woman's feet slapped against the concrete steps. There was no spring, no grace to her gait. Paleness dabbed her cheeks and left her lips as blue as death. Somberness weighed the corners of her mouth. Greasy strands of hair fell over her face. She blankly stared at the ground. Her arms fell limply from the slack of her shoulders. *Splat.* Blood trickled across her palm and dripped from the tips of her two middle fingers. *Splat.* It fell on the steps in a gentle rhythm. *Splat.* The blotches of blood struck the ground and boiled. They evaporated into a red-tinted wisp of smoke, leaving no trace of its presence.

Older by at least a couple of decades, an air of confidence spilled from the man behind the woman. He stood tall and stared straight forward without as much as a hint of worry on his face. He held a briefcase so tightly that his knuckles and fingers had turned white. Then again, his entire being was bathed in a sheen of whiteness.

Anthony blinked. He could see the wall and the steps as if the man were transparent—a mere ghost. His lungs, liver, stomach and intestines glowed like a hologram from inside his body.

The man's heart contracted. An organ as purple as necrotic meat. Shriveled like a decayed apple. It hung from a blackened web of arteries and vessels. It contracted again and then quivered in its rotting web of decay.

The group drew closer. Their steps louder. Anthony held his breath. He dared not breathe. Not make a sound. The leader's hissing voice sizzled like electricity. The heat of the man's breath skimmed over Anthony's neck. A trickle of sweat dribbled down his back. Would they notice? If they did, would he be forced to follow?

The leader was directly in front of him. Anthony could reach out and touch him. He tightened his grip on his knees. The reptilian guide didn't look down. A silent breath trickled past Anthony's trembling lips. If only the other two wouldn't notice. The college girl followed close behind. *Splat...sizzle.*

She was about to pass without as much as a tip of her chin when she snapped her head. Her eyes sprang wide open. Anthony's stomach knotted. He swallowed hard. A bitter numbness slid over his arms and legs.

Dread clung to her face. Her eyes pleaded for help. She looked at the leader and then back at Anthony. Her pale hand reached out. He started to reach for her blood-drenched fingers, but stopped. Where would he take her? Her lips fell open...

"Come now, this way. Nothing important for you to see." the leader said. The woman's head whipped forward. "Didn't your momma tell you not to talk with strangers?" Her solemn expression returned. Her gaze fell to the floor as she continued to systematically trudge down the steps. *Splat...sizzle.*

"No need to be scared. You should be proud of your-selves...proud to have chosen this direction."

The group descended the steps, slowly rounded the bend and disappeared. All that remained was their lengthening shadows. The seconds ticked by and even those shadows were eventually consumed by the daunting gray walls. The leader's voice faded deeper and deeper into the unknown depths until it became a garbled hiss. The type of hiss that escapes a steaming pipe. Silence followed. A deafening silence. So deafening that the loneliness returned and squeezed even tighter.

Anthony shimmied his back up the wall. He looked up the steps. It wasn't too far to the top. But then where? He gazed down into the abyss. What was down there? What if she truly did need help?

He cautiously snaked his way downward and tried to re-main as silent as he could. Sudden laughter pierced the still air. It wasn't joyous laughter. It was a mocking laughter. A laughter that says things aren't what they seem. One that says there is no escape. The scalpel-sliced glee cradled a dread so cold that Anthony's joints stiffened. The sweat that had trickled down his back froze. Fright-filled frost crackled across his spine. He placed his hand on the cool wall to steady himself.

As quickly as it came the laughter died. No one was talk-ing. Not even a hint of a voice. It was as if a mute button had been pressed, returning him to total quietness. Anthony's legs grew rock hard. His shoes slapped against the steps. He tried to move slower so as not to make any noise. It was no use. The sound of his leaden feet echoed off the walls and fell into the depths below. If that wasn't a dead giveaway, his scampering breath would make sure he was heard.

Anthony pulled his shirt over his mouth hoping to deaden the sound. He leaned against the wall and used it to steady his weight as he descended the steps. One step, then another. It wasn't becoming any easier. Down several more. His lungs seared like burning embers. He stopped to catch his breath. Only a few more to the bottom.

He finally reached it. The air was warm. Stuffy. Heavy with the stench of untold years of grime and a faint undertone of decaying flesh. The corridor shot straight forward and forked at the far end. A rusted red metal door sat in the middle of the hallway. Embedded in the wall to his immediate left was a large window. Someone was talking from the other side. Anthony crouched low and peeked through the bottom corner of the window.

Dressed in matching blue uniforms, two men moved back and forth as if pacing.

"Didn't I tell you he manages to get 'em here quicker than some of the others," the taller of the two men said.

The shorter, more broad-shouldered man nodded. "You're right. He's one of the better ones."

"Just watch." The taller man motioned with his hand. "By day's end he'll be back with a couple more."

"You think so?"

"I know so," the tall man said. "When he converts, he's like an animal on the hunt."

"That's fine by me. The more the merrier." The shorter man chuckled. "Did you see that look in her eyes?"

The taller man moved toward the window. "You mean when she found out where she was?"

"That was priceless." The shorter man paused. "That look never grows old."

The tall man stopped inches from the window. "It never does." He smiled exposing his fang-like molars. "I don't know how he gets 'em, but he captures 'em like he was shooting something in a...how does that saying go?" He snapped his fingers as if trying to jar his memory. "You know what I'm talking about?"

"Like shooting fish in a barrel."

The tall man laughed. "That's it. Like fish in a barrel." He laughed even harder. "The secret is to feed 'em lies and empty promises and then when they get here..."

"Welcome them to the abyss they never believed existed." The shorter man laughed so hard that he began to cough.

"How dumb can these people be? You'd think they'd catch on once they started coming down the steps." The tall man tapped on the window. Anthony crouched tighter into the corner of the window. "That smell." He crunched his face. "Damn, it's horrible." He paused. "And then there's the heat." He looked at the shorter man. "You and I are in this shit every day. We're used to it." He shook his head. "How they don't notice it is beyond me."

The shorter man scoffed. "It's because they're too self-absorbed." He pointed outside the window. "Once we tell them though, they feel it, all right."

"Amongst other things."

Anthony looked up at the gray walls. The putrid odor of moldy flesh and dank mildew grew stronger. The heat singed the hairs on his arms. Was this place really...?

Anthony lost his balance. He fell hard against the wall and grunted. A gust of air was knocked out of his lungs.

"What was that?"

"I heard it, too."

Anthony's heart knocked against his chest like a battered

piston. His legs prickled with fear. He fell forward and stumbled on his hands and knees toward the steps.

"Who's there?"

He crawled faster. The jagged concrete dug into the soft flesh of his knees. A pinpoint pain slivered into his palms.

The footsteps were rushing toward the door. *Bang.* It smashed against the wall.

"Who the hell are you?"

"You're not supposed to be here!"

Anthony slammed his hand on the step and tried to stand. Something claw-like gripped his flanks. A hook pierced his back and into his stomach. He panted in pain. He lifted his arm to turn, but the pain forced him back. It couldn't be the two men; their footsteps were still rushing toward him.

"Oh no you don't!"

"Grab him before he…"

Whatever it was that hooked him yanked him backward. The air rushed by his head. The world went dark. A hoarse cry leaped from the depths of his lungs.

Anthony gasped. He sat up. Daylight sprang through the blinds, ricocheted off the white walls, and pierced his eyes. Beads of perspiration clung to his arms and dribbled over his legs. He flung the blanket off his body. Waves of heat tumbled skyward. The cool air of the room plunged over his skin. A welcome relief. The chill that soon followed in its wake made him shiver. Anthony's head swam in a soupy fog. He rubbed his eyes and reached for his clock. Eleven thirty-five. He shook the cobwebs from his brain.

Oh Shit! I'm going to be late! His legs responded to his sudden panic, but his sense of balance hadn't purchased a ticket to his cerebellum. He bounced off several walls and smashed his shin into the coffee table. The textbook was on the table. He stuffed pens, pencils, folders and a notebook into his backpack.

Anthony threaded his legs into the crumpled jeans on the floor. His jacket was behind the couch cushion. Slipping into his shoes, he flew out the door and down the steps leading from his apartment. The crystal-clear March sky was so cool and blue that it greeted him with a crisp punch. The blow stung. It also slapped the cloud from his mind.

His nap had gone into extra innings. Burning the candle at both ends with work, school, and studying had taken its toll. Anthony needed the sleep. He unfortunately purchased it on credit and now realized he couldn't afford the interest. There was much that still needed to be done. Reading those chapters. Going over the study questions. The rough draft to the paper was due in two weeks. He ran his hand over his head and sighed.

During his walk to class he would normally think about the day's lecture. He tried, but the dream played its trump card and refused to be evicted from his memory. The strange feeling of stepping out of his body. The steps. Those people. The black eyes. What happened to the girl? Where was that place? Maybe it wasn't a dream?

Would you risk your own life and the lives of those you love to save millions marked as sinners? Get your copy of *Chain of Salt and Water* here and find out what Liana and Anthony do. If you're interested in learning about my new releases, or when my books go on sale, please follow me on BookBub, or subscribe to my newsletter.

www.timsabados.com/books

bookbub.com/authors/tim-sabados

bit.ly/timsabadosnewsletter

About Tim Sabados

Tim Sabados has been an emergency room nurse for over a decade and a part-time paramedic for over two decades. A native born Detroiter having interests in painting, sculpture and drawing it was only natural that he turned to creative writing to fulfill that artistic gap formed by the excessive amount of technical writing required of him during nursing school.

His influences in fiction have come from interests in various mystical concepts and the many unusual situations presented to him during his medical career. More importantly his writing strays from any one single genre, but instead blends them together to create a literary experience that allows a vibrant mental journey and the ability to contemplate the multi-faceted aspects of life. Something he feels the reader will find enjoyable on top of an entertaining story.

If you like unusual literary facts, trivia and the strange origin of words and phrases or you simply want to know about his latest books you can connect with him at any of the places listed below:

Facebook: facebook.com/Tim-Sabados-Author-453239271716099

Instagram: instagram.com/tim_sabados

Bookbub: bookbub.com/authors/tim-sabados

Newsletter: bit.ly/timsabadosnewsletter

Website: timsabados.com